I0738980

# The Lost Letter

## Joe Shumock

*Book Two of the
Letter Series Novel*

Silver Sage Media

Scan this QR code  to visit
www.SilverSageMedia.com

# The Lost Letter

Copyright © 2012 Joe Shumock

Cover Design and Author Photo by: Barry Hodgin
All rights reserved. No part of this book may be reproduced in any form by
any electronic or mechanical means including photocopying, recording, or
information storage and retrieval without permission in writing from the author. This book is a work of fiction. Names, characters, places, and incidents
either are products of the author's imagination or are used fictitiously.
Any resemblance to actual events or locales or person, living
or dead, is entirely coincidental.

Hardback ISBN:978-0-9837939-3-9
Trade Paper Back ISBN: 978-0-9837939-4-6
Limited Edition ISBN: 978-0-9837939-5-3
Ebook Lost Letter ISBN: 978-0-9837939-6-0

Book Web site
www.SilverSageMedia.com
E-mail: info@SilverSageMedia.com

Give feedback on the book at:
feedback@SilverSageMedia.com

Printed in the U.S.A.

To my daughter, Cindy Daniel,

and

my son, Gene Shumock,

and

as always, Kathy

# Acknowledgments

An author produces a manuscript … and then the work begins. Many others have a part in the final product. My editor for The Lost Letter is R. J. Communications - New York City. Readers read … going through the material checking those things the writer may have missed such as spelling, punctuation, story plausibility, and other obvious or not-so-obvious problems. Readers/content editors in this project included: Jackie Courtney, Barry Hodgin, Ray Lapierre, Sharon Mafredas, and Judy Ragan.

Thanks, folks. Without you, the project would have suffered.

Special thanks go to Barry Hodgin, my business partner and friend. Barry designed the book cover and is responsible for photography, websites, and much of the marketing.

If I have forgotten anyone, I am sorry. I would hope you know I thank you, too.

Last, but certainly not least, I would like to say a special thanks to all those who have encouraged me. Thanks, too, to all those who have read, A Letter to Die For, the first in the Letter Series.

We hope each of you readers, both present and future, will consider becoming a *Joe Shumock, Author – Fan Club* member as we move forward with plans to formalize the fan club. There will be benefits: discounts, coupons, prizes, surprises, and much more. Watch the websites and our blogs for current information. Also watch for us on Facebook. We will want your input, too. Get in on the ground floor and help us grow.

 # *Prologue*

The old woman heard the helicopter land at midmorning. With a list of food and other items in her pocket, she hurried out and climbed aboard the aircraft.

Earlier as she had served his breakfast, Pablo "the Merchant" Perez told her she would be accompanying him to the warehouse compound. She often flew there to bring back supplies for the main house.

She was aware her boss was one of the most ruthless drug lords in Central and South America. Though she feared him, Perez had always treated her as family. There were only a few times she could remember when he had been displeased with her. Those moments were always scary but usually passed quickly

This morning had been different. Pablo had appeared especially angry as she topped off his coffee. She had caught him glaring in her direction several times. The woman wondered if she had done something wrong. But the thought had slipped away as the Merchant finished his breakfast and left the kitchen.

She would remember his anger later—with fear in every part of her being.

Pablo and two other men were already there as she scurried aboard the helicopter and secured her seatbelt. They lifted off immediately, but the pilot didn't take the normal path south toward the warehouses. Instead, the aircraft swung eastward, heading out over the blue water below the cliffs at the edge of the compound.

A thread of concern ran through her as the shoreline slipped away. She glanced toward Perez then, and her heart doubled its pace. The Merchant's eyes were on her, and they were narrowed and angry.

She immediately thought of the letter.

~ ~ ~

The woman had practically raised Pablo's son, Juan, so she had not hesitated when he had asked her to help him compose a message—at least, not until she had realized who it was going to. Efforts to discourage Juan had been futile. Then, even as an extreme sense of foreboding had crept over her, she had relented and done what the boy had asked.

She had translated the youngster's words to English and written them on the pages. Fear had stiffened her fingers as she had listened to Juan's thoughts and realized what both had to lose.

The message was meant for a young man who worked for the Merchant. When this particular individual, an American, had arrived at the compound, Juan had quickly chosen him as a friend and companion. Pablo had seemed pleased, too, his son had a new compadre. Juan had begun to speak English very well, and his father had appeared happy with that, too. The newcomer had been tall and friendly, but he had been an American. That fact had surprised the woman.

The boy's short letter was a warning. Obviously, Juan had secretly overheard a conversation his father had had with one of his lieutenants. In the letter, Juan told his friend to disappear—or die.

She had organized the words for him, knowing as she did, if his father saw it Perez would recognize the handwriting—even in English. She had also known the letter's discovery would mean certain death for her. Yet, she had still written it.

The reason was simple: she couldn't have loved Juan more if he had been her own. She had raised him and been with him every day since his birth.

With the letter finished, the boy had asked her to slip it under the door of his friend's room in another part of the compound. Again, she had done as the boy requested.

Getting rid of the letter had been such a relief. Still she had worried her efforts for the boy would be discovered.

Ten days had gone by before she had finally felt at ease.

~ ~ ~

"Did you think I would not discover what you had done?"

Guilt and fear immediately overcame her. Tears clouded her eyes as a choking sensation constricted her throat. *He knows about the letter. He knows I wrote it for Juan.*

Suddenly Pablo was in front of her, yet she didn't see the slap coming. Her head snapped back, the left side of her face stinging. She could actually feel his handprint. Tears cascaded down her cheeks, but she didn't try to stop them. Instead, she sobbed openly, her head sagging toward her chest.

Perez reached into his pocket, unfolded some sheets, and held them in front of her. *The letter!*

"See this!" he shouted. Then he spit on her.

She suddenly smelled urine and realized she had soiled herself. Embarrassment did not enter her mind. She was too scared. A new whimper escaped her lips.

"Bind her arms!"

Perez's attention shifted to the men who had accompanied them onto the helicopter. They were already on their feet. A length of heavy cord was quickly looped around her wrists, and then they were tied in back. She could not imagine what was going to happen and did not want to try.

She heard the helicopter's door slide open and felt a rush of wind. Then she was dragged toward the opening. A longer rope was secured just under her arms as the wind tore at her. The rope was already attached to a pulley and hoist; the pulley was hooked to the end of a metal arm. One of the men swung the arm outside the aircraft and locked it in place.

Finally, she was spun around to face Perez again, her back to the opening and the blue waters beyond. He still held the letter in his hand. Anger flashed in his squinted eyes, The Merchant once more held the pages up for her to see.

He screamed, "No one betrays me and gets away with it!"

Then he spit in her face a second time … and shoved her out the door.

She heard someone screaming. It took her a moment to realize it was her. Falling a few feet, she suddenly felt a jerk and was left dangling, swinging back and forth, unable to help herself in any way. Then the hoist above engaged, and she started moving toward the water.

As she drifted closer, large shapes could be seen gliding back and forth just below the surface.

Sharks! Dear sweet Jesus. Sharks …

Something washed over her from above—a liquid. She looked up toward the helicopter. Though spinning, she caught a glimpse as one of the men emptied a second bucket of a foul-smelling substance over her. She recognized the scent—chum—food waste from the kitchen and several days old. She had seen the two white buckets at the back of the helicopter's cabin but had not given them any thought.

Pablo is baiting the sharks. Now she is covered in the same slime.

Oh, God!

Even He couldn't help her now.


From fifty feet above, the three men watched as the old woman neared the surface of the water. She was spinning and squirming.

They could see the sharks, and she could see the sharks. Still, there was no way for her to climb the rope—not with her hands and arms tied behind her. But she tried. Oh, how she tried!

The two men with Pablo laughed, pointing at the action below as one of them pushed the button on the hoist, suddenly dropping the old woman into the water. The Merchant leaned against the opening and watched. No emotion was evident.

The sharks went into a frenzy below the surface. As the woman's legs and lower body broke the water, one of the largest shadows turned directly toward her. Upon reaching the woman, its head heaved violently from side to side. It then swam away, its place quickly taken by others.

Pablo Perez looked on, a sadistic grin now on his face as he slowly moved his head back and forth. One of the men hit the button, causing the hoist to lift the woman back above the surface. A leg was missing, her torso torn and damaged.

Enough!

Perez reached out with a large knife. Beneath its blade, the rope holding the woman separated, dropping her body among the feeding and frenzied sharks. The water appeared to boil as it turned a pale crimson.

Perez stepped back into the cabin.

"Vamos!" he yelled to the pilots. "Let's go home."

 ## Chapter 1

He could hear a conversation in the distance. People were talking about him, but he couldn't make sense of what they were saying. They seemed too far away.

And his head hurt. Damn, his head hurt.

Then, everything became quiet again, and in his mind, he walked back into the fog. As he drifted away, he tried to remember what had happened.

~ ~ ~

The shot that almost killed Webster may have saved his life. His recent enemies had been close to locating him when a bullet brought him down in New Orleans. With Webster critically wounded, leaders in the U.S. Marshals Service saw a chance to get him out of immediate danger and into deeper security. Prior to being shot, he had been furnishing information to the marshals on a case involving several city leaders. Faking his death provided a perfect opportunity to hide him.

While working with the marshals, Webster had also aided Cary Anne Warren in her pursuit of those responsible for her mother's death. In a final showdown with the killers, the couple's situation became desperate. The marshals were after the same group for other illegal activities. U.S. Deputy Marshal Jack Robbins, a close friend of Webster's, had commanded the team assigned to sweep in and arrest the group's leadership while rescuing Webster and the girl.

But the marshals were almost too late.

The raid's main purpose had been to bring down local corrupt politicians who fronted and supervised a clandestine pipeline and protection racket for drugs coming into the southeastern United States from Central and South America. Over the last several years, the organization had flourished, using with impunity due to its strategically placed leadership. For the raid to be effective, the group's leader, the city's police superintendent, had to arrive before Robbins's team could move in.

After the superintendent had arrived but before the U.S. Marshals could get there, someone had gotten off a shot, taking Webster out. He had almost died before the trauma team could get him to surgery.

~ ~ ~

Robbins now stood in a darkened corner, watching as a nurse took Webster's vital signs. Webster had not regained complete consciousness since being wounded five nights ago. His trauma surgeon, Dr. Best, had operated almost immediately and had looked in on him several times each day since. The LSU Medical Center in New Orleans was a teaching hospital, so Webster was getting the best care the city could offer. The damage to his body had been extensive, though, and would have killed most men. Webster's conditioning and will to live had made the difference between life and death. The surgeon's orders were to keep him sedated and immobile. Toward that end, he had been isolated in a small, dimly lit room within the Surgical Intensive Care Unit since leaving the operating room.

However, within the last few hours, the situation had changed dramatically. Now hurried preparations were in progress in Webster's room and elsewhere in the SIC Unit. Dr. Best and others were making arrangements for his relocation. An armed officer stood at the door to Webster's room, and another was stationed at the main entrance to the intensive care unit.

Even with the security, Jack Robbins was still worried. Some violent people were searching for Webster, and it was Robbins's assignment to keep them from locating and killing his friend.

Two recent communications had everyone on edge. The latest, a note, had been intercepted in Atlanta only five hours earlier. Robbins carried a copy in his pocket. The short enigmatic message, mailed from outside the country, carried a warning for Webster. There was no signature, only the brusque four words in Spanish: "Ellos vienen, mi amigo." They are coming, my friend.

Robbins and his boss assumed the note was from someone inside the drug cartel Webster had infiltrated and where he had operated undercover until a few weeks ago. The note had come on the heels of another possible threat. Sources had recently sent word to Robbins a suspicious communication had been recorded in a telephone exchange in Central America. Although Webster's name had not been used, there was concern the discussion was about him. With those two pieces of information in hand, Robbins chose to err on the side of caution.

Webster would be out of New Orleans within the hour. His name had already been changed for security purposes. All paperwork listed the patient being transferred as Webb M. Michaels.

Robbins paced the hallway, worrying as he kept tabs on preparations for the move. For the moment, at least, everything was going as expected.

Elaborate planning had led the public, including Cary Warren, to believe Mike Webster had died as a result of the clash inside the New Orleans warehouse. There was also a concerted effort afoot to make sure old enemies knew of his "untimely demise." Misinformation had been flowing since the morning after Webster's shooting—even before the discussions about moving him.

Robbins hated lying to Cary because Webster had begun to care for her, but there had been no other way.

A short obituary in the New Orleans newspaper listed Webster as a resident of Knoxville, Tennessee. According to the article, the deceased's body would be cremated, and there would be no service.

~ ~ ~

Across the Gulf and some distance outside the city of Veracruz, Mexico, a telephone rang in the early morning.

The sprawling estate on a bluff overlooking the Bay of Campeche belonged to the head of a large drug cartel. A smooth, ten-foot concrete wall surrounded the property. The top of the barrier was capped with broken glass and three feet of razor wire. Sentries, in vehicles and on foot, patrolled the grounds 24/7.

The phone conversation was short.

"Hola?"

"I am sorry to wake you, mi amigo. Do you know my voice?"

"Si."

"My sources tell me the man you have been searching for has been shot in New Orleans. It happened last Wednesday evening. I am told he is dead." The caller provided details.

"Is your information reliable?"

"Si." There was a pause. "Usually."

"I will check it out."

"I expected you would."

"I will be in touch."

The phone clicked, and the caller was gone.

~ ~ ~

Careful measures now called for Webster to be known as Webb Michaels until he reached the medical facility where he would recuperate. On a need-to-know basis, only the U.S. Marshals Service and Webster's doctor knew the true situation.

A stretcher was wheeled into the small room where several pairs of hands lifted Webster onto it. All the necessary tubes, monitors, and machines were ready to go. Robbins watched from the doorway, aware  an ambulance waited outside of the emergency room entrance.

The two security officers and Robbins spread out and accompanied the small procession as it left the SICU. Two nurses and Dr. Best quietly walked from the building behind Webster's stretcher. Predawn darkness provided cover as they hurried him out to the ambulance.

With the patient and equipment loaded, an attendant closed the doors, tapped twice, and the vehicle drove away. Though its lights were flashing, the siren remained silent, and no official cars were used so as not to draw attention to them. Instead, three unmarked vehicles left the parking lot from separate locations, one leading the way while the others moved along in the light traffic.

The group drove out to the New Orleans Lakefront Airport where a specially equipped Lear jet sat waiting. All four vehicles pulled up close to the aircraft. Five men quickly spread out, taking up guard positions while two others helped the medical personnel load Webster onto the jet.

As the stretcher was secured, Robbins pulled one of the men aside and gave him instructions. Josh Hamlin, one of Robbins's team members and a U.S. deputy marshal himself, would accompany Webster to his destination. No one expected problems, but Robbins remained apprehensive.

"Stay with him until he's safely settled into his new facility," Robbins told Hamlin. "You're in charge, but other agents will meet you and act as security."

"Got it."

Hamlin boarded the aircraft and took a seat at the rear of the cabin. The doctor and nurses finished tending the patient and took their seats, too. As the right engine spooled up, the pilot and first officer worked through their preflight checklist. At last, the doors were closed, and the left engine screamed to life. The aircraft began to move even as the first officer requested permission to taxi.

"Lear Delta Bravo 57 Echo requesting taxi and take-off instructions."

He received an immediate response, and a couple of minutes later the crew lifted the landing gear as the aircraft clawed its way into the early morning sky over Lake Pontchartrain. A flight plan had initially been filed for Memphis but was revised with Houston Center as soon as they attained altitude. Their new destination was Charlotte, North Carolina.

~ ~ ~

Pablo Perez lifted his arm from the shoulders of the caramel-skinned beauty seated beside him. The Merchant, as he was known throughout Central and South America and the United States, was of medium height, about five eight, and slim. He wore a short beard that gave him a youthful appearance, although facial wrinkles and a receding hairline suggested middle age. The woman smiled as she stood and walked toward the extraordinarily large swimming pool that resembled a small lake. The area was striking, with its mature trees and numerous waterfalls which surrounded the indigo surface.

At poolside, several young men and women sat talking at tables and lounge chairs. Others playfully splashed each other, enjoying the water and the weather. A few of the women wore tiny bikinis, while others sported only thong bottoms. Several were totally nude. The woman who had been sitting with the Merchant was in the latter group.

Perez motioned for a man sitting alone on the opposite side of the pool to join him. Several others had been glancing his way from time to time on the chance he might require their attention.

The Merchant watched with satisfaction as the individual he had summoned strolled to his side. Casually pulling a chaise lounge close, the young man sat down and leaned in to listen.

"Do you remember much about our friend who closed down our Gulf Coast operation?"

"Si, Pablo. I remember him. The tall one."

"Yes, the tall one." Perez frowned as he continued. "I have been told he was killed in New Orleans a few days ago. I want you to go and find out if this is true."

The man stood and simply said, "I will leave today."

"Good. If he is dead, we will celebrate. But if my information is not true, find out where he is hiding." Thinking of Webster, Perez rose in anger as he talked to Mateo.

Unaffected, the young man looked back at Perez, his arms crossed at his chest. Though Mateo had proven himself many times over, Perez was continuously surprised by his protégé's total lack of fear. It was uncanny.

"My information says our friend is using the name Mike Webster," Perez said. "He was employed at Trebeck Corporation out of Knoxville, Tennessee. It also appears he was helping a woman look for her relatives in New Orleans. The woman's name is Cary Warren. She works at the same company. My sources tell me Webster was shot and killed during a raid involving this woman's search." Perez lightly jabbed the young man with his finger. "I must know if this is true."

"Si, señor. I will find out for you."

"Don't fail me, Mateo. I depend on you."

"No, señor Pablo. I will not fail." The younger man continued to stare at Perez. "If I find he is alive, what do you want me to do? Shall I kill him or bring the information back to you?"

"Let me know what you discover. If you find him alive, I will come to meet you. I want to be there when this one is finished," the Merchant said. His face was red now, attesting to his fury. "I will cut his throat and spit on him as he takes his last breath. Do you understand?"

"Si, te entiendo perfectamente."

 # Chapter 2

The sleek jet carrying Webster had pulled out of its gentle turn toward Charlotte when he opened his eyes. It was the first time he had truly been awake in five days. Turning his head toward the nurses who were talking quietly, he whispered, "Can I have something to drink?" The words were scratchy, and it hurt Webster's throat to speak. "Wh … where am I?" he asked, glancing at his surroundings.

"You're on an airplane," one of the nurses told him. Pointing to the others, she said, "That's Sarah and Dr. Best. I'm Judy." Then she gestured toward the back of the cabin. "Mr. Hamlin is riding with you, too. I believe you know him."

Deputy Marshal Hamlin had been scanning a magazine. Rising, he said, "Well, look who's decided to rejoin the world of the living."

Webster raised his head. "Hey, Josh. Why are you here?"

Hamlin stepped forward and leaned over. Whispering, he said, "Some people were asking questions about you in New Orleans and other places. We decided to move you. Jack thinks it is the group from down in Mexico. We couldn't take a chance."

Then Hamlin explained about the name change and waited for a reaction.

"You sure?" Webster's face was drawn. "I mean about those people asking questions?"

"Let's just say Robbins is concerned."

~ ~ ~

Sarah opened a small cooler, poured water over some ice, and passed it to Judy. Webster reached out but halted with a moan. In obvious pain, he grimaced as he let the nurse hold the cup to his lips. He swallowed thirstily until she moved the cup away.

"Not so fast," she told him. "There's more."

Dr. Best had risen from his seat. Hamlin moved forward to listen.

"How are you feeling?"

"Like I've been run over by a truck."

"I'm not surprised." The doctor reached for his wrist and felt for a pulse, then nodded as he released Webster's arm. "Let's get the rest of his vitals."

"How's he doing?" Hamlin asked.

"Good, given the circumstances."

"How long have I been out?" Webster asked.

Judy glanced at Dr. Best.

"Let Mr. Hamlin bring him up-to-date."

"You were shot five days ago," Josh told him. "Late Wednesday night. Today is Monday."

Webster frowned. "The last thing I recall was glancing toward Cary Warren. Nothing after that."

Sarah took the pressure cuff off his arm, entered a note in the chart, and handed it to Dr. Best. The doctor flipped through it, a scowl on his face. Tossing it aside, he moved to face Webster.

"Mr. Michaels," he said using Webster's new name, "you came close to being killed. The bullet did a lot of damage; it even nicked your aorta. A centimeter or two and you wouldn't be on this flight."

"Pretty close, huh?"

"Yeah."

"You think my reflexes saved me."

"Tell yourself that if it makes you feel better," the doctor said. "Personally, I think someone had an eye on you." Dr. Best studied him for a moment. "You a religious man, Mr. Web … ah, Mr. Michaels?"

"Not really."

"Maybe you should be." He finally smiled. "By the way, your friend Jack Robbins and I go back to our days as undergraduate students. I did your surgery."

"I think I'll rest … a little. Webster's words trailed off, and he closed his eyes.

~ ~ ~

After a short ride above the clouds, the pilot came on the intercom and told them to secure for landing. Minutes later, the jet lightly touched down and taxied to a remote area of Charlotte's Douglas International Airport.

An ambulance was waiting, along with two government automobiles. There would be an official escort this time. Two men climbed out of each vehicle and helped move Webster and the equipment into the ambulance. With the transfer finished, the men introduced themselves to Hamlin; they were federal agents from the local FBI office. Hamlin quickly gave them instructions and then they were ready to move. Everyone loaded up. Webster had slept through the transfer.

One of the automobiles pulled out, serving as lead. The ambulance and the other automobile followed closely, and the procession proceeded at a normal speed.

As they approached the gates, Hamlin, riding in the ambulance with Webster, scanned the area for threats. Seeing nothing, his thoughts moved to the future. He hoped Jack Robbins had a plan in place to protect the patient as he recuperated. Jack had indicated Webster would be left alone in the medical facility, and,

Hamlin guessed, Webster wouldn't be taking care of himself for several weeks. That could prove bad timing if the wrong people found out where he was located. Josh was concerned.

The vehicles turned on their emergency lights once they were outside the fence. With other traffic moving out of their way, the lead vehicle stepped up the convoy's speed as they headed for their destination.

A half hour later, the lead vehicle turned into an unmarked driveway. The entrance, if it could be called that, was closed in on each side by woodlands. The drive was difficult to see unless you knew it was there. The meager roadway consisted of loose gravel and was definitely in a state of disrepair.

A guardhouse and stout metal gate blocked their way about fifty yards into the woods and around a sharp curve. An armed, uniformed guard stepped out to meet them. Other men with weapons watched from both sides.

An agent in the first car spoke with the guard and produced papers for him to examine. Obviously satisfied, the guard handed the papers back and returned to the guardhouse. Hamlin watched as the man made a telephone call. Moments later, the gate slowly retracted into the stone fence on each side, and they were waved through.

The vehicles continued another quarter mile through dense brush and trees. As the ambulance came out of the woods, Hamlin could see two large buildings and a parking lot. The buildings were one story and appeared relatively new. The parking lot, only partially full now, could accommodate a large number of automobiles.

The three vehicles made their way to a covered area leading to the entrance of the first building. The ambulance backed up to a large set of glass doors and stopped. Several people dressed in medical scrubs hurried out of the building as the FBI agents opened the back of the ambulance.

The patient started to come around as he was wheeled into the building. Hamlin stood watching. Webster seemed to understand a new set of caregivers was now in charge. Dr. Best, relieved of his responsibility, brought the new doctor up to speed as a nurse settled Webster into his room.

The new doctor was a woman. "What can you tell me?" she asked, having introduced herself as Dr. Irene Dunn. She was a striking woman of medium height, blonde, and very attractive. The scrubs she wore with deck shoes couldn't hide thirty-something curves. Hamlin almost envied Webster. That was before he heard the two physicians talking.

The new doctor was obviously concerned about Webster's condition. Best answered her questions.

"Gunshot wound," he said. "A bad one."

They both glanced toward the patient as he groaned. Dr. Best continued, "It beat him up pretty badly, but we were able to repair everything." He handed Webster's chart to the woman. It was the new one they had used in New Orleans for the transfer.

Dunn flipped slowly through the pages. Speaking low, she said, "I've already received a call from Jack Robbins about the name switch." She glanced up at Dr. Best, then back at the chart.

Pausing as she examined the information, Dunn said, "Looks like you got to him just in time."

Dr. Best agreed. "Another five minutes and I don't think we could have saved him."

"We'll continue your good work," she said with confidence. "I noticed he's regained consciousness. Is he coherent?"

When the two doctors moved into the room, Hamlin edged over to the doorway. Even with the noise and activity, he caught most of the conversation.

Dr. Best said, "He's fine, just dazed from the trauma, of course, and the medication."

"Let's look." She moved to the bed. "Are you flying back to New Orleans today?"

"Yes. The plane's waiting for us. We should be home for dinner."

"Wish I could say that. I have a surgery this afternoon."

"You do surgery here?" His eyes widened in surprise.

"We do everything here," she said matter-of-factly.

"Wow." Dr. Best was obviously impressed.

One of the nurses asked if Webster wanted to try eating some Jell-O.

"Uh … sure," he grunted.

Though groggy, Webster attempted to tease Dr. Best. "I see you're trying to get rid of me so you can go back home." Then he got his first look at the new doctor as she felt for a pulse.

"This is Dr. Irene Dunn," Dr. Best told Webster. "She has the power to take you out, so you better be nice."

"I'll be on my best behavior." Turning on a boyish smile, he looked as if he meant it.

Dr. Best reached across the bed and shook his hand. "Good-bye … and good luck," he said. Then he looked at Hamlin. "You ready?"

"I need a moment with the patient and Dr. Dunn before we cut out," Hamlin said.

Dr. Best and the nurses from New Orleans headed out the door. Hamlin moved over to the bed and stood beside Webster.

Speaking softly to the doctor, he said, "Let Jack Robbins know if you see or hear anything suspicious, okay?"

She smiled. "Don't worry, Mr. Hamlin. We have high-profile patients here all the time. That's what the guard detail is for. The patient will be just fine with us."

"Yeah, Josh," Webster added, "don't worry. I'll be able to take care of myself in a day or two." His speech was slurred.

Hamlin shook his head as he started for the door. Webster tended to take things lightly; Josh could only wish he would take this threat more seriously. He also hoped Robbins would be watching things closely. He had an uneasy feeling, not unlike several he had before.

Josh had learned to pay attention to gut feelings.


When they were alone, Dr. Dunn asked, "So how are you really feeling?"

Webster watched her, more interested in what she thought than in his own opinion. He could feel the furrows on his brow—pain a constant companion. "I'm pretty sore, and it's hard to breathe."

"I'm not surprised from your chart."

"Pretty bad?" He moaned softly as he turned a little.

"Bad enough."

"Anything I can't overcome?"

"No … but it'll take a while."

She wasn't giving him much. Webster couldn't help but worry about what Hamlin had told him.

She paused and then said, "I'm guessing you'll be with us for several weeks."

"That long? But …" He left his concerns unsaid.

She smiled at him and then glanced at her watch. "I have to prepare for surgery, but I'll check on you later." Webster watched as she walked out the door.

Then Cary Warren strolled across his consciousness. He shook his head. I will probably never even see Cary again, he thought. A familiar tightness closed his throat.

Sometimes he hated this life: he was thirty-one years old, almost thirty-two, and had no one he was close to. Cary could have been that someone. He missed her.

Then his thoughts turned again to the threat Josh had whispered about. There had been a couple of situations in Central and South America that could cause bad people to search for him. The one which always came to mind was the boy,

Juan, being killed. Webster had no doubt Juan's father would search for him until one of them was dead.

Theoretically, it shouldn't be a problem now that he was out of New Orleans. Webster doubted the possibility of anyone following him to this facility, at least not very quickly. Jack planned these transfers carefully. But if anyone could find him, it would be the Merchant.

I have to get myself ready, he thought. And I have to do it fast.

When Dr. Dunn walked out of Webster's room, she paused, leaning with her back against the wall. I can't believe it, she thought. After five years, she had believed it was really over. John Dawson had hardly crossed her mind in the last year—until today.

Now he had come storming back, at least in Irene's memory. In the room behind her was someone who could have been John's twin. Webster had no way of knowing he reminded her so completely of her old lover. He even sounded like him. But John Dawson was dead and buried in Montana. The accident had almost killed Irene, too.

But, after all, that was another life—wasn't it?

Pushing out from the wall, she thought, surgery. Set your mind back on the job at hand.

Rage Doyle stood in Webster's doorway and glanced both ways before stepping into the hallway to leave; he had listened before stepping out, too. He would rather no one know he had been there. Wearing his usual fedora, shades, and leather trench coat made Doyle almost invisible in the shadows of late afternoon.

Doyle had wanted to assure himself his young friend was okay. He would monitor the situation until Webster could take care of himself. The Author had heard rumblings about the people who were searching for Webster. Rage would watch over things for a while.

Later, when a nurse brought the sleeping pill and pillow the doctor had ordered, Webster did a double take. The African American man was tall, six two or three, and had a deep voice. Webster had never seen a more formidable-looking nurse. He at once decided whatever this one told him to do would be done with no argument.

The nurse held the pill in one hand and a heart-shaped pillow in the other. "Brought you something to make your dreams technicolor tonight." He nodded toward his right hand. "That would be the sleeping pill, not the pillow," the nurse said with an eighteen-karat smile. The room seemed to shake when the man spoke.

"Man, you must sing bass in the quartet," Webster told him. "If you don't, somebody messed up bad." That got a chuckle.

"You nailed me," the big man said grinning. "I've been singing bass since I was thirteen. The voice just came along with the size, I guess."

They both laughed this time.

"Want some water with your pill?"

"Any chance of OJ instead?"

"We can do that," the nurse replied as he headed for the nurse's station. He was back momentarily and handed the juice to Webster.

"What's your name?" Webster asked trying to see the nametag.

"Bobby Ramsey, but everyone here calls me Tiny." Pausing, he added, "Not wild about the nickname, but I guess I'm stuck with it."

Webster made a snap decision. "Bob or Bobby?"

Ramsey gazed at him, appearing to make a judgment. "Bob."

"Bob, it is."

There was a quiet moment and then Bob said, "Thanks."

Webster reached out, and they bumped fists.

Friends!

## Chapter 3

Far to the south, at the Merchant's compound in Mexico, the day was especially warm. But remembering other such times, a chill ran through Mateo's body. This wasn't the first time he had felt these sensations when starting out on a mission for the Merchant. Danger was always a part of working for Pablo. That was just the way it was. A part of the uneasy feeling came from wanting to please; that was extremely important. The Merchant provided everything needed for the young man to do any job required.

Back in his quarters there were several sets of travel documents. Each appeared legal and was up-to-date. The drug lord owned many legitimate businesses in Mexico, South America, the United States, and several other locations. He had never been detained when he traveled the world for the Merchant.

Mateo was almost six two with a sturdy build. He was muscular, but not in the manner of a weight lifter. Well-built and handsome—he knew that. His dark eyes and hair complemented his olive skin, and Mateo's profile perfectly fit his other features. Several of the women around the pool watched as he approached and talked with Pablo.

Their interest was of no concern to him. Mateo used women, never the other way around. They were for his purposes and satisfaction only; then he tossed them away like everything else he no longer needed or desired.

When their conversation finished, Mateo walked away. He heard Perez get out of his chair and call for the woman to come back and join him. From a distance, he watched as Pablo kissed her. Her name was Rosa. Mateo felt a flush of heat. He watched for a moment and then glanced away, thinking and remembering.

Mateo Mendez, though relatively young, had been the Merchant's top lieutenant for three years. Mateo remembered other individuals he had found for Pablo during that time. He had been present for the last breaths of several. Now, in the quiet of night, as he dropped off to sleep, Mateo often heard the screams of a few. Some had been lucky and died quickly. Others had not. Those were the ones he could not forget.

Mateo had been taken off the streets of Mexico City by Pablo when he was nine. That was nineteen years ago. Mateo was on his own even then, with no family he remembered, a boy of the streets. Like many others, he didn't even have a real name.

Thinking of his past, Mateo walked over to the bar and asked for a Corona, all the while glancing occasionally at his mentor. Pablo had given him the name Mateo after Pablo's own father. In those early days, the boys he ran with had called him Un Perrito, a little dog. No one dared call him that now.

Sipping the beer and enjoying its bitter flavor, he thought about those days. Circumstances had been cruel and demeaning on the streets. Mateo had no memory of ever doing childhood things. Play, other than an occasional pick-up game of soccer, had not been a part of his life. Each new day had required finding ways to live: something to eat, rags to wear, and fulfilling every other need he had. Even at the age of nine, Mateo had done whatever he needed to do. Life was cruel for the young ones who had no home.

He pulled a chair to a patch of shade, all the while remembering those years. On the evening Pablo found him, an older boy, about fifteen, had taken it upon himself to humiliate and torture Un Perrito. The boy, drugged out and drunk, had beaten Mateo with his fists and then with a heavy stick until Mateo lost consciousness. When he came to, Mateo had been stripped of his clothes and tied to a rail fence near a main road. Even now, as Mateo gripped his bottle of Corona tightly, his face warmed as he remembered the shame he had felt that night. He had later vowed never to feel that way again and had kept that promise to himself.

With Mateo tied to the fence, the older boy then persuaded other street kids, both boys and girls, to do terrible things to him. One, a fifteen-year-old girl, took inordinate sexual pleasure in touching and teasing him with her fingers, then striking out, drawing blood several times.

Finally, having endured the misery for a half hour, Mateo mentally moved past the pain and indignities to focus on his hatred for his tormentor. He even warned the boy, "You should kill me now, you turd. If you don't, I will come for you."

The boy laughed and then viciously struck Mateo's privates one more time with the big stick. As a last insult, the fifteen-year-old then pissed on him before walking away.

Un Perrito watched the boy go with eyes as cold as the steel rails in the fence at his back.

*I know where you sleep,* Mateo thought.

Time passed—Mateo didn't know how long. Hot with fever, he felt like he was dreaming.

Several hours later, a car stopped and a man got out. Mateo was barely aware of him. The man walked over to where Mateo was hanging, bound to the fence. He felt his head being tilted back. Through his swollen eyes, Mateo stared up at the man with every ounce of contempt a humiliated and beaten nine-year-old could muster. Waiting, even longing for death, the boy expected the man to finish what the fifteen-year-old had started.

"Roberto," the man called back to his driver. "Bring a pair of coveralls from the trunk." Moments later, the driver came running with the clothing in his hand. The man produced a knife and cut the cords holding Mateo. Then his rescuer and the driver helped Mateo into the oversized clothes, rolling the arms and legs to fit. When they finished, the man ushered the child toward the car.

"Come with me," he said. "I will make sure this never happens to you again."

Mateo looked at him for a long moment. He was aware older men sometimes took boys to use them for sex. But, he thought, anything would be better than what he had been through.

"I have to do something first," he said.

"What?" the man asked as he locked eyes with the youngster.

Mateo sensed he could tell the truth. "I have to kill someone."

"The person who did this to you?"

"Si."

"Get in the car," the man said. "I will take you to him."

Mateo sat in the front passenger seat while his rescuer sat in the back of the car, quietly listening as Mateo gave directions.

When Mateo motioned to pull over, the man in the backseat asked, "Do you want me to come with you?"

Mateo shook his head and climbed out of the car.

The back window opened, and the man said, "You have ten minutes. After that we will leave you. Do you understand?"

Mateo nodded. He had no idea how long ten minutes was.

The man's knife was pulled from his pocket again. Wiping his own fingerprints off, the man passed the knife out the window. Mateo watched, then took the weapon and walked into the darkness. Glancing back, he saw the driver get out and stand beside the car, his big right hand inside his jacket.

Mateo went off into the gloom and found the fifteen-year-old who had tortured him. He was where Mateo expected and sleeping soundly. By the time he awoke, it was too late to run or to defend himself.

When Mateo was finished, the boy would never sleep there again—or anywhere else for that matter. Before Mateo's torturer lost consciousness, the nine-year-old caused him to rue the day he came to know Un Perrito and certainly to wish he had never removed the child's clothing or touched his private parts.

Mateo thought it ironic because, as Pablo was inclined to do, he had made sure the teenager's last breaths had not come easily.

Mateo remembered how he had felt that night. He hadn't cried or become emotional in any way. He hadn't enjoyed what he had done to his tormentor, but he wasn't repulsed by it either. In his mind that night, the actions had been necessary. Now, nineteen years later, that's how he handled things for Pablo—composed, direct, and without emotions.

Mateo hadn't rushed back to the car and the two men. He hadn't cared whether they were waiting for him or not. He hadn't worried about anything after he had killed his enemy.

But, Mateo remembered, the Merchant had cared. And Pablo loved to tell his version of what had happened that evening. According to Pablo, he and his driver had waited—six minutes, eight, then ten. Still they had remained where the boy had left them.

Pablo said he finally looked at his watch—twelve minutes. In telling what happened, he would laugh and say he had motioned to Roberto, saying, "Let's get out of—"

And at that moment, according to Pablo, "The boy came walking out of the dark and past us, opened the front door of the automobile, and climbed in. We got in, and Roberto started the engine and pulled onto the street.

"Without looking back," Pablo always embellished this part, "Mateo told me, 'I'll buy you a new knife.'"

There was always pride in Pablo's voice when he told that part of the story.

Mateo's memories included how he had changed that night. Thinking back, he remembered very few events that had brought joy in life before that incident and even less afterward. After that evening—after he had murdered his young tormentor—he seemed to have lost all emotions. Right and wrong were no longer concepts he considered; he only questioned whether a thing needed to be done. His dealings with others were now based solely on the requirements of his duties or on Mateo's personal needs. Sentiment was not involved in his decisions in any way.

Mateo stood up, draining the last of his beer as he glanced over at Pablo. That was how he had met the Merchant. Pablo had taken him into his home in Vera Cruz and treated him as his own son. The Merchant had given him a name and an identity. He had also sent him to school, even to college in the United States.

And three years ago, Pablo had made Mateo his top man. When he needed something accomplished and wanted to be sure it would get done as he directed, the Merchant sent him. Mateo seldom disappointed Pablo. Lacking emotions, Mateo considered himself to be like a dangerous animal, a pit bull perhaps, with only one master—Pablo Perez, the Merchant.

 **Chapter 4**

Mateo nodded to the Merchant across the pool as he set his empty bottle on the bar and headed into the house. Inside his quarters, Mateo called and made reservations to fly to New Orleans.

He didn't look forward to the trip. Mateo dreaded dealing with the kind of people required to get the information he needed. He would have preferred making telephone calls, but you couldn't put cash into people's hands over the phone.

He packed enough clothes for several days, then went downstairs and had one of the drivers take him to the airport.

Arriving in New Orleans late at night, Mateo hailed a taxi and instructed the driver to take him to any large hotel near the downtown area. The driver dropped him and his bags off at the entrance to a Comfort Inn & Suites located at the edge of the French Quarter.

Carrying his bags, Mateo made his way into the lobby where several people waited in line at the reservations desk. Mateo waited patiently for his turn. He registered and paid using the name Carlos Merro, for which he had a New York state driver's license and credit cards. Once again, he gathered up his bags and went upstairs to his room.

After unpacking and putting his things away, Mateo checked the news while relaxing for a few minutes. His window afforded a view of the French Quarter and its late evening party crowd. He shook his head and smiled, knowing he would not want to be among them with all he had planned for tomorrow.

Finally, he took a shower and slipped into bed. A last act of the evening was to leave a wake-up call for seven o'clock the next morning. Asleep by the time his head hit the pillow, he continued that way for the few hours available.

Showered, shaved, and dressed, Mateo walked into the hotel's restaurant for breakfast at seven thirty the next morning. The wake-up call had gone unanswered.

Back in his room after toast and two cups of coffee, Mateo phoned Hertz for a car rental and requested a vehicle, telling them to deliver it to the hotel. The car would be there in thirty minutes, they told him. He flipped on the news and waited for a call.

The phone book gave him the location of the nearest library. When his rented

Volvo arrived, he drove to the location. Inside, he chased down copies of local newspapers and looked for a current issue and those for the last couple of weeks. It was easy to pick out articles relating to the shooting that had involved Mike Webster.

The first ones he found mentioned a shooting involving federal marshals. Two people had died on the scene, and two others had been critically wounded.

Most of the other articles seemed to center around the local government. The city's police superintendent had been arrested, and the mayor of New Orleans was being forced to resign. Commentary indicated the superintendent had quietly headed up an organization that owned a number of legitimate businesses funded by drug imports from South and Central America. The superintendent had stayed in the shadows for years until a woman, Cary Warren, had come to New Orleans looking for her biological parents.

From the sketchy information given, Mike Webster had helped her and then been shot when the Feds closed in. There wasn't much on him. It was almost as though the reporter had wanted to leave him out of the story. Overall, according to the newspapers, Pablo's information had been exact.

Among the numerous articles that gave basic information, the newspapers said Mike Webster had died from his injuries while in intensive care at Louisiana State University's Medical Center.

Mateo checked the obituaries for a couple of days following the shooting and found a short write-up for Webster. It gave his age as thirty-one and said he had lived and worked in Knoxville, Tennessee. There was no family mentioned, and there would be no funeral, according to the article. The obituary spoke of a memorial service to be announced at a future date and stated that Webster's ashes would be scattered over the Smokey Mountains where he had enjoyed hiking. Mateo made copies of several articles and the obituary. Pablo would want to read them.

Determined to leave no loose ends, especially where they concerned the Merchant, Mateo went to LSU Medical Center's emergency room records office. He wanted a copy of Webster's death certificate.

Bad news—a clerk with the medical center filled him in on the details. "You'll have to go to the funeral home to get a death certificate," she said. "We don't issue them here." Strange, but Mateo didn't argue.

He checked a phone book and wrote down the address. On arrival, he entered and found the office. Everything was quiet, with only two of the parlors in use. Since it was nearly noon, he waited until just past the hour to enter. The young secretary was alone, which was exactly what Mateo wanted.

"Hello," he said and flashed his best smile. "I need your help," Mateo said in a soft Latin voice, "and I'm desperate."

The woman appeared suspicious but continued listening. "I'm not sure—"

He cut her off. "It's nothing illegal, and I don't think it will get you in trouble."

She smiled, obviously interested, and asked what she could do for him.

"I don't have much time, and I need a copy of a death certificate. I'm scheduled to fly out of the country in a few hours," he said, "and I need to take the certificate with me." He added, "I'll pay for any charges, of course, and if you help me hurry it up, it will be just between us."

He could tell by her big eyes and questioning expression that she was seeing an opportunity. She needed something.

"You might be an angel in disguise," she told him. "My car quit yesterday, and the mechanic said it would be expensive to fix."

"How expensive?"

"Nearly four hundred dollars," she told him with a questioning grimace on her face.

He had planned to offer three hundred.

"I think we can work this out," Mateo told her with a smile.

"Really?" She shuddered with excitement.

"How fast can you get it for me?"

"Do you need an original?"

"A copy would be fine—even a fax copy."

"Give me the information," she said with a giggle, "then go down to our refreshments room and have a cup of coffee. I'll probably have a fax before you get back."

Mateo gave her Webster's information and headed for the refreshments room and coffee. I could use a cup, he thought.

Fifteen minutes later, he walked back into the office. The woman handed him an envelope. Mateo peeled off four fresh one hundred-dollar bills from the roll in his pocket, handed them to her, and said, "A pleasure doing business with you. Thanks."

"No, thank you! You don't know it, but you saved my life," she said. "If your plans change and you don't have to leave town, call me." She handed him a card. "I'm Marty, and I'm off at five." She smiled then. "I've written my home number on the card … just in case." Now she giggled and leaned over the desk to shake his hand, displaying her very ample cleavage.

Mateo got the picture along with the view.

"I'll do that," he said and then headed for his vehicle. He dropped her card in his briefcase. She might serve a personal use to him at some other time. For now, there were several other things to carry out before he flew back to report to Pablo.

Mateo drove out to LSU's Medical Center for the second time that day. This time he went directly to the emergency room waiting area and sat down where he could watch the staff. Two men walked outside a few minutes later. They were wearing scrubs but definitely were not doctors. They were obviously headed for a break and maybe a smoke. Mateo gave them time to light up and then followed. These men were down the food chain a few notches. He had worked with people like them before and knew they were often open to earning some easy extra money.

"Que pasa?" Mateo said in greeting. "What's happening? How're you fellows doing?"

"Okay, man," they said, almost in unison. They watched him cautiously as he lingered there. One was African American and fairly short, maybe a hundred and thirty pounds—thin as a rail. The other looked Hispanic, like Mateo, and was taller, six feet or so, and stocky.

"I'm looking for some information," Mateo said. "I thought it might be faster if I could get around official channels."

Making sure he wasn't being watched, he pulled the roll of money from his pocket and peeled off a couple of twenties. Mateo handed one to each of them. Glancing around, they palmed the money.

The black man answered for both. "Maybe we can help you," he said. "Things haven't been so good here lately. They been cuttin' our hours." The Spanish one nodded.

"What do you need?"

As the men watched him put the roll of bills back into his pocket, Mateo said, "There's more where that came from." Smiles all around. They were ready to do what he wanted.

"A few days ago, a gunshot victim was brought in here," he explained. "Last name was Webster. He was wounded when the federal marshals arrested the police superintendent."

"Big Eddie?" the Spanish man asked as his eyes grew large.

"Yeah, Big Eddie," Mateo said. One of the articles had called the superintendent "Big Eddie."

"I need to know what happened to this Webster fellow. Did he die? Did he get well? Is he still here? Whatever you can dig up."

Mateo stared back and forth between them. "Is this something you can make happen?"

The men glanced at each other, and the black man gave his friend an almost imperceptible nod. "You got somewhere we can reach you, maybe a cell phone?" the thin man asked. "Like in a couple o' hours," he added.

Mateo gave them his cell number. They headed back inside, and Mateo went to get something to eat. If there was any information available, they'd find it. Their names, they told him, were Willie and Carlo.


An hour later, Mateo's phone rang.

"This is Willie." Mateo recognized the voice. Willie then asked, "Where are you?"

"Having a sandwich at the Dairy Queen down from the hospital."

"We'll be there in a couple o' minutes."

A few minutes later, Mateo saw the men park and watched as they came inside.

"You want something to eat?"

"No, man. Don't have the time. We jus' takin' a break."

"Another break," Carlo said grinning.

"Did you find anything?"

Willie did the talking, and Carlo handled the nodding. "Yeah. Your man died right after surgery. They couldn't save him accordin' to what we found. Records showed they took him down for an autopsy right after they pronounced him dead."

"Is that unusual?" Mateo's attention peaked.

"Nah … well, sorta'. Usually it don't happen that fast. But it's not really that big a deal. I guess they just' wanted to get it done because of the deal with Big Eddie and the mayor and all."

"Anything else?"

"That's pretty much everythin'," Willie said. Then he appeared to think of something else. "You never know how it's gonna turn out. One of the med techs told me another guy came in at about the same time as this Webster fella. The man in charge of Webster was watchin' out for this other guy, too. Accordin' to the charts, he got shot in the stomach like your man, but he pulled through. After a few days, this other guy got transferred out. Michaels was his name, I think. Anyway, he survived, and they flew him to some place up north. Guess it's who you know."

"I guess," Mateo said, wondering but not attaching too much importance to Willie's new story. He reached into his pocket and pulled two hundred dollars out for the men, a bill for each. They watched, appearing disappointed.

Carlo said, "Hey, man. We sorta put ourselves on the line to get this stuff for you. Maybe it could be worth a little more than a bill. Looks like you can afford it." Carlo motioned toward Mateo's pocket. "You got it," he whined. "We don't!"

After considering, Mateo retrieved four more bills from his pocket, handing a total of three hundred to each of the men. There were big smiles now—from both of them! Keep them happy, he thought. It's Pablo's money.

They were elated. "Thanks, man," Willie said. "That makes this break real worthwhile."

They got up and headed for their car with a wave. On the way out, Willie told him, "You need anythin' else, you get in touch with Willie and Carlo. We'll take care of you."

Mateo watched them drive away before he went out to the Volvo. Now he had some traveling to do.

He still had to visit Cary Warren in Tennessee.

# Chapter 5

Jack Robbins popped his head through the doorway a few minutes after ten in the morning.

"Well, hello," he said in greeting.

Recognizing Jack's voice, Webster looked up from his book. Dressed in dark slacks, a button-down shirt, and power tie, his friend appeared ready to attend a business conference. His brown sport coat added a touch of class. There was no sign of the big Glock .45 caliber Webster knew Robbins was carrying in a shoulder holster under the coat. Webster smiled when his friend brushed back the lock of blond hair that was always falling down over Robbins's eye. It was a running joke in the squad that he always needed a haircut.

"Hey, Chief. You lost?"

Robbins walked over to the bed where the two shook hands.

"How are you doing, buddy?" Robbins asked.

"Better this morning, except for a headache. I finally got a good night's rest. They let me have a sleeping pill last night, and it kicked my butt."

"Do they have you up and moving yet?"

"My doctor said they'd be doing that later today. I think they want the nurse who was with me last night here for that operation."

"Why a particular nurse?" Robbins asked.

"If you saw this one, you wouldn't ask." Webster grinned as he held his hand as high as he could. "Six two or six three and sturdy—real sturdy. I won't have to worry about falling. Oh, and his name's Bob."

Robbins thought about it for a second and then said, "Now I understand. Someone who can keep you straight."

"Now you're getting the picture. Oh yeah, and where were you guys when I was getting shot?"

"Long story short? We came as soon as Big Eddie Breunoux showed up. I heard the shot as we were rolling in."

"Funny thing," Webster said looking at Robbins, "I don't remember hearing the shot. I do remember winking at Cary Warren." Embarrassed, he could feel his face turning red. "That's the last thing I recall until I came to on the flight up here. Bob told me this place is somewhere outside Charlotte. What is this facility anyway?"

Robbins hesitated. "It's owned by a private company," he said. "I can't say who owns the company."

"Oh, I see. Enough said, I guess."

"Yeah, we ought to leave it at that," Robbins agreed. Then he added, "You understand—need to know and all that."

"What's in store for me?" Webster asked. "I guess I've lost my job at Trebeck Corporation."

"Yep. I'm sure they're mourning Mike Webster's untimely demise." Then he added, "The people you met in New Orleans are, too."

"What's the story on Cary Warren? Is she okay?" Webster asked, a smile leaving his face. Robbins listened as Webster went on about Cary.

"She's quite a lady, you know. Someone I could have built a life with." Then he added, "I don't know if I've ever met anyone with more persistence. She was really determined to find her mother's killer."

"I got the impression," Robbins said, "that she liked you, too, and maybe even more than a lot."

Webster tugged at his sheets as he quietly stared out the window. Robbins didn't interrupt his thoughts for several moments. Then he reminded, "You can't go back there, you know. Not if we're going to keep you in the shadows."

"I know," Webster said, letting his words trail off as he continued to look out the window. "I wish I could just let her know I'm okay. At least, I think I do. I wish we could have given the relationship a chance." There had been other women in his life—but not like Cary. Maybe he could go back there someday.

Robbins continued, drawing Webster's attention back to the present, "When the people here think you're up to it, they have another place for you. They'll tell you about it when it's time."

Webster wondered if his friend meant here as in Charlotte or here as in the medical facility. He knew he would find out in due time. For now, that would be enough.

"What's my future?" Webster asked gazing at Robbins. "Will you be finding another spot for me, something like the one at Trebeck Corporation?"

Robbins walked around and dropped into a chair. "Let me throw the question back to you," he said. "If we could offer you a job with the Marshals Service, would you be interested? We'd look for assignments we felt would keep you away from the people who are looking for you."

Webster considered the possibility. "Maybe, but I'm tired of being shot at … and hit, too," he added with emphasis. "This is the second time."

"I know," Robbins said. He reached over and touched Webster lightly on the shoulder with his fist. Webster smiled at his friend. He knew the risk involved without his friend having to say it.

Jack then said, "I'm really concerned, Mike. We think it's the Merchant who's looking for you. And Perez won't give up easily. You know that."

"Yeah, I do." Webster hoped his deep concern didn't show too much.

Robbins stood up. "I'm going to have to leave you. My plane is waiting."

"Where are you headed?"

"You didn't hear this from me, okay?" He grinned and lowered his voice as he glanced at the door. "I'm headed into DC for a meeting, another shake-up. You know how it is. After the meeting, I am going home to Leesburg. I have some time-off coming."

Webster nodded.

Jack stood up and reached over to shake hands. "I'll see you in a few days. You can reach me by cell in the meantime. Oh, by the way, your laptop and some other things are in the closet. I picked up your stuff from the place you and Cary were staying. Landie Kato's house, right?"

"Right," Webster said. "I hope they're all okay."

"They are," Robbins assured him. "Be seeing you," he said as he walked to the door, waved, and turned down the hallway.

Webster spent the next few minutes considering his circumstances. Obviously, they couldn't be worse at the moment. He could hardly move because of the wound, and Webster doubted whether he was thinking very clearly either. Not a good combination if the wrong people found him. Reasonably, he had a few weeks, at best. Tomorrow really would be the first day of the rest of his life. How long that life would be was up to him.

Webster returned to his book and read a few pages before succumbing to a nap. He realized he still had a lot of chemicals floating around in his system.

He awoke to a soft touch on his arm. Dr. Dunn was checking his pulse.

"Are you going to sleep all day?" she asked.

"Hi!" Webster glanced around the room then pushed himself up in the bed. He realized he had sounded surprised. He thought he had only closed his eyes for a moment.

"I see you're catching up on your sleep," she said. "That's a good thing. I came to see you early this morning, but you were wiped out. I checked your chart. Everyone said you're fine, so I let you snooze."

"You should have awakened me," he told her. "I think I'm probably napping more than I should. Now I'll probably be reading all night."

"Then we should try to find you some more books," she said. "Seriously, for the time being, you should sleep when you can and as much as you can. You will get back on a regular routine when your body is ready. Till then, enjoy reading and sleeping."

She reached for his chart. "Looks like everything is settling down," she told him.

The nurses had checked on him several times that morning: probing, pumping, and measuring, even weighing him once. He figured she had plenty of data to make the call.

"When can I be up and around?" he asked.

"This afternoon, I think. Tiny will get you up when he begins his shift."

"He doesn't like that name, you know."

"Tiny?" She looked surprised. "I assumed he was fine with it." She thought for a moment and then said, "Actually, come to think of it, I had never given it any thought at all." She frowned. "How stupid of me. Of course, he wouldn't like it. I wouldn't either." Dr. Dunn was obviously uncomfortable with what she considered to be a slip on her part.

"I don't think he would want you to be embarrassed," Webster said. "In fact, I probably shouldn't have told you."

"I'm glad you did. I like to treat people the way I would want them to treat me. Under the same circumstances, I wouldn't like the nickname either." She looked at Webster. "What does he want to be called?"

"Bob."

"Thanks for telling me," she said. "Now, here's what we have planned for you. Up and around this afternoon with Bob. After we get you walking and you're comfortable with that, we'll add some exercise. We'll start that in a couple of days. There's a gym and a physical therapist on site. I will have you work with her for a few sessions and then see where we go. You will like the therapist. She's very sweet and gentle."

Something about the way she looked at him when she described the therapist made him wonder, but he went along with her.

"Sounds good," he said. "I bet the soreness will ease off pretty fast once I start exercising."

She nodded in agreement. "See you later."

After the door closed, he tried to do a sit-up in bed. It did not go well.

# Chapter 6

They called it physical therapy, but that did not matter. Webster realized any exercise, at least in his condition, was physical torture. Whatever it was called, it hurt like hell.

He and the PT, Joanne, had made it to the middle of the second week. Now he was on a mat with her, and she was using every dirty trick in the book to make him suffer. To begin with, he thought she had been hired from a women's wrestling team. Webster kept this thought to himself. His new friend had some blame here, too. Bob had callously brought him in and turned this woman loose on him. Dr. Dunn was not blameless either. "Sweet and gentle"—right!

Damn, that last twist hurt. Webster was pretty sure something had torn loose. If not, he was in worse shape than he thought.

Joanne appeared to really enjoy her work. That bothered him. She smiled a lot while she was asking him to do things that hurt. He even thought he heard her chuckle once. The more he groaned and said it hurt, the more she smiled as she encouraged him to commit this sadistic form of suicide. He finally decided she just hated men and had found hurting them to be her calling in life. She really did appear to be fond of her work.

"Come on, candy ass. You can do five more." Webster had already done fifteen sit-ups. Sweat was popping out in places where he didn't even know he had sweat glands. What next? Three-hundred-pound bench presses?

"You want to rest for a minute, sweetie pie?" she asked.

Now it was sweetie pie. Webster wasn't quite sure where the names were coming from. Bob was nearby, barely suppressing his amusement.

"Why don't you go get a cup of coffee," he said to Bob, "and come back in hmm.... about a week?"

The big nurse erupted in laughter and walked out into the hallway. Webster could hear him laughing even after the door swung shut. Webster decided he had missed the funny part.

The doctor came in as they were finishing a session later in the week.

"Hi," she said to Webster. And then she turned to Joanne. "How's he doing?"

"As good as I would expect, considering," Joanne told the doctor. "And for a candy ass," she added.

Dr. Dunn looked over at Webster and winked. "I'm glad to see him getting started," she said and picked up his file. It followed him everywhere.

Bob returned and helped Webster into a wheelchair. That should have been their clue right there. A man who shows up in a wheelchair shouldn't have to do this crap, right?

Dr. Dunn carried the chart and walked with them back to Webster's room. Bob stood by as Webster showed he was capable of getting himself out of the chair and into his own bed. It hurt like hell, but he did it. He really was getting better.

"I'm impressed," Dr. Dunn said.

She did not comment about the sweat on his forehead and upper lip. If she had, he was going to say, "It's hot in here." But she didn't.

"I think you're ready to move it up a notch," she said when they were alone.

"I hope you have something in mind that doesn't involve Joanne."

Irene laughed. "What I had in mind is a long walk tomorrow for you and Bob."

"Ahh."

"I don't think you're ready for a second round of PT each day, do you?"

"Chances are, Joanne or I would kill the other."

"I agree, but a walk might be soothing," she said, a sympathetic look in her eyes. "Remember, you have a gunshot wound."

"That's not difficult to keep in mind."

"Seriously," she said, "you are coming along nicely. Your body's healing, and I can tell the soreness is easing off. We'll step things up slowly, but I think you'll do fine and be out of here before you know it."

Webster drifted into his own thoughts. There was a lot the doctor did not know. No one knew about the sit-ups and push-ups Webster was doing after the lights were turned off each night. He had started slowly but was doing sets of twenty-five sit-ups and ten push-ups at a time, a hundred of each every night. He was also running in place, twice each night, fifteen minutes each time. Webster had his own agenda. After all, it was his life on the line.

Webster considered his work with the PT to be icing on the cake. The exercises Joanne had him doing were painful and made him sore, but he could easily do them. Obviously, they were good for him. He would keep up the palaver for Joanne's benefit.

The underlying purpose of everything was always there—the Merchant could show up at any time.

When he glanced back, Dr. Dunn was watching him, perhaps trying to read his thoughts. He had questions, too.

"Speaking of getting out of here, I get the impression you'll be watching over me even after I leave this facility. Where will I be going?"

"That is a surprise," she said. "We'll tell you when it's time."

"Will I see you again today?" he asked.

"Nope." she smiled. "I have a rare afternoon off. I will not be back till morning. Bob and the others can take care of you in my absence."

"That's not what I was thinking about," he told her. Webster enjoyed their conversations. He hoped she didn't consider them to be more than they were.

Then, changing the subject, "Do you think it would be okay for me to go outside?" He motioned toward the wheelchair. No one was aware he didn't need it anymore.

"Do you need some help?"

Webster noticed she didn't ask if he needed someone to push him.

"I can do it. I'd just like to get out in the sun."

"Okay then, but be careful." She turned and headed out.

"Thanks for all you're doing," he said.

At the doorway, she turned and looked back. He could swear there were tears in her eyes. Her voice was soft when she said, "I'll see you in the morning."

Bob showed up a few minutes later. "Doctor-patient things almost never work out, you know?" He said it like he knew something.

"What … things?" Webster asked, genuinely surprised.

"You know, candy ass. Boy-girl things. She likes you."

Webster could feel his eyes widen, surprise on his face. "Huh?"

Bob shook his head slowly, disbelieving. "Dr. Dunn doesn't watch over everyone like this. She's made you a special project."

"No!" Webster said dolefully.

"Wait and see," Bob told him. Then changing the subject, "She's got us scheduled for a three-mile walk in the morning. You want to go before or after breakfast? Your choice."

"Before." She had mentioned a long walk, but a full-fledged hike was not what Webster had envisioned. And three miles? He was already dreading it.

"Before is good for me, too." Bob was already leaving. "See you later."

Webster watched him go and then he hit the floor. Might as well get some work done before I go outside. If Perez and his people were coming for him, Webster wanted to be ready.

He stretched out on his back, hands behind his head. "One, two, three …"

# Chapter 7

Cary Warren had not fared well since she returned home to Knoxville. She was having more trouble controlling her emotions than she had expected.

At work, friends treated her with deference, but it seemed the smallest things would set her off. A question about New Orleans, passing Webster's office, or something reminding her of him, and she would feel her throat tighten. Obviously, he had become more to her than even she had realized. At every opportunity Rita tried to take Cary's mind off New Orleans, but that was difficult.

"I really thought we could have had something," she had told Rita just the night before. "Webster was the best man I've ever met. He was special." She had still not told Rita about his background.

Cary thought of him constantly. She could close her eyes and feel the kiss they had shared in the French Quarter. Even amid the danger and conflict, that kiss had been meaningful for both. She had thought it was the beginning of something special—not the end. The shot that brought him down came just hours later.

She still could not believe all that had happened because of her search. Lives had been altered as she and Webster had tried to find the cause and circumstances of her birth mother's death.

Many people, her biological father included, had deserved what had happened. Yet she felt a little sorry for him. Even now, she found it difficult to think of Mayor Johnny Peroit as her father—but he was. Cary remembered how miserable he had looked as he walked away from her in the New Orleans Airport.

In the following days, Peroit had dropped out of consideration for the vice president's slot and resigned as mayor of New Orleans. Everything he had worked for was lost.

Cary had read in the newspaper that his wife and family had stayed with him. Many of their friends had remained steadfast, too. Those were good things. She admired those around him, and their loyalty spoke volumes about Peroit. Maybe there was good in him after all.

On the positive side, Cary expected management at Trebeck Corporation to offer her Webster's job. He wouldn't be returning, so that would be the logical step for them.

The kicker—she wasn't sure she would accept. Things were not the same there without him.

~ ~ ~

Mateo walked through the Atlanta airport to the rental car counters. He didn't want a paper trail showing him going to Knoxville in case problems should occur during his visit. He passed Hertz up this time.

Twenty minutes later, he was in another Volvo and checking a map for the best way north to Tennessee. I-75 would get him there. Satisfied, he headed out.

Traffic was light, and a short time later Mateo was out of the city and on his way to Knoxville. He would get some extended rest after he located Cary Warren tomorrow, but tonight he would concentrate on driving. A few hours later, he checked into a west Knoxville hotel.

Deciding against a wake-up call, Mateo slept until just after eight the next morning. Showered and dressed, he went downstairs for breakfast. While eating, he planned the day, deciding to visit Trebeck Corporation where Mike Webster had worked. He would go there on the premise of being an acquaintance of Webster's. By physically being at his old office, Mateo could judge how his colleagues were reacting to his death.

At midmorning, Mateo walked into Trebeck Corporation. He approached the reception counter and waited for a middle-aged woman to get off the phone.

"I'm looking for Mike Webster," he told her when she was finished. Using the same identity he had in New Orleans, Mateo said, "I'm Carlos Merro. Mike and I knew each other in Denver."

The woman appeared shaken and said, "Mr. Webster is no longer with us. Let me get Rita Ammons for you. She is filling in for Mr. Webster on a temporary basis. Please wait there." She motioned toward a seating alcove nearby. "I'll page Ms. Ammons."

Minutes later, a fashionably dressed woman walked over to Mateo and shook hands.

"Mr. Merro, I understand you're looking for Mike Webster." She sat in one of the chairs next to Mateo and motioned for him to sit, too. "I understand you were a friend of Mr. Webster's," she said when they were settled. "I have some news for you. Mike died a few days ago."

Feigning surprise, Mateo blurted, "What?" He held out his hands, appearing shaken. "Mike Webster? Dead … how … where?"

"He was shot … in New Orleans."

"Dios mio." Mateo rubbed a hand across his face. "I am in town on business and thought I would take him out for lunch. I'm … so sorry."

"You had no way of knowing," The woman said.

"Did they get the person who shot him?" Mateo asked.

"Oh, yes. They were arrested." She didn't elaborate.

"Where is he buried?" Mateo asked. "I'll send some flowers for his grave." A test for her.

"There's no grave," she told him. "His body was cremated and his ashes scattered over the mountains." That agreed with the New Orleans newspaper.

"Oh … well … thank you." He turned to go and then, as an afterthought, asked, "Was Webster alone when he was shot?"

The woman raised an eyebrow as she searched his face. He should not have asked the question.

After a moment, she answered anyway. "No, he was with a friend who works here at Trebeck. They were together when it happened."

"Oh." He hesitated and then asked, "Do you think I could speak with the friend? Maybe there's some way I could help."

"I doubt it," she told him, but something made her change her mind. "I suppose it couldn't hurt," she said. "Come on."


Cary Warren was on the phone when they reached her office; she waved to Rita and the man with her to come in and take a chair. Finishing her conversation, she turned her attention to the visitors. Rita introduced Merro.

They shook hands and then Rita explained, "Mr. Merro told me he and Mike were acquaintances in Denver some time ago. He hadn't heard about Webster and came by to visit and have lunch." She paused a moment before continuing, "I told him what happened."

"I was sorry to hear about Mike. He was a nice person." The man appeared sympathetic. "Since you were together when Mike was killed, I felt I should ask if there is anything I can do."

"No, nothing," Cary said, her eyes moist. "Everything has been handled."

"Then I will be on my way." He shook hands with both of them.

They said good-bye, and Merro told the women he could find his way back to the entrance.


After the man left and Rita had gone back to her own office, Cary considered the visit. Webster had never mentioned Merro, or Colorado for that matter; Cary was sure of that. He had never talked about Denver either. She had a gut feeling something was not right about Merro's visit. But what to do about it? That was the question.

Then the phone rang, startling Cary. It was the front desk.

"Miss Warren. The man who just left your office would like to speak with you. I'll put him on."

She did not have time to say no or even think about whether to talk with the man. Cary was trapped; like it or not, she would have to speak with Merro.

He immediately came on the line. "Carlos Merro, here, Miss Warren. I thought of something after I left you. I hope you don't mind."

"How can I help you, Mr. Merro?"

"Since we both knew Mike and it is almost noon, I wondered if you would go to lunch with me."

That does not make sense. Is he asking her out? Surely not!

Merro continued then, still not giving her time to consider, "We could discuss our friend. Maybe we would both learn something."

Now that was an interesting proposition. She made her decision.

"Yes, I'll go, but I have a deadline coming up." Then she thought, God is going to get you for lying! There really was nothing scheduled for the afternoon.

"I don't have much time, so let's go to the corporate restaurant here in the building."

"Ahh … okay." Now he sounded unsure of himself.

"I'll come and get you," she told him. "I'll be there in a couple of minutes." Now she would have an advantage.


Mateo had wanted to go someplace quiet; he doubted the company restaurant was it. He had questions and wanted to listen closely to her answers. He also wanted to watch her reactions to his questions. The company restaurant would be noisy, but he would have to make it work.

She tapped him on the shoulder then and smiled as he turned. Taller than him in her heels, Cary led Mateo to an elevator that they took down to the basement where they would be dining. The room was nicer than he had expected, and quieter, too. This would do, he thought.

As soon as they were seated, she asked, "When did you know Mike?"

Mateo took a moment unfolding his napkin. He needed time to think. He had not planned on questions from her.

"It has been a few years," he said, "and we only worked together for a brief time."

"Where?" Damn, she's quick!

"Denver," he said. "I lost track of Mike and then a mutual acquaintance recently told me Mike was working here at your company. I decided to drop by and say hello. That is when I learned he had been shot and killed." He had used the harsh words intentionally.

She glanced down, then back at him, a glimmer of tears in her eyes. Webster was probably dead—at least, she believed that.

"Who was the mutual friend?" she asked. "Perhaps it's someone I know, too."

"I doubt it," Mateo told her without elaborating. "A Denver woman told me."

He asked a few more questions while fashioning a couple of answers for her as they finished their salads. Then he paid for their lunches, said good-bye, and left Trebeck. Mateo was still not entirely sure Cary Warren thought Webster was dead, but he was ready to give the Merchant a report.

He returned to his vehicle and called Pablo. When the boss answered, Mateo relayed the news to him in Spanish.

"The friend we wanted to locate seems to have met with unfortunate circumstances," he told Perez. "Everything I have found backs up the information you received before you sent me here. I have made contacts in Louisiana and Tennessee. Everyone I spoke with agrees with the news you were given."

"Then come home, Mateo. We have reason to celebrate with a party. You will be the guest of honor."

"Thank you, Pablo," Mateo said. "You are most gracious. I will be there soon. I have one more thing I need to do."

"Hurry home," he heard Pablo say and then the phone went dead.

Mateo hoped he hadn't missed anything. This last thing he told Pablo he needed to do had come to mind as he left Cary Warren in the restaurant. He would have to stay in Knoxville an extra day, but he could answer a nagging question. He didn't think Miss Warren would even know.

Mateo hastily planned a couple of stops for the afternoon. The first was at a Lowe's Home Improvement store he had noticed earlier on his way to Trebeck Corporation. He had a visit in mind for the next morning and needed some special implements to open a door. The shopping didn't take long but was crucial; having the right tools for this job was a requirement.

Back in the Volvo, Mateo checked his watch and then pulled out a small notebook. He jotted down a list of items he would need for his visit the next morning to be successful. Then he settled back and relaxed to give his mind a few moments in case he had forgotten anything. Mateo then added two more items to the list, closed the notebook, and pulled out into traffic.

A few minutes before five, Mateo drove into Trebeck Corporation's parking lot and found a secluded location where he could keep an eye on the entrance. At five, the big front doors opened, and the secretaries and other clerical workers filed out of the building and headed for their vehicles.

Mateo adjusted his seat back a few inches and waited. From experience, he knew the higher echelon workers and bosses would be coming a few minutes after the first exodus. As if on cue, Mateo saw a couple of men in suits leave the building and then a few others. Then Cary Warren and the Ammons woman came out together and turned toward the area where he was parked. Mateo didn't expect them to notice him. He only hoped they were not going out for drinks or dinner.

After stopping to talk for a moment, the women waved to each other and then headed off toward their vehicles. Keeping an eye on both, Mateo started the Volvo and followed the Warren woman as she pulled out of the lot. Staying well back, he watched as her friend turned in another direction. Cary Warren moved through the afternoon traffic and, after a short drive, turned into a large living complex.

Not venturing too close, Mateo braked and watched as the woman's vehicle drove past three sets of buildings before taking a parking place. Even then, he didn't rush to her area. Instead, he waited for her to get out of the car and start toward her building.

Then slowly, he drove toward her. She didn't seem to be aware of him. She did not look his way or even glance back toward her own vehicle. She passed a set of stairs and then stopped at the first door she came to. Good, he thought. Easy to reach, easy to get out.

As Mateo looked on, an elderly man came out of the unit next to the Warren woman's. They appeared to say hello, then the man headed toward the parking lot. Mateo pulled into a visitor's slot and waited as the man drove away.

After a couple of minutes, Mateo backed out and drove to the street. He had what he needed; he knew where she lived and the kind of vehicle she drove. He would be there in the morning to watch her leave. He should then have ample time to check her apartment for any evidence that she had recently heard from Mike Webster.

There were only a couple of possible complications. One would be if someone saw him enter the apartment. He doubted that would happen because he planned to wait until the early rush was over. Anyone else? He would deal with them as necessary.

The second risk was if Cary Warren returned while he was there. Any number of possibilities could bring her back—forgotten papers, some purchase she needed to return—anything! Though unlikely, it could happen.

Mateo knew from experience that she could show up. He also knew that under no circumstances could she be allowed to discover him in the apartment. In that unlikely possibility, tomorrow would be the last day of the attractive young woman's life.

The parking lot at the complex was full when Mateo arrived. At 6:30 a.m. most everyone was still getting ready for work. He chose a different location to wait; one farther from her apartment but where he could still watch for her and see her vehicle, too.

An hour went by, then he eased up in his seat. Cary Warren had stepped out of her apartment and was locking the deadbolt. She turned to pick up a large briefcase and then headed for her car. The briefcase went in the backseat. Then she climbed in and started the vehicle. She glanced his way once and then proceeded out to the street. Others followed, and by eight o'clock the lot only had a dozen cars left in the area where he had parked.

A few people noticed Mateo, but he had prepared for that possibility. He was dressed in a suit and tie and had purchased a local newspaper. For the last hour, he had been holding it up to look like he was waiting for someone. Mateo had even nodded to several people. This could only become a liability if the Warren woman should return early and something unforeseen was required. Those outcomes could not always be avoided.

As he waited, Mateo visualized the woman whose apartment he was about to enter. He had been surprised at her understated allure when he met her the day before. Miss Warren did not seem aware of how stunning she was. She had been friendly, though guarded. He had enjoyed having lunch with her even as they talked about the shooting and her friend.

Surprised at his own thoughts, Mateo found himself wondering if she had made love to Mike Webster in New Orleans.

She had been gorgeous again that morning, even from a distance. He had gazed at her high cheekbones and the way her dark hair tossed about in the breeze. She had been dressed to the nines, too: a pale orange top over dark slacks and those heels. In them, Mateo remembered, she had been taller than him. Taller than most men, he expected.

He caught himself then. These thoughts were not productive. Back to the job at hand.

Glancing around, Mateo decided it was time to enter the apartment. He reached into the back floorboard and retrieved the plastic bag from Lowe's. Then he checked his pocket, making sure he had all the other necessities.

He waited five more minutes and then climbed out and walked to the building and her door. As he came close, Mateo pulled a pair of latex gloves from his pocket and slipped them on. Seconds later, he had several picks, tweezers, and files in his hands and had stooped to examine the deadbolt on her door.

Choosing a pick, he gently placed it in the lock and then used another to work the tumblers. Taking longer than he had expected, Mateo manipulated the lock, attempting to line it up for release.

With it almost ready to open, he heard someone inside the next apartment over, the one where the old man had been the afternoon before. Someone was coming out! The lock was still being contrary. Mateo gave it one more twist as the other door began to open.

Click! The lock surrendered—finally—and the door swung open. Mateo fell inside and carefully but quickly closed the door behind him.

There were some sounds outside, likely someone gathering things to carry. Finally, that someone walked by, heading toward the parking lot. It probably was the man he had noticed last night.

Mateo stood still for a few moments. As his heart rate returned to normal, he glanced around the room. Nice! It was tasteful, not cluttered—just nice.

Suddenly, a cat came sailing around a corner from the bedroom area. It yowled loudly when it saw him, skidded to a sweeping, scratching halt and headed back in the direction it had come from. It had surely expected Miss Warren. So much for a greeting to a visitor.

Still wearing the gloves, Mateo started his search. Drawers were opened and papers examined. Anything that could be from Webster was checked. The hunt went quickly but there were a lot of drawers and other places she could hide secrets.

As he worked, Mateo kept his senses tuned to sounds that might come from the front door. Being surprised now would not be acceptable. He really would hate to be forced to kill such a beautiful woman. Yet he would do it in a heartbeat if it became necessary. Discovery was not an option.

 **Chapter 8**

Cary didn't realize she had forgotten the dry-cleaning until she was at the office. She should have put the two pairs of slacks and the sweater on the bed when she was thinking about it. Planning to take things to the cleaners and actually doing it seemed to be two separate things lately. Oh well, there was tomorrow.

Upon opening her laptop, Cary discovered an e-mail from her attorney. He was reminding her of a meeting scheduled at eleven that day. There were still papers to sign dealing with her parent's estate. Would it never end? Then she remembered the dry cleaning; she could drop by and pick it up on the way to her attorney's office. And Sammy cat would be happy to see her.

As she prepared for the day's work, her thoughts kept easing back to the last several hours. Several times last night and this morning, Cary had thought about yesterday's visitor. In her mind, Carlos Merro had not appeared to be what he said. She wished she had gotten a business card or some other way of checking him out. Not that it would have served any reasonable purpose. Still, there should be something she could do.

Then it hit her. Cary opened a desk drawer and reached for a stack of cards she had kept from various individuals she had met over the last three years. She went through them occasionally, tossing out those that were no longer relevant. Some she kept. Cary shuffled through them.

There! She found the one she was searching for, picked up her phone, and dialed the private cell number written on the back. This was someone she had never called before. Cary had no idea if she would reach the Number Two man at the U.S. Marshals Service. It rang once.

"Jack Robbins."

"Jack, this is Cary Warren. Mike Webster's friend. … Do you remember me?"

"Of course, Cary. How are you?"

"I'm good, but something has come up. I thought you should know about it."

"Tell me." He was quick to the point.

Cary explained about Carlos Merro, leaving nothing out, including the fact that the visit might have meant absolutely nothing. She realized the man might really have known Webster.

Robbins assured Cary he would check it out and that she had been right in letting him know.

"Even though Webster was killed," he said, "we would love to get our hands on the people searching for him. These are very dangerous people."

Then he was quiet for a moment before adding a warning. "Cary, be careful. At this point, there is no reason to think this Carlos Merro is involved in anything. Still, keep your guard up. If anything, suspicious or worrisome comes up, call me. Okay?"

"All right!"

Cary felt better having let Robbins know about her suspicions. She shuddered at the thought that Merro could be one of the drug people. She had read stories of the terrible things they do to individuals they do not like. Cary was glad the man was no longer in Knoxville.

After making a couple of business calls, Cary grabbed her purse, left instructions with the secretary, and headed for her appointment. Oh yes, and to pick up the dry cleaning at her apartment.

~ ~ ~

The cat had disappeared after that first brief encounter. Mateo had expected it might run out from under something and scare the hell out of him. It hadn't. There was no sign of the feline.

The search progressed without complications. Other than some newspaper articles about the shooting and his death, there had been no sign of Mike Webster in any of her papers, or anywhere else for that matter—not even a treasure to remember him by. There was a small bottle of Cool Water men's cologne on her dressing table. That could have belonged to Webster, but there was no way to know. He set the container back where it had been—the exact location.

In most of the places Mateo searched, the owner never knew he had been there—unless there was a problem. Even then, if discovered, Mateo made sure the individual never disclosed the details.

He was almost finished when there was a disturbance outside the front of the apartment. Then came the distinct sound of a key in the lock. Someone was coming in. Got to hide!

Two steps and he was inside the closet. He left the door open. It had been that way when he entered the apartment. In almost complete silence, Mateo moved behind the woman's long coats and formal gowns at the back of the space. Careful of the boxes and shoes on the floor, he fit himself into the back corner. This was why Mateo never wore cologne and used unscented soap. He never wanted to risk detection or leave evidence behind.

He heard her call the cat a couple of times and guessed it had finally come out of its hiding place. Soon, he could tell she was in the bedroom and then at the closet. From the darkness of the back corner, he saw her push some things out of her way and remove a hanger or two. She must have taken them to the bed. Good, now she would be leaving.

Then she was back and in his area, actually taking a garment that was touching his cheek. There was no way she had not seen him. Yet she made no sign that she had.

He would give her a few seconds. If she did anything strange, he would kill her.

She took the item and left the closet. Was it possible she had not seen him? Mateo listened intently for any change in her demeanor. She was finishing whatever she had returned for. He heard soft footsteps on the carpet as she left the bedroom.

"Bye, Sammy."

The front door opened and closed. There was a sound of the key in the lock, and she was gone.

He waited a full five minutes before leaving the closet and venturing out into the bedroom. Moving as silently as possible, Mateo checked the apartment. There were three clothes hangers on the bed. The garments must have been what she was after. As he eased into the living room area, the cat looked up from a bowl of milk, saw him, and did another rapid takeoff; this time without the scream.

The Warren woman was gone, leaving no sign she had been there except the empty hangers. One final search in the bedroom netted Mateo her current diary. It was under the bed along with a small pen. He thumbed through it, finding several entries concerning Webster: her meeting him at Trebeck Corporation and then accounts of them together in New Orleans. There were also entries about the shooting and of Webster's death.

By the dates written there, all the information about New Orleans appeared to have been entered after she returned to Tennessee. There were several entries concerning her feelings for Webster; she had obviously been in love, and those emotions came out on the pages of the diary. There were stains, too. Tears, he guessed.

Nothing caused Mateo to suspect the Warren woman believed Webster was still alive. Indeed, everything he found showed the opposite.

He made one last turn around the apartment for anything he might have missed. The diary was back where he had found it. Nothing out of place was visible, so Mateo went to the door and listened. There was nothing of concern there either.

He glanced back into the room, a slight grin on his face. "Bye, Sammy."

Quietly, he opened the door, listened again, and then stepped out, leaving the regular lock engaged. There was nothing he could do about the deadbolt.

On the way to the car, Mateo removed the gloves and placed them in the bag with the tools. He would dispose of them somewhere on the way back to Georgia.

After climbing into the Volvo, Mateo took a moment to quiet his nerves. After a few deep breaths, he was ready to head for Atlanta and the airport. He found himself looking forward to the party the Merchant had mentioned on the phone.

As he pulled into the street, Mateo thought of the woman one last time. She was quite lovely. Killing her would have been a real shame!

~ ~ ~

Something bothered Cary on the way to the appointment with her attorney. At first, she couldn't put her finger on it. Then it finally came to her. She thought there had been a strange car in the parking lot at the apartments just now. Cary paid attention to that sort of thing. The same vehicle, or one like it, had been in the lot at Trebeck yesterday afternoon when she and Rita were leaving. And it had also been at the apartments when she left for work that morning. There had been someone in it then, a man, and he had been reading a newspaper. Though it had been some distance away, she was almost certain it was the same vehicle.

A shudder ran down her spine. Was someone watching her? Maybe Carlos Merro? Or was she searching for something to worry about?

The appointment only lasted a few minutes, a couple of signatures. Then she dropped the clothes off at the dry cleaners and decided to go back to the apartment for lunch; she would think about the mysterious vehicle then.

I'm hungry, she thought, as she pulled into her complex. She had made a gourmet chicken salad the night before, anticipating lunch at home one day during the week. She couldn't wait.

She checked for the strange vehicle as she parked hers. It was not there. Good! Everything was fine.

Cary had her keys out when she reached the door to the apartment. First, she unlocked the regular door lock, click, then the deadbolt. Huh? It felt open. But it could not be. She distinctly remembered locking it. She had transferred the clothes from one arm to the other to manipulate the lock. She had locked it.

She pushed, and the door opened. Damn! Now what? Maintenance, or … someone else.

Taking a step inside, Cary surveyed the room. There was nothing out of place. She went farther. Still okay!

"Sammy? Here, kitty."

He came but seemed nervous. Cary wished he could talk.

With some of the strain gone, she walked to the bedroom. Everything was in place except the hangers on the bed, but she had left those earlier. Cary peeked into the closet. Everything was good there, too. She could breathe again.

About the only other thing to check was her journal. She held up the bedspread and found the diary in its normal place, but it was placed wrong. It was facing up; she always put it face down—always. It was one of her OCD things.

Cary had written in the diary just last night, so someone had been in the apartment and moved it—Someone …

# Chapter 9

"Time to rise and shine." Bob was shaking Webster's bed at six the next morning.

"What?" Sleepily, Webster grumbled, "It can't be more than four o'clock."

"Yep, it's six o'clock and time for our walk. You wanted to go before breakfast. Here's a sweat suit," Bob said, tossing a package on the foot of the bed. "There's a pair of socks, too. Running shoes are over by your chair."

"I hope you mean walking shoes. Running would be cruel and unusual punishment. I don't think we want to go there, do we?"

"Not before tomorrow at the earliest."

Webster dressed and followed his friend outside. There was a walking track behind a stand of trees at the end of the building. Webster hadn't been able to see it from his window. He wondered what else he hadn't seen at this facility.

They started at an easy stroll, but Bob didn't walk slowly for long. Even with the extra work he'd been doing, Webster's breath was soon coming hard, and his upper body was feeling the new motion. They were getting farther from the medical building, too. The path wasn't some circular thing that led you back where you started. With each step, they were going deeper into the surrounding woods.

And Bob was talking, talking, talking. He was telling Webster about his little boy now.

"Robert is his name, but we call him Bobbie." Bob was grinning as he described his son, a proud father look on his face. "He seemed about ten years old when he was born," Bob added. "My wife—her name's Josie, after her grandmother—and I have to stay on our toes all the time to keep ahead of him."

"How old is he now?" Webster asked.

"Eleven."

"Does that include the ten years he had to start with?"

"What ten … oh yeah." Bob grinned as he peered over at Webster.

"So, he's what? … In about the fifth grade?" Webster asked

"Yeah, the fifth."

They walked on, talking and laughing. After a few minutes, Webster saw a bench coming up and breathed a sigh of relief. He flopped down and brushed the sweat off his face.

"Man, how far have we gone?"

"About two miles," Bob told him.

"Are you sure it's not farther? Feels like it."

"I'm sure."

"Can we go back now? I'm pretty tired." He was fine, but Webster still did not want anyone, even Bob, to know he had been doing his own routine.

Bob grinned. "We're already on our way back. You can't tell it, but the track doubles back to the facility. We only have a few hundred yards to go."

Bob stood and motioned for his patient to join him. Happy to be headed back, Webster predicted, "I think I can make it that far without your having to carry me."

"Lucky me," Bob said and slapped Webster on the shoulder, making him stumble.


The walking and the physical therapy continued over the next several days, with Dr. Dunn stopping in often. Webster still didn't believe Bob's predictions concerning Irene.

Cary was often on his mind as he continued to enjoy time with Irene. Webster felt a connection with Irene. She had become a friend. He hoped she didn't imagine it was more than that.

At the end of the third week, he looked up from a new book to see her whipping into his room with a pizza box in her hands. It was just after nine, and he was hungry, having had supper at five.

"I thought you could use a treat," she said. She set the pizza on his adjustable table and then went over and closed the door after hanging out the "Do Not Disturb" sign. "I don't do this for all our patients," she said as she walked to his bed.

"I figured this was just part of the services."

"Well, it's not." Irene had stopped and was digging in a rather large bag she was carrying. She smiled over at Webster as she produced a bottle of red wine. "We need something to wash down the pizza. Get out of that bed and put on your robe."


After washing his face and combing his hair, Webster splashed a little aftershave on for good measure. He hoped she wouldn't come away with the wrong impression, but the pizza smelled too good to pass up. He slipped into his robe, tying the belt as he walked back into his room. Irene was sitting in one of the chairs and had the other across the bedside table from her. The pizza box was open, and they each had wine in a plastic cup.

Webster sat down and looked over as she held her cup up for a toast. He touched his cup to hers as she said, "To your good and improving health."

His turn. "To the lovely lady who made it all possible." They took a sip.

Reaching for a slice of the pizza, Webster told her, "Did you hear about the fellow who told his waitress to cut the pizza in six slices. He said he didn't think he could eat eight."

Having already taken a bite, Irene almost choked. Laughing and with her mouth full, it took a moment to regain control.

Finally, able to breathe regularly, she said, "No, I don't think I've heard that one." She still had tears in her eyes.

They settled into routine conversation as they shared the respite. Webster sensed that Irene knew she could not ask too many questions about his work or, for that matter, his life or background. But that didn't stop him from asking about hers.

"How long have you been here?"

"Almost two years now, counting my training. I was under another doctor for about eight months."

"Are you in charge?"

"Of the medical wing, yes. There is an administrative area, too. Someone else runs that. They keep up with who comes and goes. They also keep up with the traffic at four other installations."

"Do you have family here?"

"No," she said, and got a dreamy look in her eyes. "My family lives out west. Montana, to be exact. Did you ever see the movie A River Runs through It? That's how my dad and mom's place looks."

"You're kidding!" Webster exclaimed. "If I had a place like that, I'd never leave home. I would fly-fish myself to death."

Irene laughed. "Where's home for you?" she asked.

"Wherever I happen to be," he told her. "There's no family to go back to."

"That's sad," she said with sympathy, but obviously without thinking. Then, catching herself, she reached over and touched his arm. "I'm sorry. That was thoughtless." Then she added, "But there must be times when it leaves you longing for a place to call home."

"It does … sometimes. I've learned to cope. I guess that is one of the reasons I am good at what I do. I don't have anyone to worry about." He added, "And there's no one to worry about me."

"Has there never been a Mrs. somewhere for you to come home to?"

"Nope. Came close a couple of times." He paused thoughtfully. "Actually, I met someone recently, but, as usual, I'm leaving her with a big question mark." He thought of Cary. There was a moment of regret. It must have shown in his eyes.

Irene had caught the change in his expression, but she didn't ask more. Webster hoped she didn't think he was referring to her.

He looked back at her, and his eyes brightened. "I shouldn't be talking about others when I'm here with you."

He meant it; Irene could tell. She suspected he didn't say things he didn't mean. Her emotions stirred as she got up from her chair. *I think he likes me, too,* she thought.

"I should be going. There are a couple of other patients I need to check on."

"Irene?" He said it softly, stopping her in her tracks. She turned back as he stood and reached his hand out to her. Irene studied him for a moment before placing her hand in his. He towered above her five and a half feet.

Barely above a whisper, he said, "Thanks for letting me talk tonight."

She sighed; he reminded her so much of John Dawson. Irene had tried hard to let her memories go. Since that first day when Webster had arrived, the past with John had tugged at her deepest emotions.

This was not good; she knew that. She'd never intended for anything to happen, but her best intentions gave way. She moved toward him, glancing up when they were close.

Then she was reaching up, against her own will. *This isn't me,* she thought. Her fingers flickered at his neck, her touch drawing him closer. Though he didn't help, he didn't refuse either.

She couldn't stop herself. The old love for John was in her memory, and Irene desperately wanted to kiss him. Their lips were close. Her eyes locked on his.

Then the door from the hallway burst open.

Bob, his hands full, had pushed the door with his elbow. He was carrying a tray with two cups of juice and a paper cup holding Webster's evening pills.

Seeing them in a close embrace, Bob spun on his heels and beat a hasty retreat. As the door was closing, they heard him say in his deep voice, "Oops! Sorry … wrong room."

They held the embrace for a moment, gazing at each other. Then they broke into laughter and stepped back.

Finally, nearing control, Irene said, "Bob should learn to knock."

"I think he just had his first lesson."

"I should go."

"Yeah …. you should."

One more glance and then she was gone.

After a couple of minutes, the door opened just a crack, and the "Do Not Disturb" sign sailed into the room. Webster picked it up and hung it on the back of the door.

Bob returned a few minutes later, a big grin on his face but not a word about his earlier entrance.

"Here's your medicine. I brought an extra juice. Thought I might join you."

Webster looked up from his book and said, "Are you sure you have the right room?"

"I think so," Bob said. "It's hard to tell around here, what with the "Do Not Disturb" signs and all. A fellow could go into the wrong room thinking the sign means someone's resting. There needs to be space for a written message. Then the occupant could add something like "Kissing in Progress." I think that would work, don't you?"

"I haven't the slightest idea what you're talking about."

 **Chapter 10**

On the sixth day of his vacation, Jack Robbins's cell phone rang. Robbins looked at the caller ID and then answered.

"Robbins here."

"Jack, this is Tom."

Tom Manning was Robbins's boss in Washington.

"Yeah, Tom. What can I do for you? I'm on vacation, you know."

"Yeah, I remembered, Jack. And I know I promised to leave you alone, but it's important."

"It always is, Tom. What's the problem? I don't have much time. I have this good-looking woman here who's trying to give me another drink." Monica set his tea on the tray and blew him a kiss.

"We need someone to fly to London and pick up a prisoner. It's an extradition situation. We've gotten this guy back to New Scotland Yard, and now we need someone to bring him home. I don't have anyone available who has up-to-date travel papers. I was hoping you'd have someone."

"What's the big rush? Can't you wait until one of your people is available? Scotland Yard can hold this guy for a few days, can't they?"

"Sure, they could do that," Manning said. "But we don't have the time. We have to get him arraigned in five days or we lose him. That's why I'm desperate."

Robbins watched his wife as she prepared their lunch. "Give me an hour to think about it, Tom. I'll see if I can come up with something and call you. Bye."

He picked up his tea and took a sip. Damn, she made good tea.

~ ~ ~

After Webster and Bob finished their morning walk, Webster went back to his room for a shower. Bob had worked him up to a relatively fast pace. Webster was also doing sets of a hundred sit-ups now. He could do three sets in the morning and afternoon. Various other exercises rounded out an hour of pain twice a day. He was improving quickly and thought he could be out of the medical facility soon.

Irene continued to drop by several times a day. Bob teased him, and a couple of the other nurses had commented on the concern Dr. Dunn was showing Webster. One had even wondered aloud as to what else she might be showing him.

Irene was very pleased with his progress. She had kept a degree of distance between them since the night she had brought pizza. He was okay with that.

Webster thought of Cary much more than he wished to. She would come strolling through his thoughts at the strangest times—like when Irene was checking his pulse or examining him. Cary and her memory were tough to let go.

On that particular morning, Irene hinted she might have a surprise for him. Bob was in the room at the time, and Webster noticed as he rolled his eyes and acquired a grin like he had an amusing idea of what the surprise might be.

"I think we're ready for the next phase of your care," Irene said. Bob's expression changed, as if he had thought she'd had something else in mind.

"I think we're ready to transfer you out of here," she told Webster. "Can you handle that?"

"What? Out of here? Where to?" Webster hadn't thought he was ready to leave. The Merchant and his people came to mind. With the guard unit on station, he felt protected here. In fact, he liked it here.

His objections sounded like whining, even to Webster.

"Poor baby," Irene said, as if she were talking to a child. "He doesn't want to leave home, does he?" Then she reached over and mussed his hair. He had been letting it grow, the beard, too. The hair was getting a little long, and the beard had filled out quite nicely.

Bob rolled his eyes when Webster looked at him.

"Don't you have something to do someplace else?"

Bob chuckled and headed for the door. As it closed behind him, they could hear, "poor baby," in that deep bass voice and then Bob's laughter.

Webster couldn't help smiling when Irene glanced his way. They both knew Bob was a keeper.

"So, you're going to toss me out."

"If you call a cabin three miles away tossing you out, then I suppose that's what we're doing." She smiled.

"Three miles? On the property? Still at this facility?" Sitting on the bed, he tried to get his bearings.

"Yes. Yes. And, yes."

"Oh!"

Webster grinned, finally understanding. He reached out to shake her hand. She returned the gesture, and their eyes met and held for a moment.

Then she said, "I have to go. I've got things to do."

Unexpectedly, she leaned over and kissed him on the lips. Then she was gone.

He sat on his bed and thought of her, and of Cary. The smell of Irene's perfume lingered in the room. Two special women, he thought, and I have nothing to offer either of them.

As Webster sat thinking about the two women, his cell phone rang. He looked at the caller ID. Blocked call. He put it to his ear anyway. Only a few individuals had the number.

"Webster here."

"Mike, ole buddy. It's Jack. Got a minute?"

"Sure. What's up?"

"How are you feeling? Are you up and around?"

Webster was immediately suspicious. "I'm coming along," he said. Jack Robbins seldom wasted words.

"What do you need, Jack? I know this isn't idle conversation." He began tossing out everything he could think of. "You are aware I'm injured, aren't you? I've been shot, and I'm under a doctor's care."

Webster then tried another direction. "I don't work for you anymore either. I'm in the program now, remember?"

Webster was thinking about the cabin Irene had mentioned. It was starting to sound really good. *Maybe the cabin doesn't have a phone. I could lose my cell.*

"It's just a small assignment," Robbins ventured. "No danger, and you get to see London."

"London, England?"

"No, Webster. London, Arkansas. Of course, London, England. Where did you think?"

"I didn't think. I am trying not to think. The last time I tried it, I got shot."

"You told me you got shot because you winked at the girl."

"That's not what I said. I told you I was making sure she was okay." But the truth was that the last thing he remembered about New Orleans was winking at Cary.

"Whatever," Robbins said. "What I need is for you to go to London, pick up a prisoner at New Scotland Yard, and bring him back for an indictment hearing. We only have five days, and there's no one available with the right travel credentials."

"Oh! I'm available?"

"Please."

Robbins did not use that word very often so he must be pretty desperate.

"What's it worth to you?"

"I'll let you come back and spend some more time with Dr. Dunn."

"Hmm! Okay, you got a deal, and you owe me one." He paused. "When do I leave? I'll need a set of travel papers, too."

"Let me make the arrangements and call you back. Oh, and tell Dr. Dunn you're going to be gone for a couple of days. Okay?"

"I'll handle this end. Bye." He closed the phone and started to think about what to tell Irene. It wasn't difficult. Irene understood many of her patients led strange lives.

"Bob can have the cabin ready when you get back," she told him. "Be careful, and take care of your wound. It is almost healed. We do not want to have to start again. Okay? Doctor's orders!" She reached out and gently touched his shirt above the wound.

~ ~ ~

Five hours later, Webster was walking through the Atlanta's Hartfield Airport toward the International gates. It was a Thursday afternoon. He had a set of travel papers, including a passport and other necessary items to get him to London and back. Everything had arrived at the Delta counter in the hands of a young woman who took her job very seriously.

Even with the beard and longer hair, she had identified Webster from a photograph she carried, and he'd had to answer several questions before she gave up the envelope. She had finally handed him the papers and said, "Have a nice trip, Mr. Webster."

Webster checked in and found he had a couple of hours before his flight. He walked back to the main terminal and looked for a newsstand. Locating one, he browsed the paperbacks for something to read on the flight. Finding what he wanted, he paid and shoved the book into his coat pocket. He enjoyed having something to read on these trips. This one was written by an older guy known for his fedora, shades, and long leather coat.

As Webster walked back toward the International gates, he stopped off at a men's room along the way. The door was closing behind him when a tall young woman walked out of the women's room ten feet away.

She continued toward her gate to await Delta's next flight to New Orleans. Cary Warren, attractively dressed as usual, flipped her long dark hair over her shoulder as she walked.

Cary had a long weekend and planned to spend it with Landie and the family. After the encounter with Carlos Merro earlier in the week, she wished Webster was still around and could be there with her. She wondered, too, how long she would have him constantly on her mind. Letting him go was something she really must do. The single gunshot that night in New Orleans had made him a memory.

I still miss him, though, she thought. A lot!

 # Chapter II

Everything went fine on the flight to London. At Scotland Yard they were expecting him, and his contact, Chief Inspector MacGreggor, had everything ready for the transfer. Papers were quickly signed, and the inspector then invited Webster into his office for tea.

Webster immediately liked Inspector MacGreggor. He was as tall as Webster, in his fifties, and had a full head of red hair. His beard and mustache were red, too. The mustache was waxed, long, and rolled into curls at the ends. It was striking.

When he spoke, MacGreggor rolled his R's, and, overall, seemed a happy chap. He told Webster he was from Edinburgh, Scotland, and that his grandfather still lived there.

"Lives alone, he does, and still chases the lasses."

"How old is he?" Webster asked.

"Turned ninety-two in September." The inspector paused for a moment, then told Webster, "His own father, me great-grandfather, lived to a hundred and four."

The inspector's office was small, and numerous files were scattered everywhere, making it difficult to get to the one available chair. MacGreggor left Webster to find his own way while the inspector himself went over to a small table where the makings for the tea were kept. As MacGreggor put water on to heat, he asked Webster about his trip.

"Weather good on the dash over?" he asked. "The last time I visited your country, the blasted aeroplane bounced all the way back to Great Brittan. Swore I would never go up in one of those things again. But I do, of course, from time to time. Can't travel without it, you know?"

Webster let him talk, answering his questions as they were asked.

"Well, how was your trip over here?"

"Actually, it was a very smooth ride," Webster replied. "I slept most of the way."

"I can't sleep on an aeroplane either," MacGreggor fussed. "I'm deathly afraid the thing will fall, and if I'm asleep, I won't be able to stop it. Not that I could anyway, but I feel better if I'm awake."

They had their tea and then the inspector delegated one of his men to retrieve the prisoner. MacGreggor then called for a car and escorted Webster and his captive out to Heathrow Airport and Virgin Atlantic Airways.

On the ride to the airport, the inspector surprised Webster, asking, "How is my old friend, the Author?" Webster's startled expression caused Inspector MacGregor to chuckle. "Don't look so out of sorts," he said. "I've known Rage for thirty years. Met him while he was with the CIA and I was stationed at the embassy in Prague."

"He's very proud of you." He was watching Webster's eyes. "Thinks of you as he would a son. Say hello for me when you speak."

Webster said he would and made a mental note to call Rage Doyle when he was back at the medical facility.

The inspector stayed with them through all the details of paperwork and the clearing of Webster to carry a weapon onboard the aircraft. When all was done, they were taken to an office to wait.

After everyone else had boarded, the flight attendant in charge came to the office to escort Webster and his prisoner onto the airplane. Inspector MacGreggor said good-bye and left them at the gate.

The flight attendant led them to their seats at the rear of the first-class cabin. Webster motioned his prisoner into the window seat. He then secured the man with his right hand cuffed across his body to the left armrest at the window. Webster sat in the aisle seat, his weapon holstered on his right hip. The two men then settled in for the long flight back to the States.

Most of the seats were occupied, and drinks were being served. A well-dressed man sitting about halfway back in first class had observed Webster and the detainee as they boarded the airplane. The event would not have caught his attention if he hadn't glimpsed the cuffs connecting the two men. He reached for a magazine but continued to glance at them as he sat quietly in his seat. He was sure he knew one of the men. Scratching the back of his head, he considered the possibilities. The tall one looked familiar; the location or the reason wasn't coming to him. Oh well, the plane would be in the air for several hours. Chances were good that he would have it worked out before they landed in the States.

The usual announcements were made, and the plane took off on schedule. Now thousands of feet above the ocean, passengers settled into their own routines. Some watched movies while others talked quietly with their seat mates. Several had reclined back for naps.

"Do you want to go to the restroom?" Webster asked the detainee.

"Not now, but thanks," the man said. "Later."

"Let me know."

Webster pulled out the paperback he had been reading on the way over. He was about halfway through it. If he took a few breaks and the flight attendants came around often enough, the book should last all the way back home to Atlanta.

After a few pages, his thoughts wandered, and Webster lowered the book to his lap. On the way to London, Cary Warren had been on his mind several times. Irene was there, too, but mostly the focus had been on the dark-haired Tennessee belle who had almost gotten him killed in New Orleans. There was just something about Cary … that …

Glancing out the window, Webster told himself again, I can't keep this up.

As he picked up the book again, his boyhood and the uncle who had raised him touched his memory. The old man had done the best he could under the circumstances. With no one else to turn to, Webster had thrust himself upon his mother's older brother when she boarded a bus one Saturday night and never returned. Uncle Sid had been no more enthused with the arrangement than Webster. Those years had been endured rather than lived.

Maybe I was being prepared for the way I live now, he thought.

The man watching Webster waited for over an hour to get up from his seat. Waiting until the first-class section's lavatories were in use, he headed forward and made a show of checking them. Turning, he strolled along the aisle toward the rear of the aircraft. As he passed, Webster looked up, catching his eye.

The man casually said, "Hello." Then he nodded and continued into the rear cabin.

Although he had never met the man with the prisoner, he definitely had seen photographs of him. Even with the beard and long hair, there was no mistaking he had seen him before. He didn't remember a name, but he guessed the individual was using a different one now anyway.

When he returned to his seat, the man checked his cell phone. The battery was almost gone, and he couldn't charge it until he got to his hotel. He would follow the man and his prisoner when they landed. Maybe he could learn something useful and then find a way to report what he had discovered.

The interesting part was that he had heard the man sitting a few rows behind him had been killed recently in New Orleans. Obviously, that was not true. To the contrary, he appeared to be very much alive.

Thinking about the possibilities, he hoped the reward for finding the man was still available. He was sure he now vividly remembered the information that had circulated concerning the individual. He smiled then, guessing this might be what it felt like to hold a winning lottery ticket.

The plane landed uneventfully at New York's Kennedy several hours later. Tom Manning had two of his people there to take Webster's companion off his hands and transport the man down to DC.

The fact that Webster and the detainee did not go through customs with everyone else made it difficult for the man in seat 5-C to follow. He stood in a line and watched as Webster and the other man were met by two individuals and ushered toward a set of doors at the back of the customs area.

When he had finished answering questions and his bags had been inspected, Mr. 5-C walked to a location where he hoped to see anyone leaving customs. He waited for as long as he could without arousing anyone's interest.

Finally giving up, the man retreated farther into the terminal and took a seat. As he waited, the two men who had met Webster walked out with the prisoner. Though Mr. 5-C stayed there for some time, he did not see Webster come into the terminal.

As careful as the man had been, Webster had observed his interest shortly after boarding the flight. Unsure at first, Webster became cautious and then vigilant after the man said hello to him.

When Manning's men met them, Webster discreetly pointed out Mr. 5-C to them and explained that he had seemed unusually interested in either Webster or the detainee. They kept a close watch on the man and had Webster moved to another concourse for a flight out of Kennedy.

While the man waited in the terminal, Webster was already on a plane bound for Cincinnati. There, he took a flight to the Midwest and another to Dallas for a short layover.

Webster took advantage of the time to purchase a postcard showing a panoramic night view of Houston's skyline. He might hate himself later, but Webster could no longer allow Cary to think he had been killed and that she might have been at fault. He wrote a cryptic note only she would understand, bought a stamp, and mailed it before he could change his mind. Then he boarded his flight back to Charlotte.

~ ~ ~

Tired and out of patience, the man finally gave up and left the airport. Later, in his hotel, he charged his cell phone and called an acquaintance.

When the party answered, Mr. 5-C announced, "I flew in from London tonight with a dead man." He explained the circumstances, answered a few questions, and then inquired about the reward. His colleague assured him the incentive would be available if the information proved useful.

He told the man all about the individual on the flight, including the fact that he was escorting a prisoner. Webster's long hair and the beard aroused the man's interest.

Mr. 5-C was then asked where he was staying and his room number. He was then told there would be a delivery coming his way. Hanging up, Mr. 5-C began making plans for how he would spend the money.

A couple of hours later, there was a soft knock at the door to his room. He went over and looked through the peephole into the hallway. A very attractive and smiling young woman was waiting there, and she was carrying a briefcase—the reward!

He opened the door, expecting her to pass the money to him.

That was not her purpose. When they were face to face, the smile was gone, and the briefcase she had been carrying was no longer in her hand. The young woman now held a long-barreled .22 caliber pistol equipped with a silencer.

He looked at the weapon, then back at her face. Terror gripped his being as completely as a hungry leopard grips and throttles its prey. Although the time since he had opened the door had been only a moment, it seemed much longer.

Then all time ended for him with two almost inaudible pops from the pistol. He felt the initial shock of the slugs slamming into his chest. The force of the hollow-point bullets knocked him backward, and Mr. 5-C immediately lost consciousness.

The woman kicked the two empty cartridges into the room ahead of her. Scooping up the briefcase, she glanced both ways and then stepped across the threshold. Using her foot to shove the man's leg aside, she then pushed the door shut.

A final bullet to the man's forehead completed her contract. Satisfied with that part of the mission, she walked into the bedroom while pulling on a pair of latex gloves. A quick but thorough search followed. She was looking for anything concerning the elusive individual on the flight from London.

She hadn't expected to nor did she find anything concerning Webster. After she completed the search, the woman stepped to the bedside table and picked up the man's billfold, removing all the currency. She then dropped the billfold, jewelry, and cell phone into her purse, along with the three spent shell casings. The folded money went into her coat pocket.

The body would be found by a clean-up crew, leaving the scene to suggest an armed robbery. No one would suspect the man had brought important information to her employers.

After opening the door, the gloves came off, and the woman checked her appearance in the mirror. Attention to detail, both business and personal, kept her in high demand in her profession.

There was no one in the hallway or on the elevator when she stepped over his body and left the tipster. If anyone had happened upon her, she would have wished them a pleasant evening.

Upon reaching the lobby, the woman walked confidently toward the exit while casually glancing about for anyone who might notice. Observing no special interest, she stepped out to the sidewalk and out of the memory of everyone who might have noticed as she moved through the building.

A block from the hotel, she inconspicuously opened her purse, removed the gloves and shell casings, and dropped them into two separate waste containers.

She loathed people who threw their trash on the streets.

# Chapter 12

Webster arrived back at the medical center at nine the next morning. He was waved through when he held his identification up for the guards at the gate. His taxi was not. Webster stepped out, and the driver was required to head back toward the highway after he was paid.

A guard in a souped-up golf cart transported Webster to the medical building. Another called ahead, allowing Bob to be waiting at the front door.

"Long time no see," Webster's friend said, although it had only been about forty-eight hours. They shook hands.

"Had any breakfast?" Bob asked.

"Donut and a cup of coffee."

"I'll see what I can do," Bob told him. "Can't promise anything."

"I'll get a shower. I'm gonna need some sleep, too—after breakfast."

The smell of toast was in the air when Webster left the bathroom a few minutes later. A tray awaited on his adjustable table, complete with coffee and OJ.

He sat in a chair and pulled the table over. Lifting the cover off the plate, Webster was surprised to find scrambled eggs, hash browns, grits, and bacon, with toast and jelly on the side. It was a pretty good spread given Bob's uncertainty about breakfast.

His stomach growled as if in anticipation of the feast. Webster chuckled, muttering, "Down, boy," and started shoveling it in.

As he finished, Bob and Dr. Dunn entered the room together.

"Your trip okay?" Dr. Dunn asked.

"Fine, just tiring," he told her. "Glad to be back here."

"Won't last long," Bob told him with a twinkle in his eye. "Moving you out, boy. We've enjoyed about all of you we can stand."

"To the cabin," Dr. Dunn said with a reassuring smile, lest he got the wrong impression.

"What's the deal on this cabin?" Webster asked. "Is it like a halfway house?"

"Sort of," Dr. Dunn answered. "It's a place for you to be on your own but still close enough for us to keep up with you."

"We can make sure you're doing your exercises," Bob added with a grin.

She smiled. "We send most of your meals from here, and Bob can make sure you don't do too much too quickly. We want you exercising, but we also want you to be careful."

"How long do I get to stay in the cabin?"

"That depends on your progress. Judging from what you and Bob have already been doing, I would say you'll be back to full speed soon."

"You'll have to chop your own wood and clean up after yourself, too," Bob said.

"You're kidding, right? About the wood, I mean." He knew he must have a "you've got to be kidding" look on his face.

Dr. Dunn and Bob both grinned and shook their heads.

"You're not kidding? You really mean it." His mouth fell open, his expression one of dismay.

"The only heat in the cabin is the fireplace," Dr. Dunn told him. "It's kind of primitive."

"It does have a bathroom, doesn't it?"

Bob jumped in, "Yeah, it's out back and has two holes. You've read about them. It's called a privy."

"Shit," Webster said before he could stop himself.

Bob cackled, having to hold his sides. Dr. Dunn laughed too.

"Yes, it has a bathroom," she said still smiling. "A small refrigerator and a microwave, too. You won't starve, but you'll get cold if you don't keep up with the fire."

"Chop. Chop. Chop," Bob teased.

"You're sadistic," Webster said, glaring at the big nurse.

Bob laughed again and headed for the door. "I'll come back and help you get ready for the move when Dr. Dunn is finished."

With Bob gone, Irene smiled and said, "You'll be fine." She handed him the napkin and motioned for him to wipe his mouth.

"Will you be checking on me?"

"Want me to?"

Webster gazed at her for a few moments, not quite sure what to say. Then he ventured, "Yeah … I do."

"Then I will." She reached out with her fingers and touched his cheek. Their eyes locked for a moment before she left the room.

After breakfast, Webster gathered his things and stacked them on the foot of the bed. Bob brought a couple of boxes and helped fill them. "The cabin's already made up with sheets and towels, that sort of thing. All we should do is take your stuff over there. I have a golf cart outside."

"Remind me, how far away is the cabin?" Webster asked.

"Three, maybe four miles. More like three, I think. Never measured it. Oh, and you have to walk over here every other day for a check-up."

"You're kidding again, right?" Webster did not like Bob's look. "You're not kidding," he said, shaking his head as he went to gather his toiletries.

Bob picked up a box. "Let's get going."

Webster could see his new home as they rounded a curve near the structure. It was a log cabin and looked old. Real old! It was set back into a stand of trees consisting mostly of hard woods. There was a clearing at the front of the cabin, the trees coming in close on the two sides and the rear. A firewood rack stood near the door, but only a few pieces were stacked there. Webster realized he would have to get busy this afternoon or sleep cold tonight.

Bob pulled the golf cart up near the front porch and stopped.

"Well, what do you think? Pretty nice, huh?"

"Did Daniel Boone ever sleep here?"

"No," Bob said, "but I think I read somewhere that his father did." They both grinned.

"I believe it." Webster grabbed a box and headed for the door.

The inside was clean in a rustic cabin sort of way. The bed was made, and dishes and utensils were set on a small table in the corner. Other bowls, dishes, and cooking gear lined shelves in the kitchen area.

Wood was stacked in the fireplace and ready to light. A few extra pieces were piled to the side on the hearth.

Webster checked the small bathroom and was surprised to find a medium-sized hot tub in the corner. After chopping logs for a few hours, he would need that.

He went back into the main room where Bob was placing the second box on the bed.

"All finished," Bob said. "Need anything?"

"Not at the moment."

"There's a small map of the grounds on the wall over there." Bob pointed above a table that served as a desk. "I'm going to leave you to your wood chopping," he said as he headed for the door.

Webster waved as Bob headed the golf cart back to the hospital wing. He stayed in the doorway until he could no longer hear the cart. The only sounds came from the forest around him.

I could learn to like this, he thought.

He listened to the birds calling and to the breeze blowing through the trees. In the city, sounds like these were hard to come by. He really could get used to being here.

Webster looked up at the sky and, for the first time that day, considered the weather conditions. There had been no need to before. But as he saw the clouds slowly moving in from the west, he realized rain could complicate his stay in the cabin. It was into early December now. Leaves had turned and most had already fallen. The temperature had started to dip down at night. He decided there was no choice but to spend a part of the afternoon replenishing his wood supply.

A couple of hours later, Webster had cut enough wood for several days, and he had rubbed enough blisters on his hands for a lifetime. He glanced at his watch. Three thirty. So much for getting some sleep today.

The clouds had covered the western skies now, and he could feel a chill in the wind. There was moisture in the air, too.

He decided to start a fire and get a shower. Maybe someone would feel sorry for him and bring something to eat.

Starting the fire did not go very well. It was not as easy as striking a match and holding it near the wood. It took some old newspaper and some puffing on his part to get the hint of a flame. Then there was another problem. When the fire finally caught, smoke immediately flowed into the room instead of going up the chimney.

"The damper … damn it! I forgot the damper."

Webster quickly moved the lever to let the smoke flow up the chimney. Stepping back, he fanned smoke with his hands and a piece of newspaper until the fireplace and chimney took over, clearing the room. Getting some fresh air in the house seemed a good idea, too, so he pulled the door wide open, allowing some of the smoke out that way.

Finally, with things back to normal, he checked the fireplace one last time and went to take a shower.

Hot water streaming over his body felt good after splitting wood. He stood for several minutes, letting the water soothe his aching muscles. He carefully rubbed the area where the bullet had struck him. The surgical wounds that had saved his life were tender. There was still some soreness in the chest area, too, but he was almost back to normal. The exercise had obviously helped.

Webster reluctantly cut the water and toweled off. Wrapping the towel around himself as an afterthought, he strolled out to the bedroom to get a pair of shorts.

The hair on the back of his neck was suddenly on end. Without seeing the person, he sensed another's presence in the room. Whirling to the bedside table, he reached for his weapon.

It wasn't there.

"Looking for something?" a female voice inquired.

Webster turned slowly, glancing where she pointed. His weapon was on the fireplace mantle.

"I was concerned you might be startled and use it without asking questions. Moving it was a good idea, huh?"

It was Irene.

"I brought your dinner."

"Damn it, Irene. Don't do that." Webster could feel his heart pounding. He stood still, his eyes closed for a few seconds, reining in his emotions. Finally looking at her, he said, "I'm sorry. I shouldn't talk to you like that. I'm tense. I'm trying to let that pass, too."

"I'm the one who should apologize," she said. "When I knocked, you didn't answer. I tried the door and then came on in when I heard the shower." She motioned toward the towel. "I hadn't planned on getting a show."

"Damn," Webster said looking down. He grabbed his robe and shorts and beat a hasty retreat to the bathroom. He dressed, brushed his hair, and then reached for the cologne. Remembering their feelings that night in his room, he kept it to a small touch.

Still, Irene noticed, saying, "Cool Water? Nice."

He nodded.

"What I said earlier was uncalled for," he said. "I wasn't expecting anyone."

"I realize that now. I probably should have said something when you came out of the bath." She smiled then, and tilted her head a bit, adding, "But it's your fault."

"Mine?"

"Uh huh. You come walking out with only a towel wrapped around you. I suppose I am lucky you had that. I could've been blinded."

"Blinded? Right. I really believe that."

They both laughed.

"Well, I could have," she argued.

Women and that last word! he thought.

They unpacked the food, and Irene joined him at the table.

"You brought enough for both of us," he said when he saw the amount.

"I was hoping you would invite me to stay."

"If I don't, I'll have enough for a snack later." He glanced at her, then back at the food.

"You would have me go home hungry?"

"I didn't say that. I was just naming the alternatives."

"Well ... that isn't one of them." She reached for a napkin.

"In that case, would you care to join me for dinner?"

"Love to. Pass the potatoes."

 *Chapter 13*

They enjoyed dinner together, kidding, joking, getting to know each other better. That hour was the best they had spent together since he had arrived. Nothing serious had been discussed, yet Irene believed she knew him better when they had finished eating.

Surprising herself, Irene had even told Webster a little about John, about their time together and how she had felt when she lost him in the accident. And he had opened up, just a little, about the woman he had been helping when he was shot. It was obvious he cared a great deal for her, but he said he couldn't go back there. It would be too dangerous for both of them.

They had laughed at the seriousness of their past situations and had agreed the past should be left behind them. At least, they should work at it.

Irene had included a bottle of wine with the meal, and they had each enjoyed a glass with their dinner. They had remained at the little table when the meal was over, pushing back their chairs, unwilling to let the moment end.

Webster had been heavy on Irene's mind for the last several days—or had it been memories of John? Whichever, their fingers touched as he handed her another glass of wine, and static electricity arched, shocking and startling them both. Some wine spilled, and there was more touching as they reached for napkins to blot the liquid.

Their eyes locked. His, deep and blue, captivated her and seemed to look into her very soul. Irene couldn't help herself. She wanted him desperately at that moment, and, in her heart of hearts, she believed he wanted her, too.

In her mind, Irene envisioned him making love to her. She wanted him to embrace and touch her, to wrap her in his arms and hold her that way for hours. She desired him in every way a woman could want a man.

And she needed him now.


They had cleaned up the spill and cleared the table, reserving their last glass of wine for the fireplace. After that emotive moment, Irene had gone off to the bathroom, leaving Webster to settle in front of the hearth.

The cabin was warm, and he dozed as he waited for her to join him. He heard a stirring behind him and turned to welcome her back for the last of the wine.

His first thought was that she was not there for the grapes.

Irene's clothing had been replaced by one of his towels, a small one. It barely covered everything that might need covering. She was smiling, her right pinkie beckoning him to join her there in the proximity of the bed.

He choked.

As beguiling as she was—waiting there for him to come and take her—he was not prepared for this. His face, his expression, must have told her.

Irene stared at him for the longest time. In those moments, her eyes teared up, and her face relayed the emotion of realizing she had made a huge miscalculation. Without a word, she turned back to the bathroom and closed the door. There was no slamming, no yelling, no words—nothing.

When the door opened again, she was dressed, the tears gone. She walked over to him, took his hand, and raised it up. She gave him a gentle kiss, a touch of her lips to his fingers, with a sad look into his eyes.

"I'm sorry," she murmured. "I should have realized you weren't ready for this. I should have known that you're in love with another woman."

With one more long look, she turned and was gone.

He walked out on the porch and watched her leave. He had heard her words. She had told him what he had not allowed himself to believe.

Cary.

Staying outside, Webster sat down in one of the rockers, Cary still on his mind. It bothered him to think he had just said good-bye to a beautiful, caring, and kind woman who had spent a part of her evening with him in a very intimate setting—and then Cary came walking through his mind. How did that happen?

I wonder where she is tonight and what she's doing. Let's face it, damn it; I miss her. That, he thought critically, isn't fair to either of them, Cary or Irene.

As the evening progressed, he could feel the temperature start to drop. He watched as shadows covered the area around the cabin while in the distance, on the low hills to the east, the moon was bright on the trees. It was beautiful, and he realized it had been a long time since he'd had the freedom to enjoy such a sight.

On a whim, he pulled out his phone and punched in a number. Several re-routes and connections later, Rage Doyle, the Author, answered with a simple, Southern hello. Webster hoped the Author would someday go into the details of how he had picked up the name during his years at the CIA. Webster had heard many of the rumors about his adventures there. Some were downright scary.

He inquired about his friend's days in retirement. Doyle gave a few details and bragged a little about his small log cabin in the mountains of Tennessee. Rage said the view from his deck at Coker Creek was something to see, especially the sunrises.

He also confided that he had found a new place to purchase the long leather coats he enjoyed wearing. Rage said he had become friends with the owners of the Boyd Thomas store in Maryville. In fact, he said, Bill and Marty had asked him to dinner Saturday evening.

The last thing he mentioned was that he had acquired a small interest in a gun store. Self-Defense Solutions was relatively close to Rage's cabin, and Webster was invited to come and admire the inventory anytime he got out that way.

"Now," he asked Webster, "what can I do for you?"

Webster told his friend where he had been staying for the last several weeks. He was surprised when Rage said he already knew and had even visited Webster on two occasions. Webster had been sleeping both times, he said.

With some unasked-for advice, he suggested Webster have friends outside the facility, yet in the near surrounding area, and that he have them watch for unusual activity.

"Always a good idea," Rage said. "Bad things and bad people are out there."

Rage enjoyed hearing about Webster's visit with Inspector MacGreggor. When they had time, Rage said he would tell him some interesting things about the good inspector. They had a few laughs and then hung up, both happy for the conversation.

A half hour later, Webster took one last look at the area around the cabin, then got up and went inside. He stirred the ashes in the fireplace and threw on a couple of new logs. The fire renewed itself, and Webster backed up to the warmth.

He thought about some of the things Irene had told him since he had arrived here and wondered if the place had a name. Everyone just seemed to call it "the Facility." He would ask Bob about a name and see if Bob could come up with a more complete map of the grounds. The one on the wall of the cabin did not show much detail.

He finally decided to leave his thoughts concerning the women and his situation to work themselves out in his subconscious.

After reading for a while, Webster went to sleep with a strange sensation that someone was thinking about him. Somehow, he did not have the sense that it was Cary or Irene.

He slept fitfully that night.

# Chapter 14

Several days had passed since the celebration party at the compound outside Veracruz, Mexico. Having been summoned early one morning, Mateo knocked on Pablo's office door and then quietly entered. A breeze was blowing off the water and through the open windows.

Pablo sat at his desk but was turned to the side and staring out the window toward the Bay of Campeche. When the door opened, the Merchant folded some pages he had been holding and slipped them into his shirt pocket. He glanced to see who had entered and smiled at his young friend.

"It is a good morning for you, I hope," Pablo said to Mateo.

"And to you, my friend."

Mateo gazed out at the stunning azure waters beyond the cliffs. Taking a chair across the desk from Pablo, he waited for the older man to speak.

"Are you ready to travel again?"

"Si, Pablo. Wherever you wish."

"Good," he said. "I have received disturbing new information about the tall one from America. He may not be dead after all." He gave Mateo details concerning the possible sighting of Webster.

Though surprised, Mateo listened without questions or comment.

When he finished, Pablo looked at Mateo for a few moments, obviously thinking. Then seeming to have reached a decision, he said, "Go back to New Orleans and start there." The Merchant paused, working out his plans as he gave Mateo instructions. "Find the people you talked with before, especially the one who told you about the wounded man they said was flown out of there. Do you know the one I mean?"

"Si, Pablo." Everything had been in his report to the Merchant.

"When you find him, see if he can tell you where the man was flown to." Pablo appeared to be thinking about the situation as he talked. "Also try to find the name of the man who was in charge there, the man who watched over both wounded men. Find out all you can about the circumstances of the tall one's death and of the other man being moved. I have decided something is strange there. Maybe our man was not really killed. Maybe they only made it appear that way. Oh, and when you have finished with your contact in New Orleans, it might be better if he is unable to tell others what he has said to you."

"Yes, Pablo. I understand."

"Dig deep, Mateo," Pablo got up and walked around his desk, placing a hand on Mateo's shoulder and looking into his eyes. "Find out all you can. This is important to me."

"I realize that, Pablo. I will not fail you."

"I know you won't, my friend. I am depending on you." Pablo walked back and sat down.

"Be careful what you say on the cell phone," Pablo cautioned. "Nothing should be said that would be a problem for us later."

Mateo rose out of his chair and prepared to leave. "I will be watchful."

"See that you are," Pablo told him. "And be cautious. You are important to our future." Pablo touched his forehead, a salute to his young friend.

Mateo went to his living quarters and packed for the trip. He called the airline and scheduled his flight out of Mexico City, then he went downstairs where he had arranged for transportation to the airport.

Mateo's flight landed in New Orleans late that afternoon. He rented a Volvo again and drove to a small hotel in the French Quarter where he had stayed before. Arriving there, Mateo turned the vehicle over to an attendant and took his bags inside to the registration desk.

"Hello, Mr. Merro. Welcome back to the Hotel St. Marie. It is good to see you. We hope you enjoy your stay."

"I'm sure I will," he said as he filled out the registration. "Could you give me a call at seven thirty?"

"Yes, sir. Seven thirty. Anything else? Would you like for us to call and make dinner reservations for you?"

"Do you have a suggestion? Seafood sounds good for tonight," he told the clerk.

"How about Ralph & Kacoo's. It's a few blocks down on this street," the clerk told him. "Go out the front door of the hotel and turn left. Stay on the sidewalk on this side. The address is 519 Toulouse. You won't be disappointed."

"Make a reservation for me. Eight o'clock?"

"Yes, sir." The man had a big smile as Mateo handed him a twenty-dollar bill.

"Thank you, sir."

Mateo went to his room, unpacked, and arranged things for his stay. The work would begin in the morning. Tonight would be for feasting, and a little more. He remembered the girl from the funeral home and dug around on the bottom of his briefcase for the card she had given him during his last trip to the city. He found it. Marty E'deau. He remembered she had said her name was Marty.

Dialing the home number she had written on the back of the card, he listened for the connection and waited. After three rings, she answered.

"Hello?"

"Marty?"

"Yes. … Who is this?"

"This is Carlos Merro," he said to her. "We met a few weeks ago. You helped me get a death certificate. I was in a rush."

Silence.

"Did you get your automobile repaired?" Mateo asked, jogging her memory.

"Oh! Now I remember you." She laughed. "Yes, it runs fine now. Where are you? I never heard from you. You never told me your name."

"I had to fly out that day, but I'm back in New Orleans for a brief time." Mateo hesitated for a few moments and then asked, "I am wondering if you are free for dinner?"

She sounded surprised at the invitation but quickly recovered. "Sure, I guess. … Sure. I'd love to go out with you."

"I'm staying down in the French Quarter," he told her. "Do you live far?"

"I have an apartment in the Carrolton area," she said. "It's not too far."

"Good," he said. "Do you know a restaurant called Ralph & Kacoo's, in the French Quarter?"

"Yes, I've heard of it," Marty said. "I've never been there."

"Would you like to have dinner there tonight?"

"Sure. That would be great."

"Okay, then. If you don't mind, I'm going to ask you to take a taxi to the restaurant. I'll reimburse you."

She started to protest, but Mateo told her he would take it as a business expense.

"I can do that." She sounded relieved to not be out the fare. "What time?"

"Eight o'clock."

"I'll be there," she said, and then he heard the dial tone.

Mateo could almost see her scurrying about getting dressed. He enjoyed having this certain power over women like Marty. She would love the evening ahead—and she would hate it.

Mateo dressed in dark slacks, a dark turtleneck, and a gray tweed sport jacket. Marty would like the outfit, and she would tell him.

He was waiting in a doorway several yards down from the restaurant when a taxi pulled to the curb. Marty paid the driver and went inside, but not before smoothing her short skirt and checking her reflection in the restaurant's window. He smiled.

When Mateo walked through the restaurant's door at a few minutes after eight, he told the hostess he was meeting a young lady.

"Oh, yes," the hostess said, motioning for him to follow. Marty recognized Mateo and stood to greet him.

He wrapped an arm around her, pulled her close, and said, "I hope I'm not late." Then he took her face in his hands and kissed her—hard.

When he released her, Marty struggled a little with her voice as she said, "Na … no, you're right on time. I just got here, too."

With his arm around her, Mateo turned and quietly gave his name to the hostess. They were quickly seated.

At their table—a small one, hidden and with only two chairs—Mateo watched as she unwrapped her silverware and placed the linen napkin in her lap. Her nerves were showing. A drink would help.

A waiter arrived for their bar order while another poured water. Marty watched, obviously fascinated. Mateo could tell she was not used to these kinds of surroundings.

"What would you like?" he asked. "Or would you like me to order?"

"You do it."

"Two bourbons on the rocks," Mateo told their server. "Your best. And make them doubles."

"Yes, sir."

A food waiter arrived.

"Give us a few minutes."

He could see their man carrying the drinks across the room.

Marty quietly watched Mateo take control of their evening. She had tiny upward curls at the corners of her mouth. Mateo glanced over, giving her a wink.

"Are you prepared for a very interesting evening?" he asked as they received their drinks.

Marty did not say anything until the waiter had finished and left them.

Gazing across at him, she nodded. "I think I am."

He lifted his drink and reached across to touch hers. As the glasses clinked lightly, he said, "I guarantee this will be a night you will remember." Then he gave her his most dazzling smile.

Her sigh said it all. She could have died right then; her life would have been complete.

Mateo just smiled.

Dinner was superb, the seafood extraordinarily delicious and plentiful. He kept the drinks coming, too. Marty had not noticed that Mateo changed his own drink choice to nonalcoholic after the first couple of rounds. He seemed to be having as much fun as she, but he was in control of his actions and, as she would later discover, of hers.

They finished dinner, and after a light dessert, he paid the check from a large roll of bills. Mateo made a show of leaving a large tip, too. He had already asked their waiter to call a taxi.

The roll of cash Mateo carried impressed Marty. She told him so. Marty also divulged that most of the men she dated could only afford beer when they went out.

Outside, he helped her into the taxi.

"What's your address?"

She told him.

She had been surprised when they stood up to leave the restaurant. Though tipsy during dinner, Marty was staggering now, and there was nothing, short-term, she could do about it.

Her concern was that he would simply take her to the apartment and drop her off. He probably won't even come in, she thought. Marty didn't blame him. The best date she'd had in two years and she was drunk out of her mind.

"Sh't, sh't, sh't!" she mumbled, almost a whisper. Still he heard her.

"What's wrong?"

"A'm dru'k … an' … an' … an' I don' wanna be." Her tears distorted everything. "Ah wan'd this tah be a spec'al night."

"Oh, it is," he assured her. "And it's not over yet."

That sounded good. Then she drifted off.

When Marty awoke, the taxi was in front of her apartment and he was helping her out of the backseat.

"Here, take my hand."

With almost no help on her part, they managed to get inside. Marty could not find her keys at first, then the lock proved elusive until Mateo took over. Once they made it through the door, he pushed it closed and tossed the key ring on a table near the doorway. Desperately hanging onto his arm, Marty managed to stagger toward her bedroom. Barely inside, she stumbled, then collapsed on the bed.

A moment later, or it could have been an hour as far as Marty knew, he had her top off and started to remove her bra. She wanted to help him—she really did—but couldn't. Too fa' gon'! she thought.

The next time she approached consciousness, she saw him dressed and moving around in her apartment, apparently getting ready to leave.

Marty hated herself. It always ended this way.


Mateo left her naked, spread out on the bed, when he was finished with her. He hated being with a drunk, and this one had been more than willing to go there. It was partly his fault, though. After all, he kept the drinks coming, and she was only trying to please him.

He didn't even pull the covers over her when he was finished.

After showering and dressing, he used his cell phone to call a taxi. Casting a last disdainful look at her body stretched out on the bed, Mateo left and walked through the apartment to the front door.

That was the way he liked sex—quick, nonresponsive, yet fulfilling, at least to him. He took dark pleasure in using, often even abusing women like Marty. Each of them was a stand-in for the one who had joined in on his naked torture when he was nine years old. Remembering that particular one, he thought, I should have killed her, too.

They were vulnerable, these substitutes. A few drinks, dinner, some seductive words whispered, and he could do what he wanted. Then he was free to leave. No strings, no complications, and no blood on his hands—most of the time.

He stepped outside her apartment, closing the door behind him. Inside, things would remain quiet until the morning.

She would awaken then, lamenting the fact that she could not remember his face. And she would not remember that she had mumbled "I love you"—over and over.

Marty awakened to chimes at six the next morning. She rolled toward the sound, moaned, and turned off the clock. The headache was a killer. She managed to slide off the bed and stumble into the bathroom. She was naked, having slept that way, so she stepped into the shower and turned the water on. Almost screaming when the cold water hit her, Marty threw her hair back and forced herself to endure the chilling spray. Finally, warm water flowed over her, muscles relaxed, and she bowed her head into the stream.

Twenty minutes later, she was dry and had donned her undergarments. She checked the apartment; he was gone. Alone, she skipped slipping into a robe. A strong cup of coffee would be the next step to recovery.

Today would be a long day. The hangover would last until midafternoon, at least.

Though she tried hard to remember, Marty did not even know if she had had a good time the night before. And she was pretty sure she would not hear from Carlos again. That might a good thing; somehow, she sensed a continuing relationship with her new friend could only end in a bad way.

Oh, well. Another of life's lessons learned. Hard way to do it, though!

 **Chapter 15**

Back at the Hotel St. Marie, Mateo took another shower before he crawled into bed. Looking at the clock, he realized he would only have about five hours to sleep. Closing his eyes, he started his normal process, counting backward from one-hundred. Sleep, as usual, was deep and dreamless.

When his wake-up call came, Mateo was already shaving. Thirty minutes later, he was in the Vacherie Cafe downstairs waiting for his food with a steaming cup of coffee in front of him.

After breakfast, he called for his car and drove out to the LSU Medical Center where Webster had supposedly died. Mateo parked and walked directly to the area where he had met the two men who helped him during his last trip.

He waited for several minutes before anyone came out for a break. Finally, two young black women came out of the building and sat on one of the concrete benches. They broke out their cigarettes and lit up.

Casually, Mateo approached them.

"I'm wondering if one of you could help me. I am looking for Willie and Carlo. Do you know them?"

The women both giggled as they glanced at each other. The tall one answered, "Yeah, sure, we know Willie and Carlo. Everybody does. Why are you looking for them?"

He had the women's interest. They appeared curious but cautious.

"They helped me with something recently," Mateo told them. "I need to clear up some details. That's all."

"You a cop?" the second one asked.

"No," he said chuckling. "I'm just trying to tie up some loose ends on a family member who died here. You know relatives. They want every last detail."

"Yeah. My family's like that, too," the tall one said while the other sat nodding.

The woman who had been doing most of the talking told him, "Carlo's not here today, but I saw Willie earlier. He comes on break at ten."

Mateo glanced at his watch. Nine thirty.

"Where can I get some coffee while I wait?"

"Go through that door and follow the signs to the cafeteria," the chatty one said, pointing.

"Thanks."

They were talking in hushed tones as Mateo walked away.

A little after ten, Willie came out to the break area. He saw Mateo, recognized him, and walked over, smiling.

"Hey, man. You lost?" Willie asked, reaching out to shake Mateo's hand. "We thought you were gone for good." Then his eyes lit up. "Say, you need somethin'? I'm broke as usual, and you pay really good."

"Well, actually I do need some more help," he told Willie. "What about Carlo? Are you two still a team?"

"He ain't here today," Willie said quickly. "Called in sick. Probably slept late. Way I look at it, ya' snooze, you lose."

"Okay. Here's what I need."

Willie's smile disappeared, and he got a serious look on his face as Mateo began laying out what he wanted.

"First, I need the name of the man who was in charge of the two wounded men—Mike Webster, the one who died, and the one who was flown out of New Orleans. I think you said his last name was Michaels. Second, I need all the personal information I can get about both wounded men. Names, addresses, next of kin. Everything you can find."

"That's gonna be hard," Willie said.

Mateo nodded and then continued, "Also, you said the man who survived was flown to a hospital up north. I want to know where. What city? What hospital? Again, everything you can find."

"Okay," Willie said. "This may take a couple of days. I can't go in there and just start pulling files. They'll want to know what I'm doin'. I'm just an orderly. I don't normally deal with files or charts. I get caught, I could lose my job. You gonna need to shell out big bills for this one."

"I pay top dollar for good information," Mateo told him. "You'll have too much money to spend."

"That'll be the day."

Oh, you won't need the money where you'll be going, Mateo thought.

"Call me when you have something," Mateo wrote down his cell number. Glancing up, he said, "Day or night. Okay?"

"You got it, man."

Mateo spent much of the afternoon planning the steps he would take after he heard back from Willie. Finding an isolated spot to meet with him was high on that list. Mateo would have to deal with his new comrade afterward; that required planning of a different sort.

Long-range planning was difficult because Mateo had no idea where Webster might have been transferred. He could be anywhere, given the time that had passed since the shooting. His lists detailed the gathering of people, supplies, and weapons when a location had been determined. The Merchant would be there, of course, and he would probably want to bring some people with him. Mateo had a couple more in mind, too. He wanted no more than six, total. More than that and they would be stumbling over each other.

After several hours at the desk, Mateo showered again and dressed for a walk in the French Quarter. He found a walking tour map downstairs in the lobby and struck out to see the sites.

Not far from his hotel, Mateo found the St. Louis Cathedral and Jackson Square. He sat on one of the benches inside the square and watched the people for a while. This was one of his favorite pastimes. The area was crowded with pedestrians, many of them tourists, he assumed, and some residents. Most of those around the square and cathedral seemed unhurried. Mateo sat listening to a jazz trumpet playing somewhere outside the park.

He had dinner alone at an oyster bar there in the Quarter and then returned to his hotel for the evening. After going over the information he had prepared that afternoon, Mateo called it a night.

He slept late the next morning, had a pancake breakfast near the hotel, and then went for a drive. Time behind the steering wheel always cleared his head and made his thinking sharper. An hour later, he found himself at the shoreline of a large body of water. Consulting his map, he realized he had made his way out to Lake Pontchartrain.

Mateo parked the Volvo and strolled along the seawall. The waves lapping on the steps and the clouds along the horizon were mesmerizing and the walk was comfortable in the cool weather. He returned to his car thinking of Pablo and the anger he harbored for Webster. Those depths of emotions, especially hate and anger, could be self-consuming. Thinking back to their conversation, Mateo was concerned that was happening to Pablo.

When he left the lake, Mateo drove around the old homes scattered nearby. Many were large with sprawling grounds, almost castle-like. He could see history there, not unlike that of cities in other countries. He smiled, comparing these surroundings to those of his childhood on the streets of Mexico City—a human irony in his own life.

Late in the afternoon, as he was driving back to the French Quarter and his hotel, the cell phone buzzed.

Mateo answered, "Yeah?"

"That you, man?" He recognized Willie's voice.

"Say, you got a name? I don't know what to call you."

"Carlos," he said. "Carlos Merro. Do you have something for me?"

"I'm gonna have a bunch of stuff. I had to let Carlo in on it, though. Too many questions and too many files for me to do it all by myself. We're gonna need some workin' money, too," Willie said. "We'll have to pay for some of the things you want."

"Now wait a minute," Mateo was suddenly nervous. "Don't get other people involved. You said you could get what we needed."

"Suit yourself, man. No skin off my teeth. But if you want everythin' you told me, we gonna have to pay some people."

"Keep my name out of it!"

"Oh yeah, man. If we give 'em money, they ain't gonna be askin' no names, you know what I mean? They'll just get the stuff and give it to us."

"Okay … how much?"

"Five or six hundred ought'a do it. We'll just feed 'em twenty or so at a time till we get what we want. You know, like you did Carlo and me before." Willie laughed. "Just kiddin', man."

"When do you need the money? And where can I get it to you?"

"Tonight would be good," Willie said. "If we pick up the money tonight, we may be able to have everythin' for you by tomorrow."

"Okay. Listen, there's one more thing I want."

"What is it?" Willie sounded cautious.

"Can you get a pistol and some ammo for me? Oh, and I'll want the gun to have a silencer."

"Man, you don't want much, do you? Say, you ain't gonna shoot me and Carlo with this pistol, are you?" Willie laughed again. "When do you need it? I'll see what I can do."

"You can bring it when we get together tomorrow," Mateo told him. "How much money do you need for the weapon? You'll need it tonight, too, won't you?"

"What kind of pistol do you want?"

"Twenty-two caliber semi-automatic with a long barrel and the silencer. Oh, and a box of hollow point ammo."

"Better bring fifteen hundred for all that," Willie told him. "If it's more, we'll work something out."

"Where can we meet?" Mateo asked.

"You know the donut place down in the Quarter? They got beignets and French Market chicory coffee."

"Yeah, I know the place."

"Meet us there at six."

"See you then," Mateo said and hung up.

Mateo drove back to the hotel and went up to his room. He stopped by the desk and asked if they had a plain business envelope. He took it up to his room and slipped twenty-two one hundred–dollar bills into it. Sealing it, he then slipped the envelope into his jacket pocket. With his chores out of the way, Mateo lay down on the bed and rested until it was time to meet Willie and Carlo.

At five thirty, Mateo brushed his teeth and freshened up. Thirty minutes later, he was drinking French Market coffee and waiting for his new associates. A short time later he saw them, deep in conversation, walking toward the café.

Willie and Carlo grinned as they sat down but kept their voices low as they said hello.

"You got the money?" Willie asked.

Mateo took the envelope from his jacket and slid it across the table. Willie picked it up, weighing it first in his hand, and slipped it in his jacket pocket.

"Feels about right," he said.

"It should feel a little heavy," Mateo told him. "I put in an extra bill for running around money."

"Hey, thanks, man. You a sport."

"You think you'll be able to get the items we discussed?"

"Don't worry," Carlo told him. "I already made a call. We'll have 'em when we see you again."

Willie and Carlo ordered coffee but left after taking only a couple of sips. Mateo stopped for a sandwich on his way back to the Hotel St. Marie. Back in the privacy of his room, he checked in with Pablo. They could only talk in general terms, so the conversation was short.

"I've contacted the people I spoke to when I was in New Orleans the last time," Mateo told the Merchant. They are getting the information for me, maybe as early as tomorrow evening."

"I knew I could count on you," Pablo said.

Mateo was eager to get off the phone. "I'll call as soon as I have something."

After hanging up, Mateo showered and lay in bed watching the news and then a talk show. He went to sleep thinking of ways he could close his situation with Willie and Carlo. He needed to finish it in a way that didn't come back to haunt him later.

# Chapter 16

A call came in to Robbins's cell phone just after five in the morning. He answered with a sleepy voice. Tom Manning was on the line sounding serious and excited.

"I need you to send one of your people to New Orleans. Somebody's asking questions about Webster." Manning took a breath and then continued. "We need to find out who's doing the asking."

Robbins was technically still on vacation but didn't mention it this time. Manning knew the situation, so Jack figured this must be high priority. Besides, he did not want to take a chance on anyone finding Webster.

"I'll get someone moving on it," he told Manning.

"Yesterday would be good. You follow me?"

"I'm with you. I'll get back to you when I have something working," Robbins said. "By the way, how did you find out?"

"I received a call from the LSU Med Center," Manning said. "This might be a casual inquiry, but we can't take a chance."

They needed someone sharp for the assignment, someone who could think on the move. Robbins decided the best person for the job was a woman---------, U.S. Deputy Marshal Amy Hogan.

Hogan had been with the U.S. Marshals Service for nine years, the last two spent on Robbins's field team. Physically, she could take down most men, regardless of size, before they knew what was happening. She was also a crack shot with a Glock 22 .40 caliber pistol.

She was attractive, too, with short, dark hair and big, brown puppy-dog eyes that could be hard as steel when necessary. Hogan did not take a lot of lip from anyone, including her fellow agents, so she certainly would not take it from anyone on the wrong side of the law. And at five eleven, she definitely stood out in a crowd.

Hogan climbed out of her seat before the plane stopped moving and retrieved her laptop and other belongings from the overhead compartment. She was the first person to deplane when the flight attendant opened the door. Choosing not to respond to the "Thank you for flying Delta," she walked purposefully off the plane and through the concourse.

Hogan rented a vehicle and asked for a map of the New Orleans area. She slipped the rental papers and map into her briefcase and went to locate her car. Once everything was secured in the backseat, Hogan slipped behind the wheel and unfolded the map.

She had asked the rental agent if there was a Best Western somewhere near the downtown area of New Orleans. The man had checked the yellow pages and said there was one on St. Charles Avenue, in the five hundred block. Hogan set the vehicle's GPS and headed out. An hour later, she had registered, taken her things to her room, and freshened up.

Now, with a pad and pencil in front of her, she sat at the desk. Hogan liked to get her basic plan on paper before she ventured out.

Robbins had put her in touch with Tom Manning for the assignment. She had never worked directly for Manning, but he sounded efficient and serious on the phone.

"Get in touch with Dr. Howard Best at the LSU Medical Center," Manning had told her. The tip that someone was looking for Webster had come through the medical office.

The good doctor had called looking for his old friend Jack Robbins. When told Robbins was on vacation, he had asked for Robbins's boss and been handed off to Manning.

According to their information, a Latino man had shown up at the hospital a few weeks earlier. He had inquired about one of the men shot when the New Orleans police superintendent was arrested. Recently the Latino had been seen again, this time talking to one of the orderlies in the emergency room area of the hospital. When Dr. Best heard about it, he thought Jack Robbins should be informed.

Things had happened fast after Tom Manning was told about the inquiries. The news had reached Manning about ten hours ago. Hogan was now on the ground in New Orleans.

When she called Dr. Best's office, Hogan was asked to hold while the doctor was found. He was expecting the call. Hogan listened to Cajun music for a short time before he picked up.

"Hello, Dr. Best here."

"Doctor, my name is Amy Hogan. Tom Manning asked me to come to New Orleans and visit with you. Would you have some time for me this afternoon?"

"I'll see you whenever you can get here," he said.

"I'll be there in thirty minutes." Hogan was already on the way as she ended the call.

Dr. Best looked at the phone before placing it back on the hook. He was not used to having callers hang up on him.

He buzzed his secretary, telling her to find the two nurses who had flown with him when they had taken Webb Michaels up north a few weeks back. Five minutes later Judy arrived, with Sarah a couple of minutes later. Dr. Best waved them in.

"There's someone coming to check on the Latino fellow who's asking questions about Webster and Michaels. Either of you heard anything?"

The two women looked at each other and then Judy answered, "Nothing since we talked to you last night." Sarah nodded agreement.

"Tell me again exactly what the med techs told you," Dr. Best said.

Sarah spoke up, "Maggie and Tammy said a Latino man had been here a couple of days ago. They said he was asking questions about the man who had been killed in the shootout when the police superintendent was arrested. They didn't say he used Webster's name."

"Did this fellow talk directly to the women?"

"No," Judy said. "He was looking for a couple of their friends, Willie and Carlo. I don't know their last names. They're both orderlies in the emergency room area."

Then the doctor asked, "What was the Latino looking for?"

"He was here several weeks ago and seemed to be trying to make sure Webster was really dead," Judy said. "According to the women, Willie and Carlo asked a few questions and then sneaked in later to look through some records. They got enough information to assure the Latino that Webster had died. Someone even said they saw papers about the autopsy."

Sarah then continued, "They said the Latino was satisfied on the first visit and gave Willie and Carlo some money for their efforts."

"Then he showed up again a day or two ago?" Dr. Best inquired.

"Yeah," Sarah agreed, "two days ago. This time he wanted to know about Webb Michaels, too. Who he is and where he was flown to. And he wants to know who was in charge of Webster and Michaels."

"Were the men able to get answers for him?"

"The women didn't know," Judy said. "Willie and Carlo are both off this afternoon. It will be morning before we can ask without letting them know someone's investigating."

"Okay," Dr. Best said. "This gives me what I need to talk with Webster's people. Thanks."

The nurses had just left when Amy Hogan arrived. Dr. Best introduced himself and led her into his office. "Can I get you something, coffee or water?"

"No. I'm fine," Hogan assured him. "I'll try to be brief. What can you tell me about the man who's asking questions?"

"Here's what I know," Dr. Best said. He then repeated everything Judy and Sarah had told him. When he had finished, he added, "Willie and Carlo are due back at work tomorrow morning. Do you want to interview them?"

"Actually, I'd rather try to catch up with them tonight," Hogan said. She didn't say she preferred to reach them before they had further contact with the Latino. Hogan wanted to know what information they had been asked to get for him.

"I would like to influence them to tell him what I want, but," Hogan ventured, "I'm guessing they may have already set a meeting."

"You think so? This quick? I'm not sure they could have learned anything of value the way they would have needed to go about it." Dr. Best was unsure about what records might be available to the orderlies. Then he looked at Hogan and acknowledged, "They've both worked here for several years. They may know more about where things are kept than I give them credit for."

"Would this type of information be kept under lock and key?" she asked.

"Probably not. There could be notes in the patient file. Technically and normally, no one but the doctors and nurses should be in those charts," he told her. "Of course, we're not dealing with a normal situation here."

"I agree," Hogan said. "I'm going out to the men's homes to see what I can salvage. Can you give me some addresses?"

"Let me see." Dr. Best turned to his computer. He did not have Willie's or Carlo's last names, but he traced them through their job assignments.

"Willie's last name is Johnston," he told Hogan, "and his address is 2838 Pasteur Boulevard. That's out near the University of New Orleans." Hogan wrote the information in a small notebook she carried.

"Oh, and here's Carlo. That's Carlo Alvera's. His address is 917 Prentiss Avenue, Apartment 29. It is in the same area as Willie's. Be careful," he told her. "Hurricane Katrina did a lot of damage in the area where they live. People are still living in FEMA trailers in several places. The lighting isn't good at night, so watch yourself. Are you going alone?"

"No choice," Hogan said. "I'll be careful." She closed her notebook and prepared to leave. "I'll call you tomorrow and bring you up-to-date."

Back in her car, Hogan unfolded her map again, found Willie's street, and set the GPS. She did not have a good feeling about the information she'd been given. Before pulling out onto the street, Hogan moved her purse closer and unzipped the pocket holding her Glock.

 *Chapter 17*

Early that same afternoon, Mateo received a call from Willie Johnston.

"We got what you need, man."

"Everything?"

"Yeah!"

Although he had already decided on a location, Mateo asked, "Where can we meet?"

"Up to you, man," Willie said. "Your call."

Mateo had driven around during the day and picked out a drugstore at the corner of Carrolton Avenue and Airport Highway. Near the rear of the parking lot there were some trees and, as far as he could tell, very little light once night settled in.

"I needed some things this afternoon and stopped at a drugstore on Airport Highway at Carrolton. Let's meet there, at the rear of the parking lot." Mateo didn't want to spook the two men, so he added, "We don't want anyone to see us passing the weapon around."

"I know the place." Willie said, "Yeah, man. That's good. We'll meet you there. What time?"

"Nine o'clock, okay?"

"We'll be there. And don't forget, you need to take care of us really good this time."

"Oh, I will," Mateo assured him and closed the phone.


Hogan found Willie's place without delay. It was an older house that had been converted into a duplex. Willie's apartment had its own entrance off the small front porch. She knocked three times, each one louder, and then listened to the silence inside. Obviously, no one was home.

She then decided to try Carlo's location since they lived near each other. She had the same result. A neighbor opened the door on apartment 28 and looked out.

The big woman said, "Don't matter none how hard you knock, he ain't home. Seen him leave 'bout two o'clock. Ain't been back."

"Thanks," Hogan told her. "I'll come back later."

"Won't do no good," the woman said. "When he go cattin', ain't no telling when he be home."

"Thanks, again," Hogan said as she walked to the stairs.

Back in her car, Hogan thought about eating. She hadn't had anything since the crackers on the airplane. She decided to have supper somewhere and then try again.

~ ~ ~

As Deputy Marshal Hogan headed off to eat, Mateo was driving to meet Willie and Carlo. He planned to get there early and set up the situation. In meetings like this, it was always good to know in advance how things could be expected to play out. He wanted Willie and Carlo to be walking away from the store's traffic when they returned to their vehicle.

When he arrived at the parking lot, Mateo drove slowly toward the thick row of trees growing across the rear of the space. He picked an exact spot for his own car and backed into it. Willie and Carlo would likely park farther back. At the present time, there were several cars in the lot, but most would likely be gone by nine o'clock.

With the parking issue settled, Mateo looked around for security cameras. Sure enough, there was one about half way back on the building. But … someone had obviously not wanted it there. The camera was pointing upward and damaged beyond repair. It wouldn't be a problem for Mateo and his little meeting.

Satisfied, Mateo drove out of the lot and went to get a sandwich.

At eight fifty, he was back, parked in the spot he had picked for himself, and watching for his contacts. Willie and Carlo drove in five minutes later and parked a few spaces farther back in the lot, just as Mateo had anticipated.

The men got out of their vehicles, and Mateo waited as Willie and Carlo walked over to the Volvo. Willie carried a paper bag.

"Got the weapon, man, and it's a good one." Willie held the bag out to Mateo. "Saved you a couple of bills, too."

"Okay!" Mateo exclaimed. "Sounds good. Let's take a look."

He slipped the pistol out and handed the bag to Willie.

"Show me how it works." Mateo intentionally sounded like a kid with a new toy. "Where's the silencer?"

Willie glanced at Carlo and then back at Mateo. He shook his head as though wondering whether Mateo had ever held a weapon before.

"Just hold on a minute. The silencer's in the bag." Willie said it like he was talking to a slow child.

The three of them took a quick look around to be sure no one was watching. Willie then took the suppressor and magazines out of the bag and passed the bag to Carlo.

Glancing at Mateo, he nodded toward Carlo and said, "There are two boxes of hollow points in the bag and the mags are full."

Willie took the weapon back from Mateo, handed him the magazines, and then screwed the suppressor onto the muzzle of the pistol. He then reached for one of the magazines, inserted it into the butt of the pistol, and kicked it home with the heel of his left hand. The click was audible when it locked into position.

"There now," he said to Mateo as he handed it back. "All you got to do is jack a round into the chamber, flip the safety off, and pull the trigger. Aimin' would be good, too," Willie said and chuckled.

"Where's the safety?" Mateo asked.

"There," Willie said as he pointed.

Mateo held the weapon as though it was the first time. Willie watched him for a moment and then peeked over at Carlo and rolled his eyes. He obviously hoped Mateo didn't shoot himself before they got out of the parking lot.

Mateo pointed into the trees and took aim on an imaginary target. "Bang! Bang!"

"Hey, man," Willie said excitedly. Looking back toward the drugstore, he exclaimed, "Don't go wavin' that thing around. Somebody sees us, they'll call the cops."

Mateo peered around, too, and said, "Yeah, you're right." He shoved the pistol into his belt and dropped the second magazine into his jacket pocket. The bag with the extra ammo went into another pocket.

Looking at Willie, he said, "You and Carlo split the rest of the money I gave you for the weapon. It was worth it."

"Thanks, man," they said in unison and glanced at each other, smiling.

"Now," Mateo said, taking charge of the meeting, "what have you been able to find out?" He looked at Willie, "You said you had a bunch of stuff for me."

"Well," Willie started, "we got the man that was in charge. Name's Jack Robbins. Nothin' on him but a cell phone number." Willie was reading from a folded paper he had taken from his pocket.

"What about the two men who were shot?" Mateo asked. "What did you get on them?"

"Gimme a minute," Willie said. He sounded a little put out. "I'm gettin' to them." He looked back at the paper and then at Mateo.

"First, on the one that was killed. He didn't seem to have no next of kin. The form said if somethin' happened to 'am, he wanted to be burned up—you know, creamed." Willie looked at Mateo and then at Carlo. Then he shuddered.

"I don't understan' that. Being' burned even if I'm dead don't sound like somethin' I want."

"You didn't find anything about his body being shipped to a crematorium or anything like that?" Mateo asked.

"No," Willie said and shook his head, "and we searched good, too. I even paid this broad who knows 'bout record systems to look. She couldn't find nothin' either."

"That's strange," Mateo said. He been still silent as he considered the details.

Willie continued, "Yeah, I thought it was weird, too. When I couldn't find nothin' 'bout his body bein' shipped, I paid somebody ta' look at the morgue records. Thought maybe he was still in one of them drawers down there."

"And?" Mateo was starting to get impatient.

"And Webster ain't there—nowhere."

Carlo spoke up, "I checked, too. Willie's right. His body's gone. There's no record of it anywhere."

Mateo stared at the two men. They stared back, both men shaking their heads.

"What about an address on Webster? Where did he live?"

Carlo answered again, "He lived in Tennessee, but he'd only been there for a few weeks. His record said he had moved to Knoxville from Atlanta. The Knoxville address is on the paper Willie's got."

"Okay, what about this Webb Michaels guy that got moved up north?"

"We got an address on him," Willie said quickly. "He lives in the capital—you know, DC. Works for the Agriculture Department accordin' to his transfer records. That don't make no sense neither. What would someone who works for the Agriculture Department be doin' gettin' shot down in N'awlins?" Then he said it again, "Don't make no sense."

"Did you find out where they took him? When I was here earlier, you said up north some place."

Willie looked like he didn't really want to answer that question. "The only information I found said they moved him ta' Memphis. Don't name a hospital or a doctor or nothin', and it don't say why they took him there. I woulda' thought they'd take him home to DC."

Mateo was getting disturbed. "Hell, Willie, you don't have much of anything, just more questions." Now he was angry.

"I know it ain't much, man, but we really dug around. There just ain't nothin' there."

"You got nothing else?" He paused. "This is it?"

"There's one more thing," Willie said. "The people that flew him out of here are stationed in Texas. International Air Taxi is the name o' the company, and they're out o' Dallas. The address and phone numbers are on the paper."

"Damn it!" Mateo exclaimed.

Willie shook his head again. "I know it ain't much, but it's all me and Carlo could get." Willie hesitated for a moment. Then he volunteered an opinion to Mateo, "Funny thing … the newspapers made it sound like this Webster fella was a civilian an' was just in the wrong place at the wrong time. But accordin' ta' some o' the other orderlies on the floor, Robbins was real interested in Webster an' his condition." He glanced at Carlo and said, "Ain't that right, Carlo?"

Carlo nodded but let Willie continue.

"The other thing that's funny," Willie added, "is that nobody actually seen the other guy, Michaels, till they got ready to transfer him out o' the hospital. That was on Monday after he came in late Wednesday night."

"Was the transfer a big deal?" Mateo asked.

"Yeah … accordin' ta' this friend o' mine." Willie rubbed a hand back and forth across the top of his head. "The doctors moved Michaels out early on Monday mornin' an' it was hush, hush. They rolled him out, put him in the ambulance, an' he was gone. Even his files are gone. The only thing left is a transfer record."

This interested Mateo. "Did you get the name of the place where he went?"

"Jus' said a facility in Memphis. Didn't say which one," Willie told him.

"What else?" Mateo asked.

"That's it. Everythin' I'm telling you is on this paper." He held up the sheet for Mateo to see. "I'm gonna give it to you when we finish talkin'."

Mateo gave the appearance of relenting. "Ah, hell, Willie. I know you and Carlo tried. Somebody's covering things up. It's not your fault." Mateo playfully jabbed at Willie and then at Carlo. "How much do I owe you fellows?"

"I don't know, man. How much do you think it's worth?"

Mateo thought for a moment. "How about five more bills each?"

Willie looked at Carlo and got a slight nod.

"That's fine," he said to Mateo. "Five's good."

Mateo took out the roll of money he always carried and started to strip off hundred-dollar bills. When he finished, Mateo divided them between the men.

"I gave you each six hundred. I know you took some chances."

"Thanks, Mr. Merro," Carlo said and stuck his hand out to shake.

"Me, too," Willie chimed in. He handed Mateo the notes.

They shook hands and slapped each other on the back. Then Willie and Carlo said good-bye and started back to their vehicle.

They were almost there when they heard a metallic noise close behind them.

Willie recognized the sound of a bullet being chambered even as he spun around. Mateo was in a shooting crouch a few feet away.

In a cold voice he said, "Guess what, Willie? I know how to use one of these."

Willie recognized the bad situation, but he tried. "Don't, man. Please. We ain't gonna—"

The bullet struck him above the left eye. Willie was dead before his body struck the asphalt. Mateo immediately shifted his aim to Willie's friend.

Carlo had his hands half raised as he looked down at his friend.

"Ah, man—" Then Carlo's life ended too.

Mateo stepped over and fired another round into each man's brain. Traffic on nearby streets had easily covered the slight sound of the double execution. Then he knelt and took the money he had just given them. He emptied their billfolds, too, and checked their pockets for anything that might connect them back to him. Finally, he picked up the four shell casings and dropped them into his pocket.

When he had finished, Mateo stood up and glanced around, making sure no accidental spectators had stumbled onto the scene; there were none. The parking lot was eerily quiet and empty.

Mateo slipped on latex gloves, reached into another pocket, and retrieved three small packets of cocaine he had purchased in the French Quarter the prior night. He always planned ahead. Mateo scattered the drugs near the bodies, tearing one packet and spreading its contents.

The killings had been almost soundless. Mateo was pleased; the suppressor Willie had bought for him had worked well.

As he pulled out of the parking lot, Mateo began planning the next step. He would have to talk with the pilot who flew Webb Michaels out of New Orleans. For that he would need to go to Dallas.

Mateo knew he should operate from the shadows until Webster's location was determined. Toward that end, he chose to drive to Texas.

# Chapter 18

Over the last few weeks, Webster's life had been the best he could remember for a long time. Except for almost losing his life, some really good things had come his way.

He had become friends with Irene and Bob. Both visited him regularly. Bob even helped with chopping the wood from time to time. When the rack on the porch was full, they would each take one of the big rockers and discuss world affairs or the NFL standings, whichever was more important. Bob brought a six-pack of Miller Lite at some point, and occasionally they would partake. Bob kept him stocked with chips, peanuts, and veggies, too, as required by the good doctor.

Irene brought meals when she could and sometimes stayed late if she didn't have to make rounds. Their discussions usually took place on the porch, which seemed comfortable for both of them. Neither had allowed their time together to become serious since their earlier, almost disastrous, encounter at the cabin. That was okay, too.

Webster's healing was coming along nicely. The physical therapist and Bob had conspired to make ordinary chores a part of his recovery process. They often had him carry heavy boxes of this and that back and forth between his cabin and the medical building, and there was always the need for firewood. He was, though, for all practical purposes, back to normal; the remaining soreness in his body was only a reminder of his close call with death.

Jack Robbins called him often, so Webster wasn't surprised when the cell phone rang as he relaxed in one of the big rockers. He now carried the phone 24/7.

"Yes, Jack?" Only a few individuals had his number, not even Bob or Irene.

"Evening, Mike, ah, Webb," Robbins said. "Damn, I may never get used to calling you that."

"It's okay. I'm going back to using Mike anyway. I've decided," he said matter-of-factly, not leaving it up for discussion. "Everyone will have to get used to it. Now, what's going on? Can I do something for you?"

"I need to bring you up-to-date. I'm not trying to alarm you, but this is a wake-up call," Robbins told him. "Someone has been asking questions down in Louisiana. We received information on this three days ago. The doctor who took care of you called us." Robbins sounded worried. "We've sent someone down to check it out."

"Who did you send?"

"Amy Hogan. I figured she would draw less attention."

"Yeah," Webster agreed. "They probably wouldn't be expecting a woman."

"I wanted to let you know what's happening," Robbins said. "I don't think we have to worry. We covered our path pretty well, yet we both know that we shouldn't relax too much."

"Tell me about it," Webster said. "Wink at a pretty girl and you'll get shot every time."

"Yeah, every time!" Robbins sort of skipped over the joke, then continued. "I'll keep you informed. In the meantime, you might want to make sure you're familiar with your territory."

"Speaking of my territory, how much longer do you think I'll be staying here?"

"I've talked to Tom Manning about it. There's no one needing the cabin at the moment, so we think you should stay where you are. Any problems at your end?"

"No," Webster said, maybe a little too quickly. He added, "I like it here."

"Don't get too comfortable," Robbins cautioned. "We could pull you out on an hour's notice. Oh, and be nice to the staff."

"What do you mean by that? I'm always nice."

"I hear you. Talk to you later." And Robbins was gone.

Webster closed his phone and relaxed back into the rocking chair. Maybe I'm getting lazy, he thought. I should have already checked out the territory.

He got up and headed out toward the medical building. Three miles and it's still uphill—both ways.

Webster knew Bob would be working that afternoon. When he arrived at the facility, he searched around for his friend and found him in the coffee room talking to a couple of other people. They all said hello when he joined them. Bob feigned a punch at him and laughed when he dodged.

"I think somebody's lost a step," Bob kidded. Then Bob introduced him to the man and woman. They were both nurses and worked with Bob. After a quick hello, they excused themselves and went back to their duties. Bob stayed.

"What's going on? You walk all the way here?"

"All the way. Why, didn't you think I could?"

"Oh, I figured you could walk here," Bob said. "I'm just wondering how you're going to get back. I'm not taking you," he said and laughed.

With the kidding over, Bob said in a more serious tone, "Okay, I don't figure you came all the way here for your health. What do you want?"

Webster looked at Bob and smiled. "Am I that transparent?"

"Sometimes," Bob said. "Actually, at times you're like a little boy in a man's body. Don't get me wrong. That's not necessarily a bad thing."

Webster grew reflective, and his expression must have changed. The image of Cary Warren had suddenly come to his thoughts when Bob made the comment. That's the kind of thing Cary would have said. Damn! When will I stop missing her?

The change in his expression must have made Bob think the remark had bothered Webster. Bob looked concerned.

"Oh, you didn't hurt my feelings. It's just that someone else recently said that to me. You made me remember her."

"Must have been someone that mattered."

"Yes … it was," Webster said quietly. After a moment, he added, "She still matters … I guess."

There, he thought, I've said it out loud.

They looked at each other, and each shook his head as though it was time to move on.

"Now, what do you need?" Bob asked.

"A map," Webster said. "I need a good map of the property here. The little one in the cabin's not detailed enough."

"I'll see what I can do, but it will have to wait until morning. Administration should have something, but they're closed for the day. I'll get with them early and come up with something."

"That's fine," Webster said. "I don't need it tonight. At least, I hope not."

Now Bob was curious. "Why do you need a map of the property?"

"I'd just like to know what cards I'm holding. You know, in case anything should come up. An invasion or whatever." He tried to make light of the situation.

"Look, man. I'm ex-marine," Bob told him. "This place is my second home. If there's a potential problem, I need to know. Maybe I can help."

Webster gazed at his friend thoughtfully. Maybe Bob could help.

"Can you keep this between the two of us? It's probably nothing. I just like to stay a step ahead."

"I'm not going to talk," Bob assured him, "unless it puts my patients in danger."

Webster stared at him for a few moments and then decided to bring Bob into his confidence.

"Let's take a walk."

As they strolled along the path outside, Webster told Bob about the phone call from Jack Robbins.

When he finished, Bob looked thoughtful and then asked, "How many people know you're here?"

"You guys, meaning you and Irene, and two or three on the outside. Not many. At least that's the plan."

"So … someone who had helped to get you here would have to let the cat out of the bag, so to speak."

"So to speak!"

"How likely is that?"

"Not very," Webster said. "We're a pretty tight group."

"Can't be too careful, though."

"No, you can't."

 **Chapter 19**

In New Orleans, Hogan was on the move, knocking on Willie's door at five thirty in the morning. There was no answer—still. She hoped that held no special meaning. A foreboding chill ran through her body.

Hogan returned to her vehicle and drove to Carlo's place. She got the same result—no answer when she knocked at his door either. Same song, second verse, she thought. The same feeling of dread she'd had earlier returned. She returned to her car and sat watching Carlo's door. After thirty minutes, she started the engine and went looking for breakfast.

When she had eaten, she returned to both places and still found no one home. She was definitely worried now. Hogan looked for Dr. Best's number and called him.

When he came on the line, he said he had bad news for her. "Willie and Carlo were both shot to death last night. I just found out."

Not surprised, she asked. "How? Where?"

"I don't have all the details," Dr. Best said. "The police identified them through their fingerprints."

"Who called you?"

"Carlo's sister called the medical center. The police had gone to her as next of kin. Their fingerprints were on file here because of their jobs. That got them identified quickly. The police wanted the sister to confirm Carlo's identity."

"Couldn't the police have identified them from their driver's license or ID cards in their billfolds?" Hogan inquired.

"That's the strange thing," Dr. Best answered. "Their billfolds were missing, and they didn't have any money on them. And there were several packets of cocaine scattered about on the ground where they were found." He hesitated for a moment. "Like it was a drug deal that went wrong."

"Or like someone wanted it to look that way," Hogan said. "Call me skeptical."

"I'm having some of those same thoughts," Dr. Best replied.

"I need to talk to your people," Hogan said. "With your permission, of course. And I'm going to call Jack Robbins and let him know."

"Yes, Jack should be advised. Who knows what's going on. We'll get you set up in a conference room and pull our people in as you need them. Some are off for the weekend, but we can get them here."

"You realize," she told him, "I won't be acting as a law enforcement officer. They aren't even required to talk to me. What they may tell me probably couldn't be used in court."

"I understand that," he said. "You're just trying to get ahead of whoever is trying to find out about Webster and Michaels."

"Exactly!"

"Come on out."

"I'm on my way."

~ ~ ~

Mateo's decision to drive to Dallas after the shooting solved several problems. He would need a vehicle when he arrived, and he just might need the pistol, too. Besides, by driving, he could delay anyone knowing where he was headed. Since he had used an alias, he could leave the Volvo anyplace. It could be a long time before the car was spotted.

After leaving the two bodies in the drugstore parking lot, Mateo had stopped at a food store and purchased new latex gloves and some freezer bags. Then he stopped near a construction site and gathered up a couple of medium-sized rocks. He made sure the rocks would fit into the bags and still accommodate the men's billfolds.

He had pulled over on a quiet street and made use of his purchases. Donning the gloves, he then fit three bags inside one another. Then Mateo checked the billfolds, pocketing the money inside them. No reason to waste it, he thought.

Mateo had made a package to dispose of the billfolds. He placed them in the plastic bags along with rocks to make them sink. Finished, he looked at the package and smiled, satisfied that the muddy Mississippi River would take care of the evidence.

Now, to get rid of it. He realized this was extreme, but it was better to be safe.

Earlier, he had looked at his map and studied the bridges that crossed the river. He started the Volvo and headed for his destination. A short time later, he was driving along a strand that would take him toward the west bank of the Mississippi. The traffic was light—just as he had hoped. As he reached the far side of the bridge, with the river still below, he turned on the vehicle's emergency lights and pulled to the outside lane.

He checked traffic and then climbed out of the vehicle. Mateo hoped the bridge authorities didn't show up before he could complete his chore. That would really screw up his night. The package was bulky but easy enough to carry over and slip through a hole in the protective railing at the side of the bridge. Mateo watched it fall away to the river below. Remembering the shell casings, he pulled those from his pocket and dropped them in the river, too.

Then Mateo moved back and acted as though he was examining his right front tire. Not a moment too soon either.

A bridge police vehicle pulled in behind the Volvo with lights flashing. The officer stepped around the rear of Mateo's vehicle.

"Something wrong, sir?"

"My car felt like it was pulling to the right," Mateo told him, "but I don't see anything. I guess it's okay."

"In any case, you're not supposed to stop up here. It's dangerous," the officer warned. "In the future, drive to the bottom of the bridge and then pull over." The officer started back to his vehicle and then turned. "Did I see you toss something off the bridge?"

A lump immediately materialized in Mateo's throat. "Yes, I tossed an empty drink cup over." He thought of the pistol hidden behind his hip and positioned his right hand to reach for it.

"You shouldn't litter, sir, and in the future, unless there's an emergency, drive to the bottom of the bridge to check your car."

Relaxing, he said, "Yes, Officer. I'll do that."

"Good night, and be careful."

The officer returned to his vehicle, and Mateo did the same. He pulled back on the travel lane and drove a mile or so before turning around. He crossed the river back to downtown and headed to his hotel. All the physical evidence of his meeting with Willie and Carlo was now at the dark bottom of the Mississippi River.

At the hotel, he showered and slipped into bed, hoping to get five hours sleep before leaving for Dallas. His last thoughts before dropping off were of plans to locate a certain pilot and find out where he had taken Webster on the flight up north.

# Chapter 20

Armed with news about the deaths of the two men, Deputy Marshal Hogan hurried to the LSU Medical Center and went directly to Dr. Best's office. The secretary motioned her through as the doctor was hanging up his telephone. The conference room was ready, he told her.

"Who do you want first?"

"The two young women this fellow talked to when he came looking for Willie and Carlo a couple of days ago."

"That would be Tammy Maples and Maggie Atkins," Dr. Best said. "I'll get them. Who else?"

"The two nurses who went on the flight with you."

"That's Judy and Sarah. I'll get them, too."

"That should get us started," Hogan said. "We'll see what develops from there."

A few minutes later, Hogan was seated in the conference room, and Tammy and Maggie were ushered in.

"First, let me say this is not a formal New Orleans police interrogation," Hogan told them. "I work with the U.S. Marshals Service. You don't have to answer any of my questions. Do you understand?"

"We want to help," one said.

"And you are …?"

"Tammy Maples."

"Okay, Tammy," Hogan said, "let's begin with you."

"Are we in trouble?" she asked, looking at Hogan and then at her friend.

"No," Hogan assured her, glancing at both women. "We think the man who came searching for Willie and Carlo a couple of days ago may be the same person who killed them."

"Oh lordy. Why would he do that?" Maggie asked, clearly upset.

"I thought they were shot in a drug deal," Tammy said, tears in her eyes.

"That may be true," Hogan said. "We're just trying to cover all of the possibilities.

"Now," she said, turning her attention back to Tammy, "tell me about this man. What did he say to you? What questions did he ask?"

"Well, first he asked if we knew Willie and Carlo," Tammy said. "We asked why he wanted to know, and he said they had helped him on another matter recently, something about his family. He said a family member had died here, and he wanted to clear up some things."

Maggie spoke up, "I asked him if he was a cop."

Hogan looked at her and grinned. "What did he say?"

"He said he wasn't and started laughing. I remember that because he had a nice way of laughing." Maggie smiled, remembering. "Then he said he was just trying to find out about the family member's death. He said something like, 'You know how families are about things like that.'"

"Yeah," Tammy said to Hogan. "He said they wanted every detail."

"Is that all?" Hogan asked.

"Pretty much" Tammy said. "We told him Carlo wasn't at work that day and that Willie would be out for his break a little later. Then he asked where he could get some coffee while he waited. We suggested the cafeteria and told him how to get there."

"So, you think he probably came back to meet Willie later?"

The women nodded their heads in unison.

"Do either of you know if he talked to anyone besides Willie?"

They each shook their heads.

"We probably would have heard if he had," Maggie said. "There're enough single women around here that word would have gotten around. He was sexy. You know, Latino with the dark hair and eyes and all that. He was tall, too, and good looking, really good looking." She glanced at her friend. "We would have heard, you know what I mean?" She seemed to expect that Hogan, being a woman, would understand.

Hogan nodded and said, "Thank you both. If you think of anything else, tell Dr. Best. He'll know how to reach me."

The women left, and Hogan walked to Dr. Best's office. He was gone, so she asked his secretary to contact Judy and Sarah, the nurses, and ask them to come to the conference room.

They came and tried to help, but they only repeated what Hogan and Dr. Best already knew. Hogan spoke with several other people who had been in positions where Willie might have sought information for his contact. No one knew anything. The most any of them would acknowledge was that Willie or Carlo had been seen nosing around the files. No one admitted having helped them.

When Hogan had finished the interviews, it was well into the afternoon. She got a sandwich in the cafeteria and then met with Dr. Best to discuss the situation. They agreed they had no way of concluding which records Willie and Carlo had accessed. That being the case, Hogan decided she should look through the files herself and try to determine what information might be important if someone wanted to locate Webb Michaels.

When she asked Dr. Best about security cameras, he told her he had inquired about that, too. They were all operational and in good working order, Hogan was told, but the bad news was that images were only held for forty-eight hours unless there was an incident of some sort. So much for having photos of the Latino.

With the proper questions on the table, Hogan went to the files and quickly picked out the information she thought their man might have been looking for. If he thought Webster might still be alive with a new identity, that being Webb Michaels, then where did Webster/Michaels go? To answer that question, he would have had to ask how Webster was transported to wherever they took him.

Around two fifteen in the afternoon, while flipping through the Webb Michaels's transfer file, Hogan found a form dealing with the need to move him to another facility. And there, available for anyone who cared to know, was the name and location of the flight service used for transportation: International Air Taxi out of Dallas, Texas. Damn, she thought. Why didn't someone just put a notice in the newspaper?

She leaned back with the file on her knees and considered what to do next. Where to go? What answers to look for?

Then it struck her. If she had been looking for Webster/Michaels and had been given the information she had just found, she would have hightailed it to Dallas.

Shit! I'm already several hours behind him if he's on his way to International Air Taxi.

She grabbed her phone and dialed the number for the air taxi service shown there in the records. She wanted to give notice to the people who made the flight. When it was answered, Hogan was told that the pilot on Dr. Best's recent flight had just cleared the runway on a trip up north and wouldn't be available until the next day. Thinking fast, Hogan decided rather than try to explain the situation over the phone, she would fly to Dallas and try to get ahead of the Latino.

Hogan returned the file to its slot and looked at her watch. Three ten. She had her laptop and briefcase with her. Everything else she could do without in a pinch, and this damned sure qualified as a pinch. She borrowed a phone book. Figuring Delta was a good bet to get to Dallas in a hurry, Hogan called there first and got an agent.

As luck would have it, they had a flight due out in an hour and ten minutes. She might be able to make it. She gave them her information and credit card number and told the agent she would be carrying a weapon. She was told someone would meet her at the counter to review her ID and other papers and then escort her to the gate.

Hogan hung up and hurried to Dr. Best's office. Fortunately, he was in. She quickly explained the situation and then asked if he could have his secretary do her a favor?

"I don't have time to drive out to the airport, turn in the rental car, and still make my flight. Could I leave the key and let them pick it up here? And do you have anyone who could rush me to the airport?"

"I'm scheduled off for the rest of the afternoon," Dr. Best told her. "I'll take you myself. As for the rental, leave it here. We'll take care of it."

She grabbed her things and followed the doctor to his car. They rushed to the parking garage, and just inside, he stopped at a BMW two-seater, an old one.

Cute, she thought. Now I'm going to have to try to get into this thing.

When they were on their way and rushing through the traffic on I-10, he asked, "Have you ever ridden in one of these older models?"

"Nope," she told him. She was too busy hanging on to do much talking.

"They're small inside, as you might have noticed," he said and smiled.

"Yeah," Hogan said, and glanced over at him. "I was just thinking that it's more a matter of putting the damn thing on, rather than getting into it."

Dr. Best laughed as he zigzagged around the right side of two cars. Hogan felt sure the flight to Dallas on a real airplane would be significantly safer then this mad dash to the airport.

They pulled up in front of Delta's departure entrance with twenty-five minutes to spare. Hogan thanked Dr. Best and ran for the counter. There was a supervisor waiting. She presented her ID and showed her weapon. When they were finished, the individual called for a cart and escorted her to the gate with only moments to spare. The aircraft door swung closed and was secured as a flight attendant walked Hogan to her seat.

Things were moving fast and had become deadly with the murder of the two men. Hogan could only hope she had gained some time on the killer who was looking for Webster.

## Chapter 21

Mateo drove out of New Orleans a little after four thirty in the morning. It was five hundred miles to Dallas, he knew, and Interstate all the way. Pushing it hard, he should be there in eight or nine hours—one or two o'clock in the afternoon. He could live with that.

His watch showed one ten as he pulled into a rest stop outside of Dallas and its lunch traffic. Checking a phone book inside, Mateo found a number for International Air Taxi. He called and got a location—Dallas's Love Field. Examining a map of the area, he realized Love Field was a lot closer than the main airport. Another hour and he could be there.

He got back on the road.

Just after two, Mateo walked in the front door at International Air Taxi's location.

"Can I help you, sir?" the young and pretty young thing at the counter asked. Mateo made a mental note to keep his mind on business.

"I hope so," he told her while flashing his biggest smile. "What's your name?"

She hesitated and then said, "Elaina."

"Well, Elaina, I have to get to Cleveland in a hurry. Actually, I should have been there this morning, but I just found out about it."

"You've come to the right place," she replied. "We love doing the extraordinary."

"Well … here's the problem. I hate flying. I only do it when I'm forced to."

"I understand," Elaina said, giving him a sympathetic look. "How can we make it easier for you?"

"Well, I'm not sure you can, but … hmm, maybe there is a way. I have a friend in New Orleans, Dr. Howard Best. Howard used your company recently and was very complimentary of your pilot on the flight. I don't think he mentioned a name. If the pilot was someone I sort of knew, I think I would feel a lot better." Mateo smiled at her again. "Is that even a possibility?"

"If the pilot isn't on a flight and he's rested, I think we can work something out."

"Wonderful," he said. "Wonderful."

"I'll look at the schedules," Elaina said. "Please sit down over there while I check. Want some coffee or a coke?"

"Nothing. I'm fine. I'll just wait."

Five minutes later, Elaina walked over and told Mateo everything was arranged. She had gone back to the records for the last flight for Dr. Best. The pilot was on his way, and the aircraft was being checked out.

"How long before we can take off?" he asked.

She looked at the clock behind the counter and said, "Three o'clock okay? We'll get your information and mode of payment now and have you ready to go."

"Let's do that. Then I'll get my things and be back here at three," he said.

When they were finished, Mateo drove the Volvo over to the main terminal and parked it in the long-term lot. He flagged a taxi and told the man to take him to International Air Taxi. The driver started to complain of the short fare, but Mateo passed a one hundred–dollar bill over the seat.

"Yes, sir. At your service."

When the taxi arrived at International Air Taxi, Elaina ushered Mateo through the office into a hallway leading to the hanger. She turned him over to the pilot, a serious middle-aged man she introduced as Mark Pearl.

"I understand you don't like to fly," Pearl said. "I'll try to make it easy for you. To start with, we have a perfect safety record. I have nine hundred and twenty hours in the type of plane we'll be flying today. My copilot has almost six hundred." He smiled. "We know what we're doing. You can relax and take a siesta."

"Thanks," Mateo said. "I feel better already."

"Then let's get going," Pearl replied as he motioned Mateo toward the small, sleek Learjet.

"Is this the same plane you used when you flew Dr. Best up north?" Mateo asked as Pearl closed the door.

Pearl hesitated, thinking it an odd question. "Yes, as a matter of fact, it is. Why do you ask?"

"Just curious."

Pearl introduced the copilot, a smallish man, older than Pearl, who was busy going through the preflight checklist. His name was Doug Grisham.

Five minutes later, the small jet with its two-man crew and single passenger screamed into the midafternoon sky.

Mateo, sitting alone in the cabin, smiled and gazed out the window as he thought how easy it had been to isolate his new information source. He was already satisfied that Michaels and Webster was the same person and that a switch of some sort had been made.

Before they landed, Mateo intended to know where this pilot and plane had taken Webster. He had no doubts whatsoever that the pilot would tell him.

Mateo could be very persuasive.

# Chapter 22

Bob had come up with a map the day before. Using it, he and Webster had spent most of the morning exploring the grounds at the facility. Bob knew several of the guards and introduced them. He didn't use Webster's name, introducing him only as Jack.

Using Bob's golf cart, they toured the grounds, even going to some areas that Webster doubted Bob had ever been to. Paths near the back of the property were relatively unused. Obviously, there was not much guarding going on across the rear of the facility.

At the very back, a stout ten-foot wire fence ran along a river and through the brush and dense woods. On the northern border, a trailer park was visible through the trees. Children could be seen playing.

A young boy, probably twelve or so, turned from a pick-up baseball game and curiously watched Webster and Bob as they passed near the fence. The youngster even walked a few feet to keep them in sight for a time. Remembering what Rage had suggested, Webster filed that little fact away for future consideration and possibilities.

Using the cart, Webster could survey the terrain, including the area around his cabin. He made notes on the map; defensive ideas and plans were already developing in his mind. He would need help, though, and Webster thought he knew where to get it.

They had come full circle, finishing back at the medical building, and headed inside to the cafeteria.

Dr. Dunn entered the lunch line a little behind the two men and asked if she could join them. When they were seated, she wanted to know what they had been doing. Finding out they had been riding around the grounds on a golf cart instead of walking, she had choice words for both of them.

"You're supposed to be getting him in shape," she told Bob, "not patronizing his shiftless nature." The doctor smiled as Bob and Webster tried to talk their way out of trouble.

"It won't work," Dr. Dunn told them firmly. "I want both of you in the exercise room for two hours when you leave here. I'll be checking."

It was evident that she meant it. So, after putting their trays away, the two men headed for the torture chamber.

Webster had rapidly returned to the superior condition he had been in before being wounded. His relative youth and the fact that he liked being in shape, spurred him on. Bob found himself having a difficult time keeping up. Webster had a leg up. He had never mentioned his private exercise sessions to anyone.

"My good friend," Bob said after about an hour, "do you even know that you're making me look bad?"

"Come on," Webster teased him, "let's do another ten minutes on the stair climber and then we'll goof off for a while."

"That's what you said yesterday. Today you have to promise."

"I swear."

Dr. Dunn was standing at the door when they finished the ten minutes and motioned for Webster to join her.

"I'm finishing early tonight. Would you like me to bring you some dinner?"

"Dessert too?" he asked.

"Dessert, too," Irene said and smiled. "See you when I finish here. Might be as late as eight thirty or nine," she said.

"Whenever you can. You're always welcome. You know that."

"I know," she said as she turned and walked out the door. She looked back when she was in the hallway and winked. Webster blushed and hoped Bob hadn't seen the wink or the blush. He also hoped Irene had not formed any new romantic notions concerning him.

Bob was waiting when he came walking back, "Dr. Dunn gonna bring your supper?"

"Yep."

"Think I'll go home early then. My boy's got a game. I've missed a bunch of them this year."

"Get going then," Webster said. "Hope he wins."

"Me, too. See you tomorrow."

 *Chapter 23*

Tom Manning sat at his desk with the door closed. Jack Robbins was in a chair across from him. Manning had reached Jack at Chicago's O'Hare airport and told him to return to DC as soon as he could. Manning wanted Robbins there to help coordinate the hunt for the people searching for Webster. Jack had returned on the next available flight.

The late afternoon sun was starting to come in Manning's windows. Across the desk, with a frown and a very serious expression on his face, Jack Robbins didn't want to believe what he had been told.

"Hogan had tried to locate them last night," Manning said. "She interviewed several of Dr. Best's staff yesterday afternoon and tied down that the two dead men were gathering information on Webster and Michaels." He reached for the coffee mug on the corner of his desk. "When she went to their living quarters early yesterday evening, neither of them was home. Hogan went back later, but they still hadn't shown up. Now we know why."

"Do we know when they were killed?" Robbins asked.

"Sometime around nine last night," Manning said. "A drugstore employee found them when he got off work at nine thirty."

"When did Hogan find out?"

"This morning," Manning said. "Hogan went out early, and when they still hadn't returned, she called Dr. Best. He knew about the killings by then and told Hogan."

"What was the scene like?" Robbins asked. He was a stickler for detail.

"Hogan said there was a small amount of drugs scattered around, but she doubted it was a drug deal."

"Why not?" Robbins took a sip of his coffee.

"When she went through the files on Michaels and Webster, the information on the air taxi company was there. Hogan thinks that and the other information these two gathered probably got them killed. Whoever they sold it to didn't want them to be able to say what he got or to be able to identify him."

Robbins, elbows on the chair arms, held his coffee cup in both hands, contemplating as he stared at it.

"Yeah, that could easily be what happened," he said finally. "What's Hogan's status now?"

"She's on her way to Dallas," Manning said. "She wants to try and reach the pilot before someone else does. Whoever's hunting Webster is a cold-blooded killer. Hogan said the two men in New Orleans had basically been executed."

"Damn! I hope she gets to the pilot first. Why didn't she just call rather than flying to Dallas?"

"She did, but he was on a run someplace. Hogan's trying to get a jump on our killer."

Then Robbins informed his boss that he had alerted Webster in North Carolina.

"I don't really want to stir the pot for Webster unless we have to," Robbins told Manning. Then he added, "I did tell him to be familiar with the facility where he's staying, just as a precaution."

"That's fine. I would rather let him get back to 100 percent, too."

"Who do you think these people are?" Robbins asked. "I thought we had covered everything."

Manning appeared embarrassed; he gazed down at his desk and then back at Robbins.

Jack caught the look. "What?" he asked Manning. "What did I miss?"

"You and I are probably the cause of the problem," Manning said.

"What do you mean?"

"Remember how I asked for someone to go to New Scotland Yard recently, and you sent Webster?"

"Yeah?"

"Well," Manning said, "we think someone recognized our boy on the return flight."

"Shit!"

"Yeah, that's about what I said, too."

"Are you sure about this? I mean, are we certain he's been compromised?"

"No," Manning told Robbins. "We can't be certain about anything, but here's what we do know."

Robbins uncrossed his legs and sat up straighter, listening.

"My men met Webster at Kennedy International to take charge of the prisoner. Webster told them he thought a man on the flight had paid a little too much attention to him and his detainee. He wasn't sure which of them the man was interested in. You with me so far?"

"Yeah, go ahead."

"Webster gave our men a description of the guy. When my people took the detainee out of the airport, the individual saw them but didn't bother following.

That made us think he was interested in Webster."

Robbins nodded his head and said, "Okay, so far."

"Then we moved Webster to a different concourse for his flight back to Atlanta and Charlotte. The man couldn't have seen him. As a final precaution, we followed the man to his hotel when he left the airport. When we closed the surveillance, he was in his room."

"So, maybe he didn't recognize Webster after all," Robbins said hopefully.

"Well," Manning said with a sigh, "one of our people checked with the hotel the next morning and got some disturbing news."

"What?" Robbins asked. Manning was too slow in telling the damned story.

"A maid went into the man's room to clean it that morning and found him dead. It looked like an armed robbery, but we don't think so."

"Why not?"

"We think someone didn't want to pay for the information or didn't want the man who saw Webster to talk about it. The killing was too clean. We sent a man over to look at the scene. The man's cell phone, his billfold, and the bullet casings everything was gone. It was a professional hit. I'd bet on it."

"So where does that leave us?" Robbins asked.

"Hell, who knows." Manning got up from his desk and walked around to the chair beside Robbins. He sank into it and crossed his legs. "Right now we have Amy Hogan down south trying to chase down the people asking the questions. There's no reason to think they could know where Webster is located—at least not yet. I think they're trying to find out. I say we sit tight and see what Hogan turns up in Dallas."

~ ~ ~

As always, Amy Hogan was one of the first to walk off the plane. She carried her briefcase and laptop as she hurried through the terminal. When she reached the outside, Hogan flagged the first taxi she saw and literally jumped through the door into the backseat.

"Love Field, and hurry," she told the driver. "International Air Taxi, if you know the place."

"I do," the man said. "I've been there before."

"Good," Hogan said. "Finally, something goes right."

It was almost seven when they arrived. She asked the driver to wait, left her things in the backseat, and hurried inside.

There were two people, a man and a woman, behind the counter. The man sat at a desk in a back corner reading a newspaper. The woman was working at a computer but looked up when Hogan came through the door and nodded to her.

"Can I help you?"

"I'm looking for one of your pilots," Hogan told the woman. "Your company flew a patient out of New Orleans a few weeks ago. I think the job was arranged by Dr. Howard Best at the LSU Medical Center, although it may have been handled by Jack Robbins."

The woman took all of it in but did not say anything.

"Anyway," Hogan continued, "I need to talk with the pilot who made the flight. I called earlier today but he was on a trip and expected back later."

"None of the pilots are here at this time of the evening," the woman finally said. "There's just me. I'm supposed to handle emergencies, and there's a crew of mechanics and technicians in the hanger. Sounds like what you want will have to wait until they open the office in the morning."

"Damn," Hogan said under her breath. She looked around the office and then glanced back out toward the taxi.

"Don't get mad with me," the woman said defensively.

Hogan's attention returned to her. "Sorry, I wasn't angry at you. I'm upset at the circumstances. Is there anyone I could reach tonight? This is official business." Hogan flashed her badge.

The woman looked at the badge and then up at Hogan.

"Normally, the answer would be yes," she said, "but tonight both of the people who could help seem to be out of pocket. I've already tried to reach Elaina—that's the secretary. She doesn't answer her cell or at home."

"What about the manager?"

"He's out of town," the woman told Hogan. "He'll be back early tomorrow."

She decided to try one more thing. On the way to the New Orleans airport Dr. Best had given her the name of the pilot that had flown Webster's plane.

"What about Mark Pearl. I understand he's one of your pilots. Can I reach him?"

The woman hesitated and then told Hogan, "He's on a flight and won't be back until tomorrow morning. I'm sorry."

"Could we reach him on the radio or by phone if he's on the ground?"

The woman hesitated, then told Hogan that the pilot's wife had called earlier complaining she had not been able to reach Mark by phone.

"I tried to reach him by radio then," she said, "but got no answer. The radios seem to be shut down. That wouldn't be unusual if the aircraft was parked." Gesturing, she said, "I'm afraid you'll have to wait until morning."

Seeing no other alternative, Hogan asked, "What time does the office open in the morning? I'll come back then."

"It opens at eight, but there's usually someone here who could help you by seven."

Hogan could tell the woman was trying to be obliging.

"Thanks," she told her. "I'll be here."

When Hogan climbed back into the taxi, the driver asked, "Where to now?"

"The nearest hotel," she told him and slumped down into the seat. "Oh, and if we pass a drugstore, stop and let me pick up a few things."

They swung in at a Walgreen's location where the driver waited as Hogan went inside. Then he delivered her to a Comfort Inn a short distance outside the airport. She hoped airplanes wouldn't be buzzing the hotel all night.

Hogan gathered her things again and paid the driver, giving him a very nice tip for the waiting, the side trips, and his outstanding attitude through it all. He thanked her while seeming to take it all in stride.

"Just part of the job," he said.

Inside, Hogan registered and asked for a five thirty wake-up call. Then she went up to her room. She had picked up some snacks and a T-shirt for sleeping. She showered, wolfed down the snacks, and watched the news before slipping between the covers.

Hogan planned to be standing in front of that counter at seven the next morning. She hoped the pilot would be there early, too.

# Chapter 24

The flight had started routinely that afternoon. Copilot Doug Grisham had filed a flight plan for Cleveland. After take-off, Mark Pearl flew them to cruising altitude and set their headings for the first leg of their trip. The sky was spectacular, blue to the horizon with a few large billowing clouds here and there.

After the plane was positioned as he wanted it, Pearl turned the cockpit over to Grisham. The pilot then went back into the cabin to check on their passenger. Since the man said he didn't like to fly, Pearl was a little surprised at his relaxed posture. He was stretched out with his feet up and legs crossed on the opposite seat. He smiled as Pearl approached.

"How are you making out, Mr. Merro?" Pearl asked as he sat down across the aisle.

"Fine."

"I must say, you don't look like someone who's afraid of flying," Pearl said pointedly. The man didn't seem at all distressed, Pearl thought.

"I have a little confession to make," Merro said and smiled.

"What's that?"

"I love to fly. …"

Mark Pearl was confused. "I don't understand. Then why would you tell us you're afraid?" Merro's comment had taken the pilot by surprise, and there was an edge in his voice.

Pearl was pissed now, thinking Merro had pulled him in to make this flight under false pretenses. He really didn't care if Merro knew he was angry. Pearl realized, too, that he was starting to get strange vibes from this guy. Things just didn't feel right.

"Well, I'll tell you," Merro said. "The reason I lied about my fear of flying was so I could be sure that you, Mr. Pearl, would be my pilot."

"You wanted me to … Why?" Pearl asked. His anger and concern increased with each statement the man made. He glanced toward the cockpit and realized Grisham couldn't hear any of this unless he happened to turn on the intercom, and he had no reason to do that.

The passenger's voice intruded into the Pearl's thoughts.

"You recently made a flight for the LSU Medical Center out of New Orleans," Merro said. "You flew a patient somewhere up north. I need to know where you took him."

Pearl looked at the man for a few moments and tried to decide where Merro was going with this.

"Look," Pearl said as he started to get up, "I'm not sure what you—" Pearl stopped talking as Merro drew a long pistol from his coat.

"You were saying?" Merro motioned for Pearl to sit back down.

"What do you want?" Pearl asked as he slipped into a seat. He was more concerned than angry now. He was scared, too.

"Like I said, I want to know where you took the patient. Not just the area. I want to know the airport. And I want to know who the patient was and anything else you may know about the situation."

"I can't give you that kind of information," Pearl started to argue. "Our company signs confidentiality agreements with clients like the medical center." Then he attempted to turn the situation on Merro, saying, "And do you realize what you're doing constitutes piracy and kidnapping?"

"I have the feeling you don't understand how serious I am about these questions," Merro said to Pearl. "Tell Mr. Grisham to put the aircraft on autopilot and join us here in the cabin."

Pearl looked at Merro for a moment without moving.

"Do it or you'll wish you had," Merro said in a voice that was both low and chilling. "Don't attempt to make any radio calls either," Merro warned.

Pearl didn't hesitate this time. He stood up and walked foward, telling Doug Grisham to set the autopilot and come back to the cabin. "And don't use the radio," Pearl cautioned his copilot.

Grisham looked back over his shoulder and, seeing the serious expression on Pearl's face, set the switches. He reached across the instrument panel, adjusted a couple of dials, and then carefully got out of his seat, joining Pearl and Merro in the cabin.

Grisham immediately saw the passenger's weapon. His eyes grew large and then shifted to Pearl's. The pilot made an open hands gesture, writing down the situation was beyond his control. Neither of the pilots liked the situation. Even with the aircraft on autopilot, there should be a pilot monitoring conditions and developments in the cockpit.

Merro motioned for Grisham to take the seat across from him and then said, "I've asked Mr. Pearl for some information, and he has given a number of reasons why he can't tell me what I need to know. Unfortunately, we have now reached the point where your life, Mr. Grisham, depends on Mr. Pearl's answers."

The copilot stared nervously across at Pearl and mouthed, "What?" He obviously was not sure he understood what the passenger was saying, much less what he meant. Grisham obviously hoped he had misunderstood the man.

Merro's attention turned back to the pilot.

"Now, Mr. Pearl, please answer my questions."

Grisham remained silent, glancing back and forth between Pearl and their passenger.

"Mr. Merro. My copilot has nothing to do with this," Pearl said, his voice strong, almost demanding. "I don't—"

Sputt! The sound didn't even hurt their ears, but Grisham screamed. Pearl jumped, startled, and looked at his friend. The smell of burnt gunpowder drifted through the cabin, and Grisham's left shoulder was bleeding. His uniform shirt was already showing red.

"My God, you've shot me," Grisham managed to say to Merro. He gripped his shoulder, blood visible between his fingers.

Pearl stared back and forth between them.

"Are you crazy?" Pearl exclaimed. "If a bullet penetrates the hull and we lose cabin pressure, we're all dead." Rising out of his seat, he asked, "Doug, how bad are you hurt?"

"Shoulder. Hurts like hell." Grisham started unbuttoning his shirt to examine the wound.

"Hey! Sit down!" Merro said in a loud voice, getting Pearl's attention. When the pilot was seated, he said, "I'm going to ask you one more time for some answers. If I don't get them this time, I'll shoot your friend in the head."

Everything became very still, as the two pilots stared at their passenger.

Merro slowly looked back and forth between the men before saying more. Then he spoke, in an advising way, to Doug Grisham, "Under the circumstances, you might suggest to your friend that he answer my questions." He let that sink in and then added, "Because, Mr. Grisham, the continuation of your life depends on it."

Grisham's head dropped to his chest, and he let out a sob. Then he looked at Pearl, his eyes and his voice begging, "Please, Mark. Tell him whatever he wants. Tell him!"

"Yes, Mr. Pearl. Tell me what I need to know."

Moments passed as the plane with its captive crew continued toward the horizon.

Pearl looked at Grisham and then back at Merro.

"All right, what do you want?"

Merro repeated what he had asked earlier, "You flew a patient somewhere up north. Where did your flight plan call for you to take him?"

Pearl hesitated and then said, "We filed for a flight to Memphis."

Merro asked, "Is that where you landed?" He sensed something in the way Pearl had mentioned the flight plan that there was more.

Again, Pearl hesitated. "No … we didn't go to Memphis. We changed the flight plan after takeoff. The revised one took us into Charlotte, North Carolina."

"Is that where you landed and left the patient?"

"Yes."

"Did someone meet the patient in Charlotte?"

"Yes, there were people waiting for him. They transferred him to an ambulance and drove away."

"Did they have guards or just medical people?"

"Both, I think."

As if he had just remembered, Merro asked, "Who took care of the patient on the airplane?"

As if the answer was obvious, Pearl said, "Dr. Best did, and there were two nurses."

"From New Orleans?"

"Yes."

"What was the patient's name?"

"They called him Michaels. That's all I heard."

"Okay. Did the medical people get off when Michaels was placed in the ambulance at Charlotte?"

Pearl continued watching Grisham as he answered Merro's questions. The co-pilot was pale, sweat visible on his forehead and upper lip, and he looked close to passing out.

"They went with the ambulance," Pearl told him, "but they returned a couple of hours later. We flew them back to New Orleans." Looking concerned, he asked, "Now, can I help Doug? And I need to check things in the cockpit."

"You have five minutes. We need to finish this." Merro looked at his watch and motioned for Pearl to get moving.

Pearl pulled Doug's shirt open and probed at the wound. Then he stepped to the cockpit, returning with a first-aid kit and a handful of paper towels. Pearl wiped away the blood, nodding his head as he worked.

"The bleeding stopped," he told Grisham. Then he asked, "Can you hold these towels to the wound while I check things up front.

Grisham seemed sleepy but said, "Yeah, go ahead. I'll be all right for a few minutes."

Pearl started forward to the cockpit. Merro followed him and slipped into the copilot's seat.

"I'll be keeping an eye on you," he said to Pearl. "Stay off the radio and don't get funny. I know a little about what goes on up here."

"Oh," Pearl said to him, "and you could land us if Doug and I weren't able to?"

"No, Mr. Pearl, I couldn't," Merro said very seriously. "But if I don't get the information I want, I might as well be dead, too. So, you see, I have nothing to lose by killing the two of you. And we all have a lot to gain if you tell me what I need to know and get us on the ground in Cleveland. The two of you get to keep on living, and I can go on with my job."

Pearl had satisfied himself that everything was operating as it should. He checked their course and then took the aircraft off autopilot for a few seconds to review the instruments and operations before going back on autopilot.

When he had finished, Pearl started to get out of his seat.

"Where are you going?" Merro asked, surprised.

"Back to bind up Grisham's wound."

"Oh … okay. But stay where I can see you from here," Merro said. "And hurry."

Pearl climbed out of his seat and went back to the cabin. He checked Grisham's wound again and moved the shirt back so he could tape on a dressing.

"How're you feeling, Doug?" He was still pale but seemed more alert. Pearl had worried that his friend might be going into shock earlier.

"Not good. Are you okay?" the copilot asked, watching Pearl's face.

"I'm fine. When I get this dressing on, I'm going to give you a couple of Tylenol to help you rest. See if you can get some sleep. I'll get us down."

"Mark … be careful," Grisham said, his concern causing a tremor in his voice. "This guy's crazy."

"I know. I'll watch him. You rest."

Pearl returned to the pilot's seat and then peered across the console, fixing Merro with an angry stare.

"He needs a doctor."

"Finish answering my questions. Then we'll see."

"I have answered them."

"I have more," he said. "Who was in charge of the patient's transfer?"

"I don't know?" Pearl said, his hands spread and open, gesturing honesty. "There was a man in New Orleans. Someone said his name, but I wasn't really paying attention. Roberts, Roden, something like that. I'm pretty sure it started with an R."

"Could it have been Robbins?" Merro asked, watching Pearl's expression.

"Yeah … that might have been it. Like I said before, I really wasn't paying attention."

"Did the medical people from New Orleans say anything about where they'd been when they came back?"

"No," Pearl told Merro. Then he added, "I doubt if they saw much riding in an enclosed ambulance."

"Can you remember anything else? It could help you and your friend back there."

"That's all I can tell you," Pearl said. "What are you going to do with us and the aircraft? We can't just disappear, you know."

"Where does the flight plan call for us to land?" Merro asked.

"Cleveland Hopkins International Airport."

"Do you fly into Cleveland often?" Merro inquired casually.

"Occasionally."

"Okay, let's stay with the plan. But park as far as you can from terminals or other buildings."

"I can do that," Pearl said.

"Do you have any cord or tape? I'm going to have to leave the two of you in the airplane, and I don't want anyone to find you for a while."

"What about Grisham's wound?" Pearl was becoming more concerned for his friend.

"I looked at the wound, too, when you bandaged him up. The bleeding's stopped. He'll be okay for a few hours. Now, what about cord or tape?"

"There may be something in the supply cabinet on the floor behind your seat," Pearl said.

Merro reached back and opened the box. He came up with a roll of tape and tossed it back to one of the seats in the cabin.

Appearing satisfied he had gotten all the information Pearl knew, Merro settled into the right seat and secured his seatbelt.

"All right, Mr. Pearl, fly us into Cleveland. You and your copilot may make it through this thing yet."

Pearl thought about the crazy man riding in Grisham's seat. Merro had already proved he was capable of shooting them. What if he was also capable of killing them?

Pearl realized there was nothing more he could do except get them on the ground in Cleveland and hope for the best.

# Chapter 25

The weather was gray and smelled of rain. There had been showers overnight, and it now appeared a significant storm was at hand. Hogan stepped out of the taxi and glanced across the field, wondering whether she was going to end up getting drenched.

The large clock behind the counter in International Air Taxi's office agreed exactly with Hogan's watch—seven o'clock.

A young woman approached the counter when she heard Hogan come through the door.

"May I help you?" she asked. "I'm Elaina."

"Yes, I'm Amy Hogan with the U.S. Marshals Service." She flashed her badge. "I'm looking for one of your pilots. I was here last night, but there was no one who could help me. A lady tried but said I would have to come back this morning."

"Perhaps we can do better now. What's the pilot's name?" Elaina asked. "I'll see if he's in."

"Your company flew a patient out of New Orleans recently. A Dr. Best with the LSU Medical Center handled the flight. The pilot I'm looking for made that flight. His last name is Pearl, I believe."

Elaina's eyes grew large, her expression registering surprise. "You're the second person in two days who's come in looking for Mark. His full name is Mark Pearl."

"Is Mr. Pearl in?"

"I'll see," the young woman said. "He flew Mr. Merro out yesterday afternoon around three."

"Mr. Merro?"

"Yes, that's the other person who was looking for Mark," the woman told Hogan. "He wanted to go to Cleveland. Like I said, they flew out at three yesterday afternoon, so Mark should be back."

Hogan's heart had dropped a beat when she realized her target was ahead of her by several hours and had been alone with the pilot. The sinking feeling grew worse as Elaina tried to provide an answer for the pilot's location. She stepped to a computer and typed while watching the monitor. Hogan leaned across the counter, hoping she could see the screen, too, but couldn't.

"Why did Mr. Merro want this particular pilot, Mark Pearl?" Hogan asked as the young woman searched for answers.

Without looking up, Elaina said, "He told us he was afraid of flying, but he has a friend in New Orleans, a doctor, who had used our service to transport a patient." She looked up and walked back to the counter, obviously having found what she was looking for. "I guess the doctor had given us a good recommendation, to include the pilot. Of course, the pilot was Mark. Mr. Merro said he would feel better flying with someone that the doctor had indicated was okay."

"Who was the doctor?" Hogan was holding her breath.

Elaina thought for a moment and then said, "I think it was a Dr. Best. Yes, the doctor you mentioned. I'm sure that's his name. He's with the LSU Medical Center."

Hogan lost concentration for a brief moment. Then, motioning toward the computer, she asked, "What did you find out? Is the pilot back?"

"No," Elaina replied. "But they could have stayed over." She hesitated. "Here's the strange part. There's a record of them landing at Cleveland, but the aircraft isn't parked in its usual location. And there's no record of a return flight plan or any sign of a takeoff from Cleveland to Dallas."

Hogan stared at Elaina, her thoughts dark and filled with dread.

Elaina broke the silence. "Something's wrong, isn't there?"

"I'm afraid so," Hogan told her. "We need to find that aircraft as fast as we can."

Elaina, her mouth agape, looked open to suggestions.

"Do you have anyone at Cleveland who can look for your airplane?" Hogan asked. "If it landed and hasn't flown out, then it has to be parked there somewhere."

Elaina nodded. "There's a company that does the same thing we do. We can call them."

"You better let your manager know what's going on and then call Cleveland," Hogan told her.

"Mr. Blake won't be in until about eight."

"Does he have a cell or can you call him at home? If you can't reach him, go ahead and call Cleveland. If there's a problem, tell your manager I ordered you to do it."

Elaina's face was pale, and she looked ready to cry as she picked up the phone and dialed.

Hogan pulled out her cell phone and punched in Jack Robbins's number.

When he answered, Hogan explained the situation. They discussed a couple of points, then he told her to keep him informed and broke the connection.

As she hung up, Hogan heard Elaina talking and understood she was on the line with someone in Cleveland. The young woman put her hand over the phone and said, "Mr. Blake told me to get a call in to Cleveland. He said he's on his way here and to tell you not to get lost. He wants to talk with you."

She took her hand away from the phone and said, "So, you can look for us. Okay!" She gave them the aircraft ID along with other information and then hung up.

"Is there anything else I should be doing?" Elaina asked.

"Wait and hope. A prayer might not be out of place." They shared worried looks.

A few minutes later, as they waited, a man walked through the front door. He was dressed casually, as were most of the people who had been moving through the office since Hogan had arrived that morning. The new arrival came right over to the two women.

"Heard anything?" he asked Elaina.

"No, sir. Nothing yet." Then she turned to Hogan. "Mr. Blake, this is Deputy Marshal Amy Hogan. She's with the U.S. Marshals Service."

He nodded. "Ms. Hogan."

Elaina said, "This is Mr. Blake," motioning toward her boss.

"Hello, Deputy Marshal Hogan or … Ms. Hogan … Which is it?"

"Amy would be fine. Amy Hogan."

They shook hands. "Hi, Amy. Sounds like we have a problem here. What's your connection?"

"Well, for starters, we're concerned that the man who had your crew and aircraft fly him to Cleveland may be someone we are looking for. We think he may have done some really bad things in New Orleans."

"You're not really getting my morning off to a good start here."

"Sorry. Wish I could."

"What did he do down there? Can you say?"

"I can't tell you much," Hogan said. "He seems to be looking for someone we don't want him to find, and a couple of people have been killed along the way. He's a suspect for the murders. That's about all I can say."

Blake's expression settled into a frown. His eyebrows bunched together, and the corners of his mouth turned down. "You really have me scared now. Are you sure this is the same man who's out with one of my crews and several million dollars' worth of equipment."

"Pretty sure," Hogan said.

"Damn the luck. Mark and Doug don't deserve this kind of danger."

The office phone rang. Elaina answered and looked at Blake, nodding. "Just a moment," she said and handed the phone to her boss. "It's Cleveland."

"Yeah, Blake here. Whatcha got?" He listened for a moment and then said, "What kind of authorization you need? Can I tell you it's okay and follow up with something written? We can fax it to you." He listened again. Then, "Shit, yeah, okay. Give me a fax number." As he talked, Blake reached for a pen and a sheet of paper. He started taking notes. "In the meantime, get ready to open it. You had better get a locksmith out there to bore the lock on the handle for you. Have you already called the police? Good, okay. You'll have it in a few minutes. Thanks. Bye." Blake handed the phone back to Elaina.

"They found our jet. But it's locked, and they won't open it without written authorization." Motioning to his secretary, he said, "Type something that says it's okay for them to break the lock on our plane. Be sure and include the wing number. I'll sign it, and here's the fax number. Let's see if there's anything in the plane. They said the windows are all covered, and they can't see anything through the cockpit.

"Why wasn't it parked in its usual place?" Hogan asked him.

"I didn't think to ask." He seemed worried and angry. "I just hope Mark and Doug are okay."

The coffeemaker was popular as they waited. Hogan drank one cup and went back for a second as Blake went through three cups. Elaina also had one as she prepared and typed the permission letter that needed to go to Cleveland.

Gossip about the situation had been picked up by several different people in the hanger. Everyone who had come into the office over the last half hour had heard some bit of the conversation. Now everyone on the premises knew that there was a problem involving Pearl and Grisham.

Elaina worked diligently and soon had a permission letter for Blake. He read it and signed off. She faxed the letter, and the waiting continued. The coffeepot was working overtime.

Hogan's cell phone rang. She looked at her watch, five after eight. She wasn't supposed to call Jack Robbins until ten. She opened the phone and looked at the screen, Tom Manning.

"Hello?" she said as she walked outside.

"Hogan, this is Tom Manning." As if she didn't already know.

"Yeah, Tom?"

"What's happening? Jack Robbins and I have talked, but I couldn't wait any longer."

"The aircraft's been located in Cleveland," Hogan told him. "It's locked, and they needed permission to open it. A permission letter was faxed a few minutes ago. They should be getting into the plane's cabin any time now."

"What do they expect to find?" Manning asked.

Hogan hesitated to say it, but she might as well get things out in the open. "Everyone here is worried about the crew. No one has heard from them since the aircraft left Dallas. I think everyone is concerned they're still in the cabin."

"I hope not, damn it," Manning said.

Then, as if thinking to himself, he said to Hogan, "You're probably going to need to go up there." She knew he meant Cleveland. "We need to get our hands on this guy … and fast."

"Yeah, I know."

Elaina stuck her head out the door. Hogan told Manning she would call him right back and closed her phone.

"They've opened the cabin," Elaina said. She had tears in her eyes. "Mark and Doug were inside. They've both been shot," she said. Then she broke down. "They're dead," she sobbed. "The son of a bitch."

Hogan moved closer and put an arm around her shoulders.

"They were nice guys," Elaina said. "They both had families. Doug even had grandchildren."

Hogan guided the young woman back inside. Elaina poured another cup of coffee and went to her desk. Hogan joined Blake who was just getting off the phone.

He turned to Hogan and said, "Elaina told you?" Blake was pale and suddenly looked very tired.

"Yes. She said they were in the cabin and both had been shot." Hogan was angry. She agreed with Elaina. "The son of a bitch."

Blake was angry, too. "He taped their hands and feet. He even taped their mouths so they couldn't call out. And then he shot them. No one heard or saw anything. But I guess all he had to do is wait for another aircraft to taxi by and cover whatever sound there was."

"What are you going to do?" Hogan asked. "Are you sending someone up there?"

"I have to go see Mark's and Doug's families first. I need to do that before it gets out on the news."

"Are you convinced it's them, I mean, before you tell the families?"

"It's them," Blake said. "The people who found them gave me descriptions and both had identification in their pockets when they were found. So, yeah, we're sure."

"After you go see the families, then what?"

"I'm going to send a plane up there. My assistant will go to make positive identification and handle any paperwork. I'm sure Mark's aircraft will be held as a crime scene. We'll get it back later." A thought struck him. "Do you need to go up there? You can go on our plane."

"Thanks." Hogan thought for a moment. "I'll probably want to take you up on that. I need to call my people first. I'll let you know in a few minutes."

She walked outside to call Manning back. She also needed to call Jack Robbins. There was a lot to report; over the last twenty-four hours, things had gone to hell in the proverbial hand basket.

# Chapter 26

Seven fifteen that morning saw Jack Robbins leaving his home for a scheduled session on the pistol range. He tried to go for an hour a month, but time permitting, he stayed longer. His team was required to do the same.

Robbins had fired off five magazines of ammo from his .45 caliber Glock pistol when his cell phone rang. It was blaring out a marching tune that Monica had set as his ringtone. He kept forgetting to reset it to something more appropriate for his line of work.

Da-da-da, da-ta-da, da-ta-daaa. Oh, hell! He hoped no one could hear.

"Hello?" he shouted into the phone. The range noise always made him speak loud at first. There were shots being fired in the background.

"Damn, Jack! Somebody shooting at you?" It was Manning.

"Nah, I'm at the range," he replied, bringing his voice down an octave or two. "What's the latest?"

"I'm waiting on Hogan to call me back now. They've found the aircraft at Cleveland International. It's locked up, and they're trying to get permission to enter. Everyone's afraid of what they're going to find. They still haven't heard from the pilots."

"Are you sending Hogan up to Cleveland?"

"Yeah," Manning said, "and probably you and me. This idiot is killing people as he goes. And he's looking for one of ours, so we have some responsibility here."

"I agree. You want me to take some of my team?"

"Nah, I don't think so," Manning replied. "More than the three of us and we'll just end up getting in each other's way. So, it's just you, me, and Hogan."

"Okay. I'll finish here unless I hear from you first. Why don't I call when I'm ready to leave?"

"That works."

~ ~ ~

Webster awoke early and lay in bed stretching and yawning for a few minutes. He thought about Cary and wished he could go see her. He thought about the card he had mailed her and wondered if he ever crossed her mind. He doubted it since they had been together such a short time.

After a few minutes, Webster climbed out of bed and slipped into his robe. Walking outside, he listened to the sounds surrounding the cabin. There were all kinds of birds, more than he could count, and squirrels—at least three—and even a woodpecker or two. They were fun to watch. Webster smiled. Now there was a facet of his character he hadn't realized he possessed—nature lover. Wow!

He took a short walk and then he went back inside and made some coffee. He pulled out the cereal and poured a bowl. After breakfast, he opted for a couple of hours of exercise. He could walk and maybe throw in some jogging, too.

Webster was back at full strength, and he was becoming bored. He wondered when Robbins would give him another assignment. He should ask and save them the trouble.

~ ~ ~

Unnoticed and avoiding buildings and security cameras, Mateo had walked away from International Air Taxi's Learjet around seven the prior evening. He had used devious methods to gain information from the pilot. Threats and promises had been made, and in the end Mateo believed he had gotten all that Mark Pearl knew about Webster's transfer.

As a final act, Mateo had killed both pilots, carrying out what was necessary to slow those searching for him. Pearl and his copilot had known too much about Mateo and his mission to let them live. Now, depending on how careful the two men in New Orleans had been before they were shot, maybe no one knew where he would be headed next. The odds for that were slim, though, Mateo realized.

Now he knew Webster had really been transferred to Charlotte, not Memphis. The pilot had also told Mateo about the doctor and the two nurses who had accompanied Webster. If Willie and Carlo had mentioned the medical personnel, he could have approached one of them for information while he was in New Orleans. Hmm.... Maybe Willie and Carlo hadn't known about them either.

Mateo had walked all the way to the main terminal before taking a taxi to a Hampton Inn near downtown. Once there, he called Avis and, using a new identity, rented a vehicle. Mateo had them bring the car to him. He couldn't chance flying out of Cleveland. He needed to disappear and then move on from some other place.

Finally, on the road, he drove several miles before stopping at a Walmart for a road atlas. Finding one, he flipped through it and then paid and walked back out to his vehicle.

About five hundred miles was right—that's how far it would be to drive to Charlotte. It was easier and safer to drive, he decided, than to jump through the hoops to fly. Besides, anyone searching for him would be watching the airports. As it was, he would be ahead of anyone looking for him.

Mateo threaded his way out to I-77. The Interstate would take him directly to Charlotte. He headed south, watching his speed. After driving for a couple of hours, he got off the Interstate south of Akron and looked for a small local motel. Finding what he wanted, Mateo pulled in.

After registering, he drove a couple of blocks to a mom-and-pop restaurant that was open. They still had the makings for one of their specials. The ham was cold, and the dressing needed more seasoning; otherwise, the food was awful. Being hungry, though, he ate it.

Later, back in his room, Mateo showered and fell into bed. Though it was already late, he wanted to drive the rest of the way to North Carolina the next day. He fell asleep quickly and didn't awaken until early morning.

Seven o'clock and sunrise found him on I-77 again. He continued to be careful of his speed. Rain started falling just after he crossed into West Virginia. It continued for the next couple of hours and was hard at times, making driving difficult. At one point, Mateo pulled into a rest stop and, along with other travelers, waited for several minutes.

An hour later, he noticed his fuel was low and pulled off at the next exit. Finding a large truck stop, he filled the tank and bought some snacks. He planned to stay on the road. If he arrived early enough, he could check out Charlotte that afternoon. Mateo also needed to report to Pablo.

About thirty minutes after the fuel stop, the traffic ahead abruptly slowed and then stopped. Emergency lights were visible in the distance, but he had no idea what was happening. Several drivers left their vehicles and walked toward the problem.

Mateo remained in the Volvo. This was a good time to look at Charlotte and the surrounding area in the atlas. Charlotte's a big city, he thought. And Webster could be anywhere. Damn!

An hour passed before Mateo noticed people hurrying back to their vehicles. Shortly after that, traffic started to move—ever so slowly. As he reached the emergency vehicles, Mateo could see an overturned truck and a small car beyond the truck. The car was crushed on the front end, and there were several people standing near two ambulances. Sheets covered two bodies on the grass.

Mateo felt sorry for the relatives, yet realized he had never given a second thought as to how he had affected several other families over the last couple of days.

He drove on. In the late afternoon, Mateo entered the outlying areas of Charlotte. He had decided earlier to go out to the airport and leave the Volvo in the parking lot. Then he would get a different car.

The airport, located out on the west side of the city, was easy to find. The atlas was open on the seat beside Mateo. He easily made the exit for the airport, and thirty minutes later, the Volvo hidden deep in long-term parking, he was filling out the papers to rent a different vehicle.

It was into the evening, almost seven thirty, by the time he checked into a hotel. He was tired and hungry following the long drive. After tossing his things on the bed, he went across the street to a Waffle House. He ordered and sat considering ways to find Webster in a city the size of Charlotte. It wouldn't be easy he knew. Still, he had his ways.

Back at the hotel, Mateo decided to check in with Pablo. He didn't worry about phoning him because Pablo had his incoming calls routed through three different stations and then to a cell phone that he only switched on periodically.

Pablo answered after five rings.

"Hola?"

"This is your friend in the United States," Mateo said. Pablo didn't like to use names on the phone.

"And how is my young friend doing? Have you been able to find the person you went to search for?"

"Not yet," Mateo told him. "I am still looking, but four obstacles that stood in my way have been lost."

Pablo understood what Mateo was telling him.

"Losses sometimes are unavoidable in our line of work. Otherwise, are you getting closer?"

"I will know in a few days. I will keep you informed."

"Don't forget," Pablo said, "I must be there when you close the deal."

"I will not forget," Mateo said and then he heard a click as Pablo hung up his phone.

He had trouble sleeping, but when he awoke the next morning, Mateo had a plan. It would require a flight back to New Orleans, but no one should be expecting him there. The doctor who had flown to Charlotte with Webster would know where they had taken him.

Yes, the doctor would know!

# Chapter 27

Hogan called Jack Robbins and gave him the news. "They're in the plane now. The pilot and copilot are both inside. They've been shot," she told him, "and both are dead."

"Damn!" Robbins exclaimed. "This guy is killing people after he gets what he wants. He's trying to keep us from knowing where he's going next."

"What makes you say that?" Hogan asked.

"Think about it, Amy. With him going after this pilot, I think our guy wanted to know Webster's destination when we flew him out of New Orleans."

"If that's true," Hogan argued, "why go to all the trouble to track down the pilot. Why not grab the doctor or one of the nurses who went on the flight and find out from them?"

"Good point," Robbins agreed, "but maybe he didn't find out about them being on the flight. Hell, he's probably still hoping we don't know he's after Webster. That would explain why he's not leaving any witnesses."

Robbins was thinking as they talked. "Okay, let's assume he got the destination city out of the pilot, and he goes to Charlotte. He still doesn't know where to find our boy. Webster's in a private facility. Someone would have to tell him and then give him directions. The pilot didn't have that information."

Hogan moved the conversation back to what she would need to do.

"The manager here at International Air Taxi is sending his assistant up to Cleveland to identify the two men. I can fly up with them."

"What's your next step?" Robbins asked.

"I need to get up there and figure out how to follow this guy," she told him.

"Hmm.... yeah, that's probably a good next step," Robbins said. "Let me know when you get there and have a strategy. Tom Manning and I were planning to meet you there, but I'll put a hold on that until you check things out."

"Sounds good. I'll keep you informed."

Blake walked out of his office as Hogan put her phone away. She waved him down.

"I'll take you up on that ride to Cleveland. When do you expect your plane to leave?"

"Tentatively, around eleven," he said. "Earlier if we can get a few things done here."

"I'll get my things and be ready."

"We have a courtesy car. Tell Elaina to give you the keys."

"Thanks."

~ ~ ~

Webster had walked and jogged almost to the medical building when his cell phone rang. He looked at the caller ID.

"Morning, Jack. How are you doing?"

"Things could be a lot better."

"That bad, huh?"

"And going downhill with each phone call," Robbins said.

"Is there anything I can do to help?"

"Not really," Robbins said. "I need to bring you up to speed on some things."

"Okay."

"There's someone out there looking for you. I've told you that."

"I'm listening," Webster said.

"Whoever's looking is very serious, and he doesn't want anyone to know what he's found out."

"How's he doing that?"

"By eliminating witnesses. Four, so far."

"Damn! What are you doing about it?"

"Hogan's chasing him. She's on her way to Cleveland this morning," Robbins said. "He's staying a few steps ahead of us so far."

"Why Cleveland?"

"The guy chartered a private jet out of Dallas to get to the pilot. This is the same pilot that brought you to your present location. When the people in Cleveland broke into the aircraft this morning, they found the pilot and copilot bound and shot, both dead."

"You think he knows where I am?"

"I wouldn't be surprised if he knows the city," Robbins told him. "Obviously he's very persuasive."

"Keep me up-to-date," Webster said. "I'm mobile now. I can help if I need to."

"Stay where you are," Robbins told him. "Let me work it from this end. I'll call if I need you."

"Will do."

~ ~ ~

The young killer walked off a plane at Louis Armstrong airport in New Orleans that evening. He had traveled several hours and covered a significant part of the southeastern United States since leaving Charlotte. Using three IDs, he had gone from Charlotte to Cincinnati, where he had purchased a ticket under a new name, and then flown to DC.

When he was sure he hadn't been followed, Mateo flew to Atlanta and moved around the terminal for another two hours. He purchased a ticket for New Orleans this time. Arriving there, he rented a car and drove to the LSU Medical Center.

Mateo was hoping Dr. Best, like many doctors, worked from early morning to late in the evening. He went to the entrance area, found a pay phone, and looked up the number for the medical center. Mateo dialed the number on his cell and then asked for Dr. Howard Best.

"I'll see if he's still in his office," the operator replied.

After a few moments, a male voice said, "Dr. Best."

Mateo closed his phone when he heard the doctor's voice and walked over to the information desk. It was crowded; there was only one woman on duty. She was trying to explain to a visitor where a patient's room was found.

Mateo tapped the old man on the shoulder and said, "Excuse me." Then to the lady at the desk he asked, "Could you direct me to Dr. Howard Best's office?"

Normally, she would have called before sending someone up to the offices, but this time she hesitated because of the crowd and her being preoccupied with trying to make sure the old man understood her instructions.

She looked at Mateo. He smiled a big smile and rolled his eyes toward the man who was demanding her attention again. She smiled back and, after a moment, nodded toward the elevators and said, "Second floor. Turn right when you get off. It's about halfway down the hall. Name's on the door."

As the elevator started to close, Mateo heard a voice say, "Could you hold that, please?" He stood away from the door, not really wanting anyone to see him going toward Dr. Best's office, but a foot reached in from the hallway and snagged the door as it started to close.

A nurse, her arms loaded with boxes of supplies, sort of hopped around and into the elevator as she held the door with her leading foot.

"Didn't you hear me?" She threw an angry glance in his direction and then said in a calmer tone, "Would you punch the third floor for me."

"Sorry," Mateo told her as he stepped around and pushed the button.

She didn't look back or speak, not even a thank you. Obviously, she had no memory of him, but he knew her. He was good with faces. She was one of the nurses who worked with Dr. Best. Willie had mentioned that fact and pointed her out when Mateo had been at the hospital a few days earlier.

Maybe she had made the trip to Charlotte too!

When the elevator stopped on two, he remained in place. The nurse glanced toward him and stepped over to the side.

"Punched the wrong button when I got on," he said in explanation.

"Oh."

The elevator moved up to the next floor and opened again. The nurse stepped off, and Mateo followed. She started down the hallway with her load of boxes. Mateo followed a few steps behind. Things were quiet, and activity was scarce.

The nurse stopped at a door marked "Employees Only." She struggled with the handle.

"Let me get that for you?"

"Thanks," she said and stepped back.

He opened the door and held it for her. She started through and then glanced at him again. There was a flicker of recognition and then an effort to pull in a breath. A scream in the making—she had recognized him!

Mateo grabbed her. With his hand covering her mouth, he shoved her into the room and let the door close behind them.

Her eyes were wide, and her voice was rasping in her throat. A look of sheer terror was controlling her expression. Everything she carried fell as she tore at Mateo's hands. She had almost escaped his grip when he hammered a fist into her face. Her hands fell away, all hope of escape now gone. He quickly dragged her toward the back of the small supply room and knelt beside her. His face was close, and his breath hot.

A small knife appeared, the blade immediately inches from the nurse's face where she could see it when she regained her senses. As she came around, Mateo showed her the gleaming blade, slowly moving it back and forth. Her eyes followed it. Mateo lowered the point to touch her throat, drawing a tiny dot of blood. Her moan was the only sound in the room.

"Keep quiet," he told her in a soft harsh voice, "and you'll go home to your family."

His promise understood, she watched Mateo with tears clouding her eyes.

"Do you believe me?"

She nodded.

Hesitating for a moment to make sure she was with him, he said, "I'm going to ask you some questions,"

She nodded again and then grimaced as the knife bit into the skin at her neck. Her eyes were wide and filled with terror.

"You work with Dr. Best." It was a statement, not a question.

She nodded.

He slowly took his hand from her mouth. Mateo then moved the knife back from her neck just a bit and waited.

"Yes," she whispered, keeping her eyes locked on his.

"A few weeks ago, Dr. Best and two nurses flew out of New Orleans with a patient. Were you one of those nurses?"

Tears welled in her eyes as she tried unsuccessfully to hold back a sob. "Please don't hurt me."

"Were you on that flight?" he asked in a harsh manner, touching her neck again with the sharp blade.

She flinched and gave out a little cry before nodding again.

"Where did you fly to?"

"Charlotte! … Charlotte, North Carolina."

The responses were coming easier. Mateo could tell she was ready to answer whatever questions he asked.

"Where did you take the patient to in Charlotte? Was it a hospital?" He shook her just enough to keep her attention.

"Not a hospital," she said. "It was some sort of private facility. Small," she hesitated, thinking, remembering, "and there were guards."

"What was the place called?" he asked.

"I don't know," she replied. "I never saw a name. There wasn't a sign. We just turned off the road into a driveway and drove into the woods. No one mentioned a name."

"There must have been a sign of some sort," he said. "Think!"

Tears again. "There wasn't," she pleaded. There was now a new drop of blood on her neck. "I would have seen it. I was looking out the front of the ambulance when we got there, and there was no sign. I remember thinking that was strange."

"What do you remember about the trip from the airport?"

"Not much," she said. "We were busy with Mr. Webster most of the time. You know," she said looking up, "the patient?"

She had used Webster's name, not Michaels. Everyone else had called him Michaels.

"Yes," he said without calling attention to the slip. "What about road signs, things like that?"

"I don't remember anything particular," she said. Then, "Wait! I do remember one. We were on Highway 16; it was four lanes."

"Good," Mateo encouraged her. "Now you're being helpful. What else?"

She thought for a moment and then continued. "We turned off the four-lane road onto a smaller one. It only had two lanes."

He interrupted her, "How long did you drive after you left the four-lane road?"

The answers were coming fast now. "Ten, maybe fifteen minutes."

"And then you reached the medical facility?"

"Yes."

"You said there were guards. Where were they and how many?"

"There was a gatehouse," she told Mateo. "They stopped us; the driver showed some papers to the guard. A couple of them looked into the ambulance before the gate opened, then they let us drive inside."

"How many guards at the gatehouse?" he asked.

"Two," she said. "No, wait. Three. One was inside."

"Did you see any others?" he asked. "Outside? Or in the woods. You said you were in the woods when you turned off the road. You mentioned a driveway?"

"No," she told him, "I didn't see anyone else."

Mateo could tell her mind was trying to keep up with the action. He noticed a change in her expression. She had probably decided that he had no reason to let her live when he was finished asking her questions. She looked around for something to use as a weapon. He could tell she wanted to strike out at him. But the knife was still at her throat.

"What happened when the ambulance arrived at the facility? Were there doctors and nurses there?"

"Yes," she said. She was obviously afraid to move now. "They came out and met us, just like a regular trauma center."

"What was the doctor's name? Do you remember any names?" Mateo was getting close. If he only had a name. With a name he could find the facility.

Mateo detected a change in her expression, in her eyes. She had remembered something.

"What?" he asked. "What did you remember?"

"The doctor!"

"Tell me," he said forcefully, "or I'm going to cut you.

She sobbed and then said, "Dr. Dunn ... Dr. Irene Dunn." Tears ran down her cheeks.

He decided to try and verify one more thing.

"You called the patient Webster," he said, "not Michaels. I thought his name was Webb Michaels."

A shocked look came to her eyes, and they grew wide. She had made a mistake.

"Tell me," he said. "You do want to go home, don't you?"

She nodded. He had given her a glimmer of hope.

"The patient's name was really Webster," she said. "They were trying to slip him out using another name—Webb Michaels." Her eyes closed, and she started to sob.

Mateo had what he needed. Before the nurse could realize she had now outlived her usefulness, Mateo let the knife slip away. He was quickly around her neck with his fingers and began to strangle her. She fought, but she couldn't reach his face or pull his hands away. The struggle lasted only seconds. All life left her.

To confuse those who would find her, Mateo then made some changes to the scene. He reached for her blouse and ripped at the buttons, tearing them away. Once her bra was exposed, he tore that, too, leaving her upper body naked, exposed, appearing used. Then he reached under the blouse tails and tugged her pants and her panties down to her ankles.

Satisfied, he picked up the knife, closed it, and returned it to his pocket. He took a couple of steps toward the door and then looked back. She appeared to have been the victim of an attacker who had been scared away. Mateo would be gone long before anyone figured out what had really happened.

# Chapter 28

Leaving the chaos behind, Mateo slipped out of the supply room. He walked to the door leading into the stairway and opened it with tissues he had used to wipe any fingerprints from the scene. He hurried to the first floor. Peering through the glass in the door and seeing no one nearby, Mateo eased out and walked to the hospital's entrance. Having considered security cameras since his arrival, Mateo had tried to avoid them or to walk alongside others keeping him from direct view of the cameras.

Back in his vehicle, he started the engine and pulled out of the parking lot. Driving away from the hospital, Mateo thought about his next move. He needed to get back to Charlotte quickly now that he had information about the doctor and the facility where Webster was taken.

He wouldn't return to the airport. There was a chance someone would find the nurse and remember him being in the hospital. He decided to drive to another city for a flight.

He stopped in the parking lot of a convenience store and got the atlas out of his suitcase. After looking at the possibilities, he headed for Alabama. A flight out of Mobile should be safe.

His destination was only 150 miles away; driving at night didn't bother him. He would pull in at a rest stop along the way and catch a quick nap if he needed one. Before leaving the area, Mateo swung into a McDonald's and ordered food at the drive-thru. He arranged the burger and fries so he could reach them and headed for the Interstate.

When he was finished eating, Mateo used his cell to make a call to Mexico. After a shorter than usual wait, Pablo was on the line.

"Have you found our friend?" Pablo went directly to the subject.

"Yes," Mateo told him. "I know the city, and I have the name of someone who can get us in."

"Good job, my friend. Is it time for me to come and join you?" Pablo asked.

"Si … yes. Can you meet me in Atlanta? I'm headed there now. I will wait for you. And we should have others with us. At least three or four. We can drive to our destination from Atlanta."

"I will call you when I have the arrival time," Pablo replied. "I will bring a couple of our people and arrange for two others to meet us in Atlanta." The phone clicked off.

Mateo was used to that.

The ride along I-10 through Louisiana and Mississippi was uneventful, even with a short stop to nap. Mobile was only a few miles from the Mississippi state line. Mateo followed the signs, taking him from I-10 to I-65 and then to Airport Boulevard. He glanced at the clock on the dash. It was almost five in the morning. He had slept longer than he intended at the rest stop just inside the Alabama state line.

There were several hotels visible as Mateo exited I-65 to Airport Boulevard. He drove to one with a full parking lot and slowly cruised among the spaces. Automobiles were parked one after another. Mateo searched for a vacant spot. As he did, a Honda SUV backed out of its location about 100 yards from the covered entrance. He waved thanks to the driver and then backed into the slot.

Mateo removed his things from the back of the car. Then he returned to the driver's seat and carefully wiped down the vehicle to remove his prints. Finished, he locked the doors on the vehicle. Next, he unlocked the trunk and, using a coin from his pocket, removed the screws securing the license plate. They were tight, but he managed to get them out and slip the plate from its position.

He looked around to make sure he was not being watched. Feeling safe, he tossed the plate into the trunk and closed the lid. He hoped the vehicle would not be discovered right away.

Dusting his hands, Mateo walked back to his luggage. He gathered everything up and went into the hotel's lobby. Dropping his bags and briefcase in front of the reservations desk, he asked to use a phone. The clerk set a phone on the counter and asked if he needed a phone book. He nodded, and she tossed one up beside the phone.

Even at this early hour, the desk was busy. People were getting on the road as others headed for early flights.

Mateo called for a taxi. Ten minutes later he was on his way to the airport. On arrival, he used one of his IDs to pay for a flight to Atlanta. His timing was good, and he was able to grab some coffee and a sweet roll before the flight. He finished and went back for seconds, having not eaten for several hours.

Finally, on the plane, he stashed his bags in the overhead compartment and dropped into the seat, making himself comfortable. He was almost asleep by the time the plane started rumbling down the runway. His last thoughts were of what should happen when they got back to North Carolina. And, he thought, Pablo should be a part of that decision. Pablo would be joining him for this last part. He believed they were ready to go after Webster now.

~ ~ ~

Hogan slept most of the way to Cleveland. International Air Taxi's people kept their voices low, and she dozed off as soon as they were airborne. The aircraft was on final approach when someone touched her shoulder, saying she needed to fasten her seatbelt.

They taxied as near as possible to the area where their airplane and crew had been found. The company's jet and the immediate area around it were obviously off-limits. Their pilot positioned his aircraft in a tie-down area nearby and shut down the engines.

Hogan stretched when she got outside. The pilot had unloaded their bags, setting them on the tarmac beside the aircraft. Hogan grabbed hers and walked toward the yellow tape surrounding the Lear. As she neared the area, a young police officer held up his hand to stop her.

Hogan set her bags down and pulled her badge cover out of her handbag. She motioned the officer over as she flipped the cover back, holding her ID out for him to see.

"Officer, I'm Deputy Marshal Hogan with the U.S. Marshals Service. We're after the individual responsible for killing the two men found in this aircraft."

The young officer checked out Hogan's badge.

"Who's in charge?" she asked, looking over his shoulder.

The officer glanced at Hogan and then turned toward the aircraft, saying with a little grin, "Take your pick, Miss. There are about four different people over there who seem to think they are in charge."

She noticed him checking out her figure.

"If you're finished examining everything," she said pointedly, "may I go over to the aircraft?"

He blushed significantly as he said, "Sorry, but you're just about the nicest-looking law enforcement officer I've ever met. I guess all the blood ran to my brain."

"As long as that's the only place it ran to," Hogan told him with a grin.

"What ...?" Catching her meaning, he turned a bright red again and stammered, "Oh, yes ma'am. It was just my brain, I can assure you, and you can go right on over to the plane."

"Thank you, Officer." Leaving her bags near the tape, she ducked underneath and walked toward a group of men standing near the aircraft. She figured the young officer would keep an eye on her things.

He was still trying to apologize as she walked away. "Sorry, ma'am, I really didn't mean anything."

Hogan waved dismissively without looking back.

One of the men standing near the aircraft watched her approach.

"Can I help you?"

"I'm Deputy Marshal Amy Hogan of the U.S. Marshals Service," she said, holding her badge out for his benefit.

"Special Agent Jeff Thompson, FBI. What's your connection here?" he asked.

"We think we may have some information on the person who did this." Hogan nodded toward the plane.

"I'm listening," Agent Thompson said.

"We think he's trying to locate an individual we have in the Witness Security Program. We also think he killed at least two other people after he found out what they knew. That was in New Orleans. The people on this aircraft would make it four."

"So, you have a loose cannon out there. Do you have a description or a name? Anything?"

"Nothing we've been able to pin down," Hogan told him. "He's wiping down everything he touches, and he uses fake IDs everywhere he goes. We're still trying to come up with a set of prints."

"What about a description?" Thompson asked again.

"Thirtyish, around six feet, nice looking with dark hair, and probably South American heritage. Maybe just a touch of a Spanish accent if you listen for it. A couple of the people who have talked with him mentioned the accent."

"Pretty vanilla description these days," he said, "with all the illegals we have from south of the border."

"Yeah, I know." Hogan looked at the aircraft. "Anything there that can help us?"

"Not really," Thompson replied. "He tapped each of them point blank and then a shot to the head. One of them also had a shoulder wound. They both had tape covering their mouths. They couldn't even scream. Small entry wounds and no exit. Probably a .22 caliber with hollow points. We'll know more after the medical examiner finishes his work."

" Obviously, he forced them to fly here and killed them after they were parked on the tarmac," Hogan said it almost to herself.

Thompson nodded.

"No one saw him leave the aircraft?"

"Busy time of the day," Thompson said. "The tower brought them in and let them park where they requested. The pilot did everything by the book, except their location." He pointed toward a hanger in the distance. "They're about a quarter of a mile from their normal area. The pilot even thanked the tower. That was the last anyone heard from them."

Hogan considered what Thompson told her and then asked, "So no one noticed anything suspicious until International Air Taxi inquired about their aircraft this morning?"

"That's right."

"Damn!"

"That sums it up pretty succinctly," Thompson said as he watched a small airplane on final approach.

"I need to call my boss," Hogan said to no one in particular. She opened her phone, dialed, and slowly walked away from Thompson.

"Jack? I'm standing near the aircraft where he killed the pilots from Dallas. FBI Special Agent Jeff Thompson has been bringing me up-to-date." Hogan briefed Robbins.

"Any guess on where he's headed now?" Robbins asked.

"I expect the pilot gave our man the city where he flew Webster. That's all he had to give unless he heard something in conversation. He would have stayed with the aircraft while Dr. Best and the nurses transferred Webster to the medical facility outside Charlotte. Afterward, they dropped the medical personnel off in New Orleans and flew the plane back to the home base at Dallas." She kicked at a rock as she talked.

"So, given what you've told me and when he left there, he is probably headed for Charlotte."

"Yeah, I think he would have gone to North Carolina," Hogan said. "But I don't think he can find the facility unless he's real lucky. The only people who know where it's located are the employees, and they require a special clearance to work there."

"Yeah, but you know information like that gets out."

"Maybe," Hogan replied. "But I'm guessing he's run into a problem on location, at least one that'll slow him down. He'll have to find someone on the inside."

"Tom Manning is on my back," Robbins said. "He's ready for us to jump on his plane and come up there."

"I think you'd be wasting your time. He wouldn't stay here after he killed the pilots. He got what he wanted from them, or he didn't. Either way, he's gone."

"Yeah, you're right."

"How's Webster? Is he mobile? Could we get him to a new location with only a few people knowing?" Hogan was throwing up possibilities.

"Sure, we could do that, but this guy would still be out there. We need to put him away." Robbins was quiet for a moment and then said, "He's looking for one of our people. That makes him our responsibility."

"Then we need a way to close him down," Hogan said. "A way to close him down for good."

"Hmm, he may not be alone," Robbins said, as though thinking out loud, "and he's probably working for someone."

"Do we have any idea who?"

"Not really, but Webster's made a lot of enemies over the years. Some of them are really bad people."

"What about the guy in Bogotá?" Hogan said. "He lost a young son in a raid by the federal police down there. Isn't he the one who put the reward out for Webster?"

"Yeah … he's certainly a possibility. And this fits with the way he does things."

"How do you mean?" Hogan asked.

"Webster slipped into the Merchant's organization. His name is Pablo Perez. It took us two years to infiltrate them. One of the things Webster told me is that Perez sends his people out to find whoever he's looking for. Then Perez shows up for the finale. Webster said you don't want to be the object of Perez's attention at that point."

"Maybe this Merchant fellow is searching for Webster?"

"Could be."

"So, what should we do?" Hogan was open to suggestions.

After a few moments, Robbins said, "Let me talk to Tom Manning and Webster. Then I'll call you back. In the meantime, see if you've missed anything there."

They finished and cut the connection.

As she was talking with Robbins, she had watched Thompson return to a group of men standing near the aircraft. Hogan suspected he had explained her presence to them. Now he walked back out to meet her.

"Anything new?" she asked him.

"No," he said. "Let me introduce you to these people." There were three other men standing near the wing of the aircraft.

"Gentleman," Thompson said, commanding their attention, "this is Deputy Marshal Amy Hogan of the U.S. Marshals Service."

She gave them a wave.

Thompson motioned toward the man on his right, a tall, slim, casually dressed individual, and said, "Deputy Marshal Hogan, this is Sheriff John Duncan."

The sheriff reached out and shook hands, firmly but with a warm touch. "Nice to meet you."

The second man was Jackson Howard. Thompson said Howard was a Fed and in charge of airport security. He didn't offer to shake.

The last man to be introduced was Lt. George Payler. "Lt. Payler is the chief detective for the Cleveland Police Department," Thompson said.

Payler shook hands with Hogan and said, "Welcome to Cleveland, Deputy Marshal Hogan."

"Please," Hogan said, including each of them with her eyes, "call me Amy."

Waving toward the airplane, the sheriff said, "Well, Amy, Special Agent Thompson tells us you're on the tail of the man who did this."

"Yes, we think so," she said.

Before she could say anything else, Howard, the airport security man spoke up. "If you people had done your job, maybe we wouldn't be standing beside an airplane where we unloaded two dead people earlier today."

"Shit, Jackson. That's not a fair statement, and you know it." The sheriff said, confronting Howard. "Hell, you've been in law enforcement long enough to know you can't always get 'em before they do something bad."

"It's okay, Sheriff," Hogan said speaking up for herself and the Marshals Service. "I've been after this SOB for several days now and through three states. If Mr. Howard has some better ideas on how stop him, I'm happy to listen."

"Yeah, Jackson," The detective now chimed in, "tell her how to do it."

"Ah, hell. I didn't mean anything," Howard said, shaking his head and scraping his toe along the tarmac. "I'm just frustrated. This looks bad for the airport. I'm sorry, Deputy … Ah … Amy."

"No problem," she said as she caught his eye. Then looking back and forth at the four of them, she said, "Did anyone out here see anything? How about the tower? Was there anything strange in their transmissions? Someone must have seen the guy leave the airplane." She was touching on all the possibilities.

"No, no one actually saw him leave the plane," the sheriff said "nor anything else, for that matter. A security camera picked up someone walking in the area around seven last night but the distance was too great for anything worthwhile. There was nothing strange in their transmissions either."

Special Agent Thompson spoke up, "One of our people is over at the FAA office now going over tapes of radio conversations with the aircraft. He's listening to their transmissions in the air and after they landed. Maybe he'll turn up something."

"Let's hope," Hogan said wistfully.

## Chapter 29

Webster had spent most of the morning exercising with Bob at the medical facility. His cell phone buzzed as he was walking back to the cabin.

Webster checked the ID. "Hey, Jack. What's the latest?"

"A lot."

"Tell me."

"Hogan's in Cleveland," Robbins said. "She's talked with the FBI, the sheriff, and the chief of detectives for Cleveland PD. Oh, the Fed in charge of security for the airport is there, too. They've coordinated their efforts but didn't come up with anything on our man. He's disappeared."

"Like you said before, he probably knows I'm in Charlotte." Webster hesitated before continuing, "Jack, if this fellow is looking for me, and we're pretty sure he is, then we need to stop him."

Robbins seemed out of ideas. "Help me here."

Webster had a plan. He gave Robbins the shortened version.

"Let him find me."

"Huh?" Robbins wasn't sure he had heard correctly.

"Let him run me to ground."

"What the hell are you talking about? What does 'Let him run me to ground' mean?"

"It's an old hunting term," Webster answered. "It has to do with chasing an animal to its den for the kill."

They were both quiet for a moment.

Then Robbins asked, "So, what happens then?"

"It's usually curtains for the animal," Webster said. "But …"

"But what? Don't keep me hanging."

"Sometimes, with nothing more to lose, the cornered creature puts up a ferocious last stand that can be deadly. Normally, the hunter isn't prepared for that.

Then Robbins said, "How do you suggest we get them to come to your den, short of taking out an ad in the Charlotte newspaper? Maybe we could include a map showing the location of the medical facility." ,

Webster realized Robbins had become agitated.

"Let me give it some thought. In the meantime, I'll make some preparations in case he shows up."

"Watch it. Obviously, he's cold-blooded … and he's smart," Robbins said. "Be careful."

"I will," Webster told him. "Keep me informed. It would be nice if I knew when he was coming."

"I'll let you know anything that comes my way."

They said good-bye, and Webster closed his phone. He stood for a moment, still and contemplative while slowly rubbing at the whiskers on his chin. Then, determined, he turned and headed back toward the medical building again. He needed another talk with Bob. Webster thought he remembered Bob mentioning the marines.

Webster found him in the break room, a cup of coffee in one hand and a book in his lap. Bob seemed to read a lot.

The big nurse saw Webster looking at the book and said, "Alex Cross novel by James Patterson. Black detective. Smarter than the average bear." Bob stuck his chest out and grinned. "I like to think I have some of his traits."

"I'm familiar with those guys," Webster said while nodding toward the book approvingly.

"You read?" Bob asked.

"Anytime I can. Listen, I need to talk to you."

"So, talk."

"Not here," Webster told him. "Let's take a walk."

Bob closed his book, tossed it on the table, and followed Webster outside.

When they were on the walking path, Webster looked at Bob. "I've got a problem."

"Something I can help you with?"

"Maybe … well, probably. But I'll have to tell you some things you won't be able to talk about. Some things about me and about what I do—or, to be more correct, what I used to do."

"I can handle that," Bob said, his smile now gone. "I didn't figure you for a postal carrier when they brought you here." He grinned again now and tapped Webster on the shoulder with his big ham of a fist. Even the small tap threw Webster off stride.

"Everything I tell you is confidential. Understand?"

"I understand."

"I was with the DEA until recently," Webster started. "Now I'm with the U.S. Marshals Service."

Bob glanced over but remained silent.

"A lot of my work over the last several years has been undercover. I've dealt with some pretty nasty people." He glanced toward his friend.

"Go on," Bob told him. "I'm listening. If you get to a scary part, I may break and run."

Webster doubted that.

"Now someone is looking for me. They're looking hard. Four people have been killed along the way including the pilot who flew me up here. That's four we know about. There could be others."

"Damn!"

"Sure you want to help?"

"Why not? Everybody's gotta die doing something." He grinned. "I think I heard that on TV."

They had come to a bench, and Webster indicated they should sit. Bob parked his big frame and then gestured for Webster to continue.

"Since this guy is so determined to find me," Webster said "we're probably going to let him. We have to stop the killings."

"Who's 'we'?"

"The people I work for … and me … and maybe you."

"Here?"

"Yeah, here," Webster said. "That's if our people don't find him before he gets here."

Bob nodded and remained quiet.

Webster was left to continue. "Hopefully, we'll know if and when he's coming and be ready for him. Maybe even have a little welcome party."

Webster peered at Bob again and said, "That's where you come in."

Bob was quick with a joke. "And you need me to bake the cake, right?"

Webster couldn't help laughing. "Yeah, the cake and the party. Right!"

They both became pensive again.

"Seriously now. Do you have a weapon?" Webster asked his recently acquired friend.

That brought a stern glance from Bob.

"Yeah … I got a Ruger Mini-14 rifle I bought at a gun show. It has a night scope too," Bob told him. "I also have a couple of 9 mm semi-automatic pistols, a Glock, and a Smith & Wesson."

"You have ammo for all of those?"

"A thousand rounds or so, total."

"That should do. Now the big question," Webster said. "Do you know how to shoot?"

"Sure do," Bob said proudly. "Got a place to practice in my own back yard. I live kinda out in the woods, but my neighbors still get their shorts in a wad some-times. The lady next door raises cats. She says the noise scares them. Says every time I shoot; the cats run and hide and don't come out for hours."

"Bob, I appreciate this. You realize you can't even tell your wife. Are you okay with that?"

"I'll just tell her I'm working overtime."

"What happens when you don't bring home extra money for the overtime?"

"I'm salaried. There's never any extra for overtime."

"That sucks," Webster observed.

"When does this action take place?" Bob asked.

"Soon, probably. If they come at all. Nothing is certain. You better bring a couple of weapons and some ammo in tomorrow," Webster told him. "Bring plenty of ammo for yourself. I have three loaded clips for mine. It's a .45 caliber. I could use a few extra rounds. Got any?"

"I'll take care of it."

"I should have more information in the morning," Webster told him and stood up. "See you then."

Bob headed back toward the facility and Webster walked along the path into the woods.

When he was back in the cabin, Webster retrieved his Glock pistol from its hidden location in his briefcase. He put his cleaning kit on the table. With everything at hand, he sat down and stripped the weapon, cleaning and oiling each piece as though his life depended on it.

~ ~ ~

Dr. Irene Dunn's mother flew into Charlotte midafternoon. The trip from Montana had been tiring. Irene waited for her just outside the security area. Sandra Dunn heard her daughter call out and hurried over. There were hugs and kisses all around while the two women giggled like schoolgirls.

"How's Dad?" Irene asked. "And, how are you?"

"Fine," her mother replied, "but your dad broke his arm playing tennis. The doctor had to do surgery. They used a screw to hold part of the bones together and then inserted a pin to secure something else."

"Mom! You should have called me."

"Why? So you could worry, too?"

Irene spread her arms. "I give up. I thought you'd have wanted to call your daughter, the doctor. Maybe get a second opinion on what was happening with Dad." She laughed again. "I really do give up. Is he okay?"

"He's fine," Sandra said. "And by the way, it was your dad who wouldn't let me call you. He didn't want to worry you."

"Now that I understand." Irene shook her head and started walking through the terminal. "Let's get your bags."

Pablo flew into Atlanta at midafternoon with two of his men from the Veracruz compound. Two other individuals, Charlie Potts from Los Angeles and Tommy Raspallo from Philadelphia, met them there. All were dressed in business suits and appeared comfortable in their surroundings.

Mateo had orchestrated the gathering. He had also made arrangements for the equipment they would need over the next several days.

Pablo and the others met him in a sports bar at the airport. Mateo had picked that particular location when he arrived that morning. The Merchant and his young protégée sat at one table, the others at a second. Everyone grabbed a quick snack as Mateo briefed Pablo. Thirty minutes later, the group had collected their luggage and was following Mateo out to a large GMC Suburban he had rented. Gear was tossed into the back; Mateo drove with Pablo in the front passenger's seat.

They left the airport and headed northeast. There would be one short stopover before leaving the Atlanta area. Charlotte, about five hours away, was their destination.

The stopover was to pick up equipment they would need in Charlotte. Mateo eased off the expressway at Exit 37 and pulled around to the rear of a large McDonald's. He backed into a space next to a Jeep Laredo. Two men got out of the Jeep and walked to the rear of their vehicle. Mateo and Tommy Raspallo climbed out. Pablo handed Mateo a thick envelope before he closed the door. Mateo exchanged a few words with the men from the Jeep as they each opened the backs of their vehicles.

Two bags were unzipped in the rear of the Jeep, and Tommy examined the contents. When he was satisfied, Tommy nodded to Mateo. After a brief discussion about the equipment, Mateo passed Pablo's envelope to one of the men. He opened it, did a brief count, and then nodded his head. The bags were then transferred to the Suburban. Everyone shook hands and returned to their vehicles.

When Mateo opened his door, Pablo was staring at some pages he was holding. As though caught with something he shouldn't have, the Merchant quickly folded the papers up and slipped them into a pocket. Nothing was said by either man.

Mateo started the GMC and drove out of the parking lot. They headed back to the Interstate and charlotte.

When they had settled into traffic, Pablo turned in his seat and asked Tommy, "Did we get everything we needed?"

"Yes, Pablo. They even threw in a couple of pistols, .22 caliber with silencers."

"Did they ask for more money?"

"No, señor. They said it was nice doing business with us. Everything was there. Six Kerr 9 mm, and six AK-47s, plus the two pistols. There are extra magazines for all the weapons and plenty of ammo. They also threw in a hunting knife for each of us."

Pablo turned to Mateo and said, "Good work, my friend. You are a good organizer in addition to your other talents."

Mateo glanced over, nodding slightly.

The men arrived on the outskirts of Charlotte a little after ten that night. They drove to the airport and let Charlie out near the entrance where the rental car counters were found. His chore was to lease a second vehicle for some of their travels. Thirty minutes later, Charlie, in a late model Ford, followed the big GMC to a large Comfort Inn. Their base was located off Derita Road at the northeastern edge of the city.

Mateo had reserved six adjoining rooms at the end of the hallway on the first floor. They moved their luggage inside, along with the equipment bags, stashing those in the room Mateo had taken for himself. After a short meeting to check out the weapons, everyone settled in for the night.

Alone at last, Mateo thumbed through the phone book for Dr. Irene Dunn's name. Sure enough, there was a listing for the good doctor, complete with her address. Now that he knew where she lived, Mateo was confident that he could deliver Webster to the Merchant. The doctor would give him Webster's location. Mateo would persuade her.

Then Pablo could deal with Webster. Mateo had no doubt his own presence would be required. He remembered the Merchant's words: "I will cut his throat and spit on him as he takes his last breath."

Mateo slept fitfully that night.

~ ~ ~

Irene and her mother left the airport and drove out to her home. It was big, much larger than Irene needed, but she had fallen in love with it the moment she saw it.

It was a ranch—four bedrooms and three baths—all on one level. Located on two acres, the property had sprawling lawns that rolled gently away from the house in all directions. There was a sunporch where Irene enjoyed her coffee and read the newspaper on mornings when she had the time. And there was a cozy pool, complete with a small waterfall, at the back of the house and out past a secluded shaded patio. The home and grounds, in its entirety, reminded Irene of her parent's place in Montana.

Her mom liked it, too.

After they had Sandra settled into one of the bedrooms and Irene had shown her around the place, she asked if her mother would like to go out for dinner.

"Sure," the older woman agreed. The sun was already nearing the horizon.

"There's a family place I like," Irene said. "It's not far, and the food's great. I think you'll enjoy it, too." And they were off.

Seated, and with drinks on the way, the women's conversation turned to Irene's life in Charlotte.

"I really do like your place," her mother said. Then concerned, she asked, "You don't think your house is too secluded, do you?"

"Oh, no. I love the privacy, and I have a great security system. I thought I'd be afraid, but I'm not."

"Is there a man in your life?" her mother asked out of the blue. She did that a lot.

Caught unprepared, Irene stammered at first, thought about it, and then said, "Well, no and yes."

"What does that mean? Either there is or there's not. Which is it?" Sandra grinned. Irene smiled. Her mother loved putting her daughter, the doctor, on the spot.

Just then Irene's cell phone rang. Saved by the bell.

~ ~ ~

Webster finished cleaning his weapon and placed it on the bedside table. He then prepared one of his favorite light meals, a grilled cheese with a bowl of tomato soup. The news was on, so he watched for a time. Minutes later, already tired of the same old thing, he punched the off button, gathered his dishes in the sink, and washed them. Webster hated to leave things sitting.

With the housekeeping chore out of the way, he glanced around the cabin. Picking up his cell, he punched in Irene's number. He knew her mother had been due to fly into Charlotte and wanted to see if she had arrived.

Irene answered after the second ring.

"Hello?"

"Hello, yourself," he said to her. "Did your mother get here okay?"

"On time and in good spirits," Irene told him. "As a matter of fact, we were just talking about you."

"Can't you find a better topic of conversation?"

"Yes, we could have," she said, "but my mother decided to talk about you anyway."

Webster didn't know if Irene was joking with him or if she was a little annoyed with her mother.

"What are the two of you doing?" he asked.

"Having dinner and conversation. We're eating out tonight."

"Oh. Sorry. I'll let you go so you can enjoy the evening. I'll call tomorrow," Webster said and closed his phone. Irene had told him earlier that she would be taking a few days off while her mother was in town.

Webster felt uneasy when he went to bed that night. Sleep didn't come quickly or easily. As he lay there, he thought of ways he and Bob and the regular guards could go about defending themselves if someone should try to reach him in the compound. Webster figured he and Bob could take care of themselves. He worried about the staff and the few other patients who were in the medical center. Bob's advice would be crucial for any solution.

~ ~ ~

Hogan visited all the rental car agencies at the Cleveland airport. No one remembered renting a vehicle to anyone matching the description she gave them.

She concentrated on the six hours after the Lear had landed. She knew he could have taken a taxi to an agency elsewhere in the city or to a hotel, having a car delivered there. He could be anywhere in Cleveland, but she guessed he had left the city within hours of killing the two men on the plane.

But where had he gone? That was the question.

Hogan dialed Jeff Thompson, the FBI agent. He answered immediately.

"Special Agent Thompson, this is Amy Hogan."

"Yes, Amy. How did you make out with the rental agencies?"

"Not good," she told him. "No leads on anyone of his description, but people come and go on duty. Anything on your end?"

"Nothing," Thompson said. "We've hit all the airlines. No one remembers him."

"I think if I stay any longer, I'll be wasting my time," she told Thompson. "I'm going to catch a flight out."

"Can I reach you at this cell number?"

"Sure. Call me if you find anything."

After Hogan hung up with Thompson, she punched in Jack Robbins's number. She told him what she had been doing in Cleveland and about her lack of success. She told Robbins that the airline reservations agents had been checked, too—also without success.

"Unless you have a better idea," she explained to Robbins, "I'm going to fly to

Charlotte and make some inquiries. This is a dead end here. I think he left after he got whatever information the pilots had."

"Why don't you come on back to headquarters," Robbins told her. "It would be a total accident if you stumbled on him in Charlotte. We'll get together with Tom and plan our next move. I'll talk with you here in the office tomorrow morning."

# Chapter 31

The Suburban Mateo had rented in Atlanta had a GPS device. He had gone out before daybreak and entered Dr. Dunn's address into the system. Moments later, it gave starting directions to the doctor's house. Mateo smiled. Then he shut everything down and returned to his room.

A few minutes after five, Pablo knocked on Mateo's door. He was at the small desk watching the news on TV as he made notes on a pad.

Looking up, he said, "Buenos días, Pablo. Did you sleep well?"

"No," Pablo told him, "I did not have my woman to keep me warm." He rubbed his face and the back of his neck.

The prior night Mateo and Pablo had talked about what they were going to do in Charlotte. Mateo explained the bits and pieces of information he had tortured from the nurse in New Orleans.

The doctor's name would lead them to Webster, and now they had her address. Mateo would park down the street from her house this morning and wait for her to go to work. He expected her to lead him to Webster's location.

"And you will find him today?" Pablo asked.

"Yes," Mateo said. "I was about to leave for the doctor's home. Do you wish to come with me?"

"No. I will stay here. I have calls to make, and I want to talk with the Americans who are with us."

"Okay," Mateo said. "I need to be there before the doctor leaves for work so I can follow her."

"Go," Pablo told him. "We will talk when you return. Besides, I am ready for breakfast now." Pablo turned and started for the door.

"I am happy with what you have done for me," Pablo said as he reached the doorway. "You will be rewarded." He smiled and walked into the hall, closing the door behind him.

Mateo gathered the things he would carry and went out to his vehicle. Twenty-five minutes later, in the early morning half-light, he was sitting a safe distance from the doctor's house.

An hour passed with no activity. He became anxious, talking to himself and asking questions. Mateo was troubled that the doctor had not shown herself. He became concerned that she may have gone early and he had missed her. From his location he could see the doors to her garage.

Relief was slow in coming.

Finally, as he watched, the garage door started up, and he could see a woman walk around to open the passenger door on a dark automobile. The person—he assumed it was the doctor—held the door as another woman climbed into the vehicle. Mateo watched them, his interest growing.

The automobile backed out and slowly came down the driveway, turning in his direction. Mateo held up the newspaper he had been reading, hiding his face as the car passed him. The women paid him no attention. They hadn't even looked his way. That was good. They were driving slowly; there was plenty of time for him to turn and follow them.

He started the engine, drove to the cross street, and made a slow U-turn. He could still see the women's car; they were signaling a left turn. He gunned the Suburban and then slowed and pulled up to the intersection.

They were a block ahead as he turned. He followed, careful of the distance between them. Their game of hide-and-seek went on for twenty minutes.

As he was wondering about the destination, their automobile, a BMW sedan, pulled into the parking lot at a large strip mall. Mateo drove to the parking area and hung back to watch.

The women parked near a large grocery store and then got out and walked toward the building. They were laughing and talking, in no hurry. Mateo parked and followed them into the store.

To appear inconspicuous, Mateo picked up a shopping basket as he entered. He walked through the produce section, choosing an apple and a bunch of bananas that he dropped into his basket. He shadowed the women now, watching the younger one as he memorized her features. She was five seven or eight with blonde hair of medium length and was quite pretty. She seemed happy; he could hear her laugh from where he was standing. Both women were dressed casually, the doctor in jeans. Now that he could recognize her, Mateo walked to the cashiers at the front of the store and paid for his purchases.

Returning to the Suburban, Mateo climbed in, tossing the fruit on the passenger seat. The store had been busy, and the parking lot was packed. Keeping a close eye on the store, he started the engine and eased through the rows of vehicles to the edge of the lot where he positioned himself behind a large construction truck. He could watch the doors where the women would come out, but it would be difficult for them to see him. He could still see their automobile too.

Cutting the engine, Mateo settled back and peeled a banana. Now they would come to him.

Minutes later, Mateo watched as the women came out of the store pushing a cart loaded with bags. He remained still until the women pulled out onto the street. When they were well on their way, Mateo followed. The young, clean-cut killer stayed two hundred yards back, moving closer at times, and then dropping back again.

As they neared the doctor's neighborhood, Mateo pulled into a convenience store's parking lot and stopped. He waited for a couple of minutes before continuing and driving past the doctor's house. The women were unloading groceries. He drove to the intersection, then onto the side street, and turned around.

He drove slowly back toward the corner and stopped. Climbing out of the vehicle, Mateo walked along the sidewalk until he could see the doctor's house. The garage door was starting to close. He could still see the automobile; the women had obviously gone inside.

Mateo walked back to his vehicle and found a place to park a couple of blocks from the doctor's house. He knew which driveway was hers and he leaned back to watch and wait.

Reaching for the snacks, he felt for the apple and wiped it off on the sleeve of his jacket. Taking a big bite, he settled back into the seat. Mateo wasn't ready to push the situation.

Not yet, anyway.

~ ~ ~

The women had sauntered through the aisles, talking and reminiscing as they shopped. They gathered ingredients for meals they planned to prepare during Sandra's stay.

"Spaghetti and a salad okay for tonight?" Irene asked. "I'll need to pick up some French bread. Oh, and maybe some Italian sausage."

Her mother nodded and then asked, "Would you like me to fry some chicken for you while I'm here? You always loved my fried chicken."

Irene beamed. "Oh, Mom. Would you? I can almost taste it now."

They walked on, gathering treats and chatting as they caught up on things that had occurred in their lives.

When they were finished shopping, Irene paid, and they walked out to the car. With their purchases in the trunk, Irene returned their cart while her mother climbed in.

When she returned, Sandra looked worried. The corners of her mouth had turned down, and lines gathered on her forehead. Irene asked if there was a problem.

"I worry about you," Sandra said. "Big cities all have crime problems, and you live all alone in that big house."

Irene laughed as she put a hand on her mother's arm. "Don't get yourself in a state, Mom. My community's quiet; we even have a neighborhood watch that patrols after ten. I've never heard of a break-in."

Irene started the car. "I'm safe—I promise."

"I hope so," Sandra said, "and I'll hush."

They chuckled. Really, what could happen?

As they pulled out of the parking lot, Irene asked her mother, "Want to stop anyplace?"

"No, but do you need to go to out to the clinic? I'll be fine if you do."

"I may want to go in and see a couple of patients later this week," Irene said. "For now, I'll call and check on everything."

Back at Irene's, they put away the food and then Irene called the medical facility to check with the head nurse.

"Anything I need to know?"

"Everything's quiet."

"Is Bob available?" Irene used Bob to keep up with Webster's condition and progress. He could tell her things Webster wouldn't.

The nurse checked and came back on the phone, "He's out walking with Mr. Michaels. Do you want him to call you when he comes back in?"

"Only if he thinks there's a problem. Tell Bob I'll come by in a couple of days to check on things. If anything comes up and you need me, call. Tell Bob, too."

She hung up and began preparing lunch.

~ ~ ~

The afternoon hours passed slowly. No activity was visible at the doctor's house. Several people had walked past Mateo on the sidewalk, a few obviously exercising, and there was an old man with his dog. One woman passed a second time and gave him a suspicious look. It was time to change locations.

Mateo drove past the doctor's place to a cross street. Turning, he parked where he could still see her driveway. With the bananas gone, he remained there until midafternoon before giving up. The doctor must not be going out again that day.

Driving back to the hotel, Mateo decided on a new plan of action. He had spoken with Pablo a couple of times during the day, mostly to keep him informed. The Merchant was starting to get antsy the last time Mateo called.

Back at the Comfort Inn, he went directly to Pablo's room. He knocked and heard a shout for him to enter.

"Tell me you have results," Pablo said when Mateo walked through the door.

He sat in a chair near the window. Pablo was at the desk, the pages, possibly a letter, that Mateo had noticed earlier, were at the Merchant's finger tips. When Pablo noticed Mateo looking, he folded them and slipped them into a pocket without commenting.

"The women stayed at the house after the grocery store trip," Mateo told the Merchant.

"What about her work?"

Mateo repeated what he had said on the phone. "I don't know why she didn't go to work."

"If she doesn't go tomorrow, we will pay her a visit," Pablo told him. "It won't be pleasant, but she will talk to me. I want to find the bastard who killed my son, and she can tell us where he is."

Mateo met Pablo's eyes and nodded. He knew Pablo's methods for getting information and agreed—it would not be pleasant.

 **Chapter 32**

When Bob walked in from the parking lot the next morning, Webster was wait-ing.

"Did you bring the weapons?"

"They're in the back of the car," Bob said.

"Do you have much going on today?"

"Just you. I've scheduled some weight training and some jogging," Bob told him. "We could throw in some hiking. That's always helpful."

"You're trying to kill me," Webster said sarcastically. "Are you sure you're not working for the people who are looking for me?"

Bob chuckled and motioned for Webster to follow him. "Let's get the stuff," he said as he led Webster out to the golf cart.

Bob went tearing out to the parking lot. Webster wondered if he drove his car the way he operated the cart. He held on tight as Bob skidded to a stop.

Webster waited anxiously as the big nurse opened the trunk. He took a canvas bag out and set it gently on the back of the cart. It didn't seem too heavy, although Webster could hear the solid sound of metal bumping against metal.

Bob guided them along the driveway to the rear of the medical building. From there, they took the path to Webster's cabin. Bob was moving a little slower on the twisting trail. Webster sat admiring the view. Having been in the cabin now for nearly three weeks, it was starting to feel like a home of sorts.

They parked near the porch, and Bob carried the bag inside, placing it on the table. Webster was eager to see the weapons.

As Bob reached inside and placed the first pistol on the table, Webster looked on and said with admiration, "Okay! The big Glock." Though black in color, the weapon gleamed, obviously clean and well oiled.

"I bought it because it was hard to get my big hand around the smaller ones. I got it after I bought the Smith & Wesson. By that time, I had figured out I needed something larger."

Bob pulled another pistol from the bag and handed it to Webster. In tip-top shape like the first one, the Smith & Wesson was a little smaller. It looked almost new.

Bob reached back and this time came up with a rifle. Webster examined it and wondered if Bob kept all his tools and equipment in as good shape as these three weapons. The rifle was a .30 caliber M-3 carbine, military style. Though an older vintage, going back to 1945, the rifle looked new. Webster suspected it had been fired relatively few times. He hoped that would continue to be true.

Bob handed him the night scope; it was in great condition, too. Webster really hoped they wouldn't have to use any of Bob's equipment.

After watching Webster admire the weapons for a few moments, Bob turned and finished emptying the bag. There were two green ammo boxes and three extra magazines for each of the pistols. Bob also brought out two pairs of night-vision goggles. They were still in their boxes.

Webster eyed the goggles and then glanced at Bob. "I bought them for me and my son to play with," he said. "I thought you and I could break them in if your friends show up after dark."

"Damn, Bob. We can make a pretty good stand with what we have here."

"I think so, too," Bob said with pride.

Webster had placed his pistol on the table with Bob's weapons as they were talking.

"Let's work out some plans," Webster said as he motioned for Bob to sit at the table. He pulled each of them a small OJ from the refrigerator.

They pushed the weapons and other equipment back and Webster picked up a pencil. He began making notes as they talked. Bob watched as he popped the top on his juice and took a swallow.

Six hours later, with a break for lunch at the medical facility, they completed what each of them thought was a workable set of plans. They needed a few supplies. Webster sent Bob off to Lowe's and a couple of other places to buy them.

With Bob gone, Webster settled in one of the rockers to make some additional notes. They intended having some surprises for anyone who might come looking for Webster. After much discussion, they decided any action would likely take place at night. They were preparing for that possibility but still not overlooking a day raid of some sort.

As he waited and to cover all the bases, Webster's thoughts turned to the forest behind the cabin and he tried to think if there was anything he should consider about that area. Then, remembering something from a couple of days earlier, he got up and headed for the path the guards took during the night. He followed one that ran toward the back and to the eastern edge of the property. When he reached the fence, he could distinguish the area where he had seen the young boy. The youngster had watched him and Bob with interest as they'd surveyed the clinic's grounds.

Suddenly, the same kid raised his head up from behind some bushes twenty yards away, over near the ball field. He was silent, watchful, and curious. Webster took the initiative.

"Hi." He waved at the boy.

After a few moments, the youngster waved back. "Hi." He stayed where Webster first saw him.

"You live nearby?"

The boy gestured over his left shoulder.

Webster approached the fence and was pleased to see the boy take a few steps in his direction, but he stopped several feet short of the fence. But within minutes, the two of them were chatting and laughing like buddies. The kid's name was Kenney Dawkin. He had recently turned twelve and lived nearby with his mother and a younger sister.

By the time Webster was ready to return to the cabin, his young friend had agreed to a couple of suggestions Webster made. Pleased, Webster had promised something in return.

On his way back to the cabin, the cell phone rang; Rage Doyle was calling. He was curious whether Webster had taken his advice and turned up someone outside the medical facility to watch his back. Webster laughed, explaining that he was just returning to his living quarters after handling that chore. He also told Rage that his coconspirator was a twelve-year-old boy, thinking Rage might consider it a bad idea. Instead, the Author was delighted.

"Wonderful!" he said. "Who would suspect a kid to be involved?"

When Webster explained what he had promised in return for the boy's help, Rage commented, "Boy, you pay your help well."

Then Webster said he might have to take the cost out of his own pocket. He didn't know whether the bosses would okay such an expenditure. The Author told him to hold off asking for a day or two.

"I have some favors due. Maybe I can help."

They left it at that and hung up, with Webster promising to let Rage know if the unwanted visitors showed up anytime soon.


Bob returned with the golf cart loaded with supplies. The two friends spent the next two-and-a-half hours getting things prepared. When they finished, Bob went home to clean up and get a little rest. He would be back at ten that evening.

After he left, Webster went inside the cabin and took a shower. Afterward, he brought in some wood and built a small fire. The heat it generated warmed the cabin quickly.

For dinner, Webster made a couple of sandwiches and poured a glass of milk for himself. He put the food on a tray along with an apple and took it out on the porch to one of the rockers.

The sandwiches satisfied his hunger, and the apple was his dessert. He had just finished and downed the milk when his cell phone rang.

"Hello?"

"Good evening, Mr. Webster." It was Irene. He had relinquished and given her the number. It was nice to talk with her as a friend.

"Where are you two ladies dining tonight?" he asked. "As for me, I've just finished a three-course meal at Webster's deli. Four courses if you count the milk."

Irene chuckled and said he had a weird sense of humor.

"We're eating in tonight, too," she said. "Spaghetti with salad on the side."

"Umm," he said. "Sounds good."

"What's going on out there? I called this morning. The duty nurse said Bob was with you. Are you two boys staying out of trouble?"

"Yes, teacher," he said in a little-boy voice.

"You'd better. Otherwise, I may have to take you over my knee and spank you."

"Oh yes, teacher!" He exclaimed in a breathless big-boy voice this time.

She broke into a fit of laughter. "Things must be okay if you have the energy to joke with your doctor."

"Everything's fine." He spoke seriously this time. Webster didn't think it necessary to worry her with what he anticipated. "You and your mother have some fun. Enjoy your spaghetti. We can talk tomorrow."

"Sounds good," she said. "I'll be in touch."

~ ~ ~

Hogan had arrived back at Dulles Airport the previous night at ten thirty. She was still tired and wasn't ready to get up when the alarm went off at six fifteen in the morning. Stretching and yawning, she made her way into the bathroom and prepared to meet the day.

Later, glancing at her reflection in the entrance door of her building, she was proud of what she had accomplished in putting herself together. She was still smiling as she walked into her office.

There was a note on her desk that instructed her to go directly to Tom Manning's office. When she got there, Manning was sitting behind his desk with his feet up. Jack Robbins sat across from him. Tom motioned toward an empty chair.

"We're trying to figure out what to do about Webster," Manning said as she settled into the chair. "Jack brought me up-to-date on Cleveland. Is there anything we don't know yet?"

"Nothing," she answered. Then she asked, "Are you going to pull him out of his present location?"

"We were discussing that possibility and we're thinking of leaving him there," Robbins said. "With this guy killing people left and right as he tries to find Webster, we have to find a way to stop him. Letting him come to Webster is one of the possibilities."

"What about the ambulance service?" Hogan asked.

Manning and Robbins looked at each other. "What about it?" Manning asked.

"I have an idea," Hogan replied. "If I was looking for Webster and didn't know where he had been taken, I'd try to find out what ambulance service transported him."

The two men exchanged glances again. Manning asked Jack Robbins, "Did the medical center have its own ambulance? You went out there."

"I have no idea," Robbins replied with a frown on his face. "Let me call them." He opened his briefcase and pulled out a notebook. Flipping through it, he came up with a number, opened his cell, dialed and put the phone to his ear.

"This is Deputy Marshal Jack Robbins with the U.S. Marshals Service. We have a man in your facility." He paused, listening. "Yeah, Michaels. Okay, here's the thing. I have a simple question, maybe two. Do you people have your own ambulance?" He listened. "Okay, do you have a contract with one of the local services?" Another pause. "Which one and who should I talk with? Give me a number, too." Robbins wrote something in his book. "Oh, and if you will, call and tell him I'll be trying to reach him in about five minutes. Thanks." Robbins broke the connection.

Manning tilted his head and waited for Jack to relay what he had found out. Robbins said, "It's too expensive to have their own ambulance, so they use a service. Only one driver knows where they're located. He makes all their runs."

Manning looked at Hogan again and said, "Okay, Amy, this was your idea. Where do we go from here?"

She thought about it. "We send a couple of our people to Charlotte, to the ambulance service, and insert them there as soon as possible. In a best-case scenario, our people will arrest this guy if he comes looking for the driver that transported Webster."

Robbins was nodding his head when Manning looked at him.

"Any downside?" Manning asked.

Hogan and Robbins exchanged glances, then remained quiet.

"Okay … we go with it." He nodded at Robbins. "Pick someone to go with Hogan and send them down to Charlotte on our plane. We need them on the ground ASAP."

"I'll go with Hogan," Robbins volunteered.

"No, send someone else," Manning replied. "I want you here to run this operation. Who knows where he could turn up before he goes to Charlotte.

Manning stood up then, signaling the end of the meeting.

Four hours later, Hogan and Deputy Marshal Jerry Jackson were in place at the ambulance service in Charlotte. Everyone there was instructed to refer anyone looking for a certain driver to Hogan and Jackson. The two of them would be residing in the on-call quarters until further notice.

 **Chapter 33**

Mateo and the Merchant prepared for the next day. If the doctor went to work, Mateo would follow in the Ford they had rented. Using a different vehicle would give him an entirely new look. They couldn't chance being noticed.

As Mateo and Pablo talked, the four other men were making plans, too. With some instruction, they had come up with basic guidelines. A decision was made that the group should work in two-man teams. Mateo and Pablo would work as one team. José and Pedro, the men who had come with the Merchant from the compound, would work together. And finally, Tommy and Charlie, the two Americans, would form the third team. The plan was presented to Pablo and Mateo as a suggestion.

Pablo made it clear that Mateo had his trust and was in charge of the overall operation. Pablo also made it clear that when they found Webster, Pablo alone would decide how to deal with him. Everyone could tell that whatever Pablo had in store for Webster would not be pleasant.

The words they heard and remembered were, "He will suffer first; then I will carve out his throat … slowly."

The group became quiet, pondering the confrontation that loomed before them.

Mateo asked Charlie to see what everyone wanted to eat and go for some take-out food. He did not want them to be seen out as a group, possibly drawing attention to the operation. Someone might remember.

Everyone had finished their supper and was back in their own rooms by nine o'clock. Mateo wanted them rested. He had a gut feeling they would confront their quarry sometime the next day—day or night.

~ ~ ~

The women finished their dinner and cleared the dishes from the table. Sandra sat at the small table in the breakfast nook where they'd had their meal. They talked as Irene cleaned up the kitchen and stacked the dishwasher.

"Do you want to watch TV or read this evening?" Irene asked. Then she added, "I saw you brought a book with you."

"Let's talk first," her mother said. "Your dad and I have made some tentative decisions, and we want to be sure you're okay with them. We've already had papers drawn up, and we've signed them. We could change them if you think something else would be better."

Irene smiled. They were going to talk about whatever decision her mom and dad had made after the fact.

As she put the last pot away, Irene said, "Let's go sit by the fire. It's nice there."

Her mother followed as Irene headed for the den. In front of the fireplace was a large sofa that faced it. On each side, between the sofa and the fireplace, were two sets of chairs. All the seating was grouped on a large and colorful Oriental rug. There were small tables between each set of chairs and a large, round wooden coffee table in front of the sofa.

"I love this table," Sandra said as she settled into one of the chairs. "It's so unusual."

Irene curled up on the sofa, pulling her legs up under her.

"It came from Holland. At least that's what they told me when I bought it."

"It must weigh a ton," her mother observed. "The top has to be three or four inches thick."

"It's heavy," Irene agreed. "The movers rolled it into the house. After they had it in place, they started calling me the 'Flintstones lady.' I saw one of them in the drugstore the other day, and he remembered me immediately because of the table. I laughed and kept walking."

"I like it."

"Now, what did you want to talk about?" Irene was curious.

Her mother looked at her for a moment.

"We've updated our wills," she said. "The problem is this. You expected us to give the foreman's house to Jacob. We know how you feel about him." She was stating Irene's case for her. "We all tend to think of Jacob as family. He's been around forever, over thirty years. He's like your dad's brother." Sandra paused. "But he really isn't family. Your dad and I decided if you want him to have the place, you can give it to him after we're gone. We don't want to make that decision."

Irene looked at her mother, concerned. "There isn't anything wrong, is there? Should I know something you haven't told me?"

"No, of course not."

Sandra smiled at Irene and then said, "We've left everything to you. That's just what we wanted to do."

Irene was quiet. She looked into the fire. Her mother did, too. After several minutes, she looked back at Sandra.

"I understand. Is Jacob aware of your decision?"

"No. We didn't want to tell him, but we don't think he expects it. He would probably be happy to live out his years working around the place. He has his So-cial Security and your dad pays him a good salary in cash. He does okay."

"Maybe I could sign some sort of document giving him a life estate on the house and a couple of acres." She waited for her mother's reaction.

"When your dad and I are gone," she said, "that would be up to you. Like I said, I don't think he expects anything."

They talked into the night. Finally, sometime after midnight, Irene's mother called it quits.

"I'm exhausted. Your dad and I don't usually stay up this late." She yawned. "I'll see you in the morning."

~ ~ ~

After his phone conversation with Irene, Webster had straightened up the cabin, picking up a few things here and there. He also moved a couple of new additions to exact locations where he wanted them. Finished, he had strolled outside and sat on the porch, relaxing, even napping a little.

When he awoke, Webster sat still, listening to the sounds around the cabin. He had trained himself to pay attention to the ordinary in any given situation. If he knew what was common, he would be able to discern sounds that were unusual. It was a little trick that had proved beneficial on several occasions. Rage had taught him about sounds along with many other useful mental tools.

At ten that evening, Webster was still on the porch. The lights were out, and the moon had not yet presented itself.

Webster was now familiar with the normal sounds in the area. Listening with renewed interest, he picked up the soft sounds of someone walking. Drawing his weapon, he rested it across his knees. There was just the least bit of light, enough to see a few yards.

Remaining very still, Webster watched as a man quietly walked off the trail and toward the cabin. He recognized Bob, and his friend was only a dozen feet away when Webster spoke.

"You could get shot slipping up on a fellow like that."

Bob jumped, startled, and dropped something he had been carrying.

"Shit, man. You could make a man pee on himself."

Webster laughed and then said, "Marines, huh? You must have been in the Little Girl Platoon."

"Funny," Bob commented sarcastically. "I might have shot you, too, you know?"

"No, you couldn't," Webster told him. "You left your weapons here, remember?"

"Oh … yeah." Bob grinned, a little embarrassed.

"See anything on the way over from the facility?"

"Nothing but a rabbit headed toward the river."

"Any sign it was packing?"

"Not that I noticed," Bob said with a chuckle.

"Let's take our positions," Webster suggested. "Come on. We'll get our things." Webster opened the door to the cabin, leading Bob inside.

"Things look good," Bob commented, examining some of Webster's preparations.

"Everything should work as long as it's dark in here."

They each picked up weapons and equipment they would use in case Webster's enemies showed up. Each of them took a set of the night vision goggles. Bob took both of his pistols, leaving Webster the rifle, the night scope, and his own handgun. They had decided earlier that Webster should take the rifle because he had significant time night firing on the shooting range with weapons like Bob's M-3 carbine. He had also used a night scope. They each picked up several items they had fabricated that afternoon.

Prepared, they turned off the lights and headed outside. Bob moved off to the left front of the cabin and Webster to the right. They took up the positions they had agreed upon that afternoon. When they reached their assigned locations, each man picked up a brown string and tied it loosely around his left forearm. The string ran along the ground between their two locations. They could alert each other with just a tug.

By agreement, Bob would be the first to sleep. At midnight, Webster would tug on the string, and it would be his turn to rest while Bob kept watch.

The two hours passed slowly. Webster strained to hear anything that was not normal to the forest where he and Bob were waiting. He quietly slipped the night goggles over his eyes and viewed the surroundings. It was always surprising to realize how much could be seen using the apparatus. Even with a green tint, the scene was clear and bright.

Webster removed the goggles after a few minutes and picked up the rifle with its attached night scope. Again, once he had adjusted to the scope, he realized he could zero in on a target with little effort. With the two of them in place, an enemy coming to the cabin would be receiving gunfire from two separate locations.

Bob and Webster could each fire from their main location and then immediately roll to another spot without getting to their feet. They could quickly make the moves without exposing themselves to return fire.

At midnight, Webster gently tugged on the string to awaken Bob. He, at once, felt two quick pulls, acknowledging his friend was ready to take the watch. Webster knew Bob was already trying out the goggles.

The rest of the night was uneventful. The two men used the hidden string to trade shifts every two hours. That proved to be their only activity for the night.

At about five forty, Webster came awake at the sound of someone walking toward him; it was Bob. Dawn was bringing light to their surroundings.

Webster got to his feet and stretched. Both men were tired, and each had joints that ached. Neither of them was used to sleeping on the cold ground.

"I guess I'm getting old," Bob observed.

"Me, too."

"We gonna do this until they come?"

Webster nodded. "Or until they're caught. I don't see any other way," Webster said. "If the regular guards can protect the facility, you and I should be able to take care of two or three thugs out here. I just hope they find out about the cabin and don't think I'm in the medical center."

"Me, too," Bob said as he surveyed the woods and cabin. "There's only one door in the cabin. That forces them to come to us."

"Yeah. It does simplify things."

They carried the equipment to the cabin and then came back outside and brushed up the areas where they had spent the night. Only with close examination would it be possible to tell someone had been there.

Bob had the day off, so he headed home for some rest. He said he would come out and check on things at the medical center during the afternoon and then see Webster that night.

Webster showered and then cooked breakfast for himself. A short time later, he fell into bed.

Maybe the killers will come tonight, he thought in the moments before sleep claimed him.

# Chapter 34

At five thirty in the morning, Mateo parked at a new location that allowed him to watch for Dr. Dunn. He was in the Ford this time and had picked up donuts, coffee, and a USA Today newspaper. He had also used the restroom at the donut shop.

As he sat waiting, Mateo put the finishing touches on the morning's plans. If Dr. Dunn didn't lead him to her work location by ten o'clock, he was prepared to take new measures. Pablo would join him for that.

Mateo moved the car every thirty minutes before ten o'clock. Each time he remained as far as possible from the doctor's house while still being able to see it.

There had been no discernible activity by midmorning.

Mateo started the car and drove slowly by the house one last time. She must be taking another day off, and the older woman obviously must be visiting from out of town. That could explain the doctor not going to work.

When he was clear of the house, Mateo sped up and hurried to his first destination. He went inside and told the salesperson what he wanted. He could pick it up in an hour, she said. He thanked her and headed for his second stop. Five minutes after arriving, he walked out with his purchase.

Mateo's next stop was to switch vehicles and pick up Pablo. He had called, and the Merchant was ready and waiting. Mateo moved the things he had purchased over to the Suburban, and they drove away, leaving the other men on stand-by.

The items Mateo had ordered at his first stop were ready when he returned. He paid and took the package out and tossed it onto the backseat. They had everything needed for the last step.

On their way out to the doctor's house, Mateo stopped in an empty parking lot to make a slight change to the appearance of the GMC. Then they drove to their destination.

~ ~ ~

The doctor and her mother had slept late that morning. When Irene finally climbed out of bed at eight thirty, she could smell coffee. Sandra hadn't waited for her. She took a few minutes in the bathroom and then joined her mom in the kitchen.

"Good afternoon," Sandra teased sarcastically but with a smile.

"I don't usually sleep this late. I must have been more tired than I thought."

"It's good for you to do that sometimes," her mother said. "It reminds you that you're human. That's especially true for you doctors."

Irene chuckled. Her mother was bringing her down a notch or two … again.

"What would you like to do today?" Irene asked.

"Let's take it easy," her mother suggested. We can talk and read. Maybe we could go out for dinner—my treat."

"Okay. I have a few calls I need to make, and maybe we could phone Dad."

"Yes," her mother agreed. "I had planned to call him anyway. He will be glad to hear from you."

They had breakfast, took care of the dishes, and then Irene headed for her study while Sandra retreated to the family room with her book.

Irene checked in with the duty nurse and then called Webster.

"Hello."

He sounded as if he'd been asleep. Not like him, she thought.

"Are we napping?" Irene kidded.

"Yep. I didn't sleep much last night," he said.

He didn't tell her why, and she thought of asking but decided against it. If he had wanted her to know, he'd have told her.

"How about you? What are you and your mother up to? Are the two of you burning up the streets?"

She expected he was only partially kidding, but he probably had a pretty good idea of how women liked to shop.

"Would you believe we're having lunch at home and then resting, gossiping, and reading? We are going out for dinner this evening, though. Why don't you come with us?"

"I'd like that," Webster said, "but I can't." He had decided against telling her what was going on. "I have orders to be available for a conference call sometime this the evening. It will probably be a long one, too. Sorry, wish I could. I'd like to meet your mother."

"She wants to meet you, too. Even after all I've told her." She laughed and then said seriously, "I really do want to get the two of you together while she's here."

"Sounds good. Have a good time when you go out."

"We will. I hope you sleep better tonight."

After she hung up, Irene sat for several minutes contemplating Webster and how he reminded her of John. As she remembered him, she thought of her loss there. But that was yesterday. She really believed there could be something for her with Webster now, but there was that other woman in his past. If only …

Irene called her mother into the study and dialed her father in Montana. They got him on the first try. Glancing at Sandra, she punched the button to put it on the speaker.

"Dad, it's Irene. Mom's here, too. We have you on the speaker." She grinned at her mom. "How are you doing? And, how's the arm, Mr. Agassi?"

"Your mom told you about the tennis accident, huh?"

She could almost see his face. He didn't like to talk about himself or things that happened to him.

"It's okay," he volunteered. "Still a little swollen, though."

"Did you have physical therapy?"

"Nine sessions. I'm continuing some things they told me to do after I finished the therapy. It seems okay, except it's still a little weak." He paused. "Did your mom's trip go all right?"

"It went fine," Sandra said. "Didn't have any delays at all." She changed subjects. "Are you feeding Sam like you should? And the birds?"

Sam was their twelve-year-old German shepherd. He knew Irene on sight and considered her a friend.

"No, dear. I'm letting them all starve," he kidded. "Of course, I'm feeding the animals and the wildlife."

Irene asked a couple of things about the Montana weather and then told her dad good-bye, leaving her parents to talk. They were seldom apart, so they had some catching up to do.

Irene went in to start lunch. She had decided a Caesar salad would be nice, and maybe a bowl of soup.

After a few minutes, her mother joined Irene in the kitchen. They talked as she prepared their food and warmed some French bread to go with the soup and salad. When it was ready, they sat down to eat. Everything was good, and they enjoyed themselves. They were just finishing when the doorbell rang.

Irene got up, leaving her mother at the table, and went through the house to see who was there. Through the sidelights, she could see a dark, van-like vehicle parked in the driveway. It had a sign of some sort on the side. And there was a young man on the porch with a bouquet of roses in his arms.

Webster! He must have sent them. How sweet!

With pleasant thoughts on her mind, Irene then opened her door to a killer.

 # Chapter 35

"Dr. Dunn?"

"Yes," she said, pushing the door aside, her eyes on the bouquet.

The delivery man took a step toward her. That's when she saw the handgun.

He said something and motioned for her to move back into the house. Irene caught part of what he was saying, and it sent a chill over her.

"… an older woman. Where is she?"

She struggled to find her voice. The words came out choked, halting. "Sh … she's in the kitchen."

First, he told her to move back into the foyer. She watched as he motioned her back with the gun. He closed the door with his foot.

Then he told her to go to the kitchen.

Irene hated scaring her mother, but she had no choice.


It had worked like a dream.

Mateo smiled as he heard Dr. Dunn unlock and open the door. He knew he had her.

He held the bouquet where she could see it at once. The roses really were pretty. She probably even thought she knew who had sent them. Whomever the doctor had guessed, she was wrong.

While she was still admiring the flowers, he showed her the weapon. He heard her gasp as she reevaluated the delivery. She'd realized he wasn't from the florist's shop after all.

"Step back into the house," Mateo said softly. "I know there is someone else here with you, an older woman. Where is she?" He could tell she hadn't understood all that he had said.

The doctor's mouth was agape, and now her eyes were wide, her voice stammering. She still hadn't taken her eyes off the gun.

"Sh … she's in the kitchen."

"Let's go in there," Mateo ordered as he tossed the roses on the foyer table.


As Irene started through the house, a thought crossed her mind. The roses aren't from Webster after all.

The man followed her closely until they reached the kitchen. As they walked through the doorway, her mother looked up and saw the pistol.

Living in Montana, Mom had grown up with guns. Irene knew the weapon wouldn't scare her, but the intruder would. She could see fear in her mom's eyes as she turned her gaze to Irene.

"Sit down at the table with the other woman," the man told Irene. Then he asked if she had some rope or cord.

"In the garage," Irene said, "on a shelf in front of the car. Why are you doing this?"

"You'll find out. Where's the garage?" he asked, waving the pistol at her. "Walk me there, both of you."


Mateo watched the women closely, especially the young one. He didn't want to hurt them—not yet.

The doctor got up first, then the other one. With Dr. Dunn leading the way, they left the kitchen and trudged through the utility room to the garage.

Mateo could tell by the way she glared back at him that the doctor would make things difficult if there was an opportunity. Tough! She would have to do whatever he wanted, whether she liked it or not. The older woman was his ace in the hole.

When they reached the garage, Mateo said, "Raise the door and motion for my friend to drive the Suburban inside."

He placed a hand on the older woman's shoulder and guided her to an area where they wouldn't be seen. Dr. Dunn watched them, obviously hoping her mother would be safe, then she hit the button to open the garage door.

Mateo had told Pablo to watch for them and to drive the van in beside the BMW. When the vehicle was parked, the doctor closed the garage door. Pablo climbed out of the Suburban and joined them.

"Let's go inside," Mateo told the women. He motioned for Pablo to bring the rope.

Then he asked Dr. Dunn, "Are you expecting visitors?"


She needed to do something to throw them off, to gain time.

Irene said, "My sister's probably coming over." Her mother glanced at her only child without a change of expression.

"When?"

"Any time now."

"You better hope she changes her mind," he said.

Irene hoped she didn't regret the deception.

"What do you want?" she asked, unable to keep her anger at bay though her voice was a little weaker now. She was worried about her mother.

"We'll get to that in a minute," the younger man told her as he reached for the rope.

The other man passed him the rope and spoke up. "Is this your madre … ah … your mother?" He spoke with a heavy Latin accent.

Irene's mother answered for herself, "Yes, I'm her mother. You can call me Mrs. Dunn." Then she asked, "Who are you? And why are you in my daughter's house?"

The man laughed. Obviously, he liked spirited women.

"You don't need to know who I am," he said. "Jus' do what we tell you."

"Stand up, both of you," the young one said, "and hold your arms behind you."

"If we are going to be tied up, I'll have to go to the bathroom first," Sandra declared.

"Both of us," Irene chimed in.

The young one considered their requests and then agreed. "Okay, but one at a time, and this man will stand at the door. He will give you one minute. Then he's coming in. Understand?"

They each nodded. Irene could see that both men had a pistol in his belt.

"Lead the way, señora y señorita."


Mateo used the time to familiarize himself with the house. When Pablo brought them back, Mateo had the women stand with their arms behind them. He tied them with the rope and then had them sit in small chairs near the fireplace. Once they were seated, he and Pablo tied the older woman's feet to the legs of her chair. She would be able to move around a little but couldn't walk away.

Mateo had explained his plan to Pablo at the hotel last night. Now that he had surveyed the house, there would be little to change. Having the mother separated would make the situation easier. The doctor would be more inclined to do what Mateo required. What he wanted was information on how to get his hands on Webster.

He took Dr. Dunn by the arm and guided her into the formal dining room where he pulled out a captain's chair and placed her in it. Mateo slid out a chair for himself, moving it in front of the doctor with their legs touching, his knees inside hers. He had learned from Pablo how intimidating it could be to impose oneself in another's personal space.

Scooting even closer, he said, "I have some questions for you." He looked into the doctor's eyes, his face inches from hers. "You will answer my questions. Do you understand?"

"Why should I?"

His voice low and menacing, Mateo said, "Because … my friend will inflict much pain on your mother if you don't. Is that a good reason?"

A thin film of tears clouded the doctor's eyes. The tears couldn't hide her fear, but the strain she was exerting on the rope conveyed her anger. Obviously, she was afraid for her mother, yet furious at the intruders, too.

"What do you want?" she asked again. There appeared to be less outrage now and more concern.

Mateo looked at her for a long moment and then said, "You treated a patient at the facility where you work. He came to you from New Orleans a few weeks ago. I need to know where he is now."

He gazed at her, waiting. He was good at this. Pablo had taught him well. He watched her eyes. When he asked the question, she had flinched and raised her eyebrows. She knows where he is.

"Where?" He asked the question again, this time not only with his voice but also with his expression and the tone of his voice. "You are going to tell me. Your mother wants you to." He let her consider that one. He could almost see her thoughts as he waited. She didn't want to tell him, but, even more, she didn't want them to hurt her mother.

It came out slow, reluctantly, "He … he's at … the facility." She looked distressed, yet somehow relieved.

She thinks this will help her mother, Mateo thought.

"Where is this facility?"

Tears were slowly making their way down her cheeks now, yet her eyes were narrowed—focused with anger. She wore a darkening frown, and her lips were pulled tight. Mateo realized he would not want their rolls to be reversed at this moment.

Snapping out the words, she said, "I can't."

"But you have to … don't you? For your mother … So the man won't hurt her. Right?" Mateo nodded his head. "Right?"

Lowering her eyes, the doctor nodded her head, too. Mateo was getting there. Slowly, but they were getting there.

"Now, I'm going to ask you again." He touched her chin, raising her head and bringing her eyes up to meet his. He could feel her breath on his face.

Quickly but gently, with the curled index finger of his right hand still touching her cheek, he softly asked, "Where is the facility?"

Dr. Dunn squeezed her eyes shut for a moment, tears now chasing one another down her cheeks. Under her breath, Mateo could hear her mumbling.

"Damn it all to hell!" Then louder, "It … it's out Brookshire Boulevard, on Long Road."

"Are there any signs for your facility?"

"No," she told him. "The people who run it don't want anyone to know what's there. Only the employees know what is located there."

"Can you get me in?"

"No." Everything she was telling him came out slowly. She shook her head. "You would need special documents and authorization to get in."

"Can you get the patient out?"

"No. He has to have special authorization from DC to leave the grounds." She had hesitated for a brief moment. He suspected she was lying about Webster but there wasn't time to check it out.

"What about guards?"

She told him about the entrance and about the hourly rounds at night.

"Is there a map of the grounds?" That seemed to surprise her?

"Is there?"

After a moment of thought, she said, "There's only one. I'm not aware of anything else."

"You're sure?"

"Yes, damn it!"

Mateo believed her, but he decided to push.

"Go ahead," he shouted to Pablo.

A scream came from the next room and then angry words that couldn't be understood. There was no way for the doctor to know what the man was doing to her mother. Then there was a shout and a resounding slap.

Then there was silence.

# Chapter 36

In reality, her mother had screamed more from surprise than from the pain. Pablo had reached over and pinched the skin on the inside of her upper arm. It had been painful but did not amount to a real injury. But it had ticked the woman off royally.

"You dirty little bastard," she said with hatred in her voice. Then she spit in his face.

"No gringo spits on Pablo," he yelled at her. Then he slapped Sandra with such force her chair almost overturned. It leaned precariously to the side on two legs. Pablo caught it and pulled it back upright.

The woman's head slumped to her chest, her eyes closed. She was unconscious. Pablo thought he might have broken her neck but didn't care. The old bag shouldn't have spit on him.

Irene and Mateo easily heard the blow in the next room.

"Mother?" Irene screamed. "Mother?" she called again. There was no response.

Irene tried to scramble to her feet. With her hands tied behind her, she had difficulty getting up. Mateo easily pushed her back into the chair. She hated the feel of his hand on her breast as he shoved her down.

"She's okay," they heard Pablo say from the other room.

Mateo put his face close to Irene's and said, "I'm going to ask you again. Can you get me into the place where you work?"

"No, damn it, I can't. I just told you. You would need special orders from the government to get into the facility. That's the only way." She looked at Mateo with total hatred in her eyes and then added, "And if you bastards hurt my mother again, I swear I'll kill you if it's the last thing I do."

"I think you would," he said as he grinned at her.

"You better write it down somewhere," she told him in a blistering tone. "It's damn well a promise."

"Okay," Mateo said, thinking aloud. "If we can't get in through the gate, what are the other possibilities?" He looked at Irene, his eyebrows raised in a questioning expression.

"I can't help you," she said.

"You can't, or you won't?" He smiled an evil smile and said, "Remember your mother.”

The doctor lowered her eyes and shook her head.

“How many guards are there?”

“I don’t know.” She probably didn’t know.

“Do the guards just stop people from coming in at the front where the entrance is located?”

“I have no idea what the guards do,” she told him. “We’ve never had anyone try to get in since I’ve worked there.”

Ignoring her comment, he asked, “Do they patrol the entire site?”

“What part of ‘I don’t know’ don’t you understand?”

His backhand across her face stunned Irene.

He could tell that the slap had come as a surprise. It must have stung. Her eyes started to water as the anger boiled up through her body. She tried to head-butt him but he moved too fast.

“That’s going to cost your mother,” Mateo told her. “Hurt the old woman!” he yelled at Pablo.

“You want me to cut her?” came the reply.

“Yeah. Cut her some.”

“No! Don’t!” It was Irene’s mother, and she sounded scared.

Dr. Dunn tried to stand up again. “Stop! I’ll tell you what you want to know,” she pleaded as Mateo pushed her down again.

“Go ahead!” Mateo shouted at Pablo. He grinned, his face six inches from the doctor’s. “Cut her.”

“Eeeeaaahhh!!!” The piercing scream came from the next room and then everything became quiet, except the doctor’s breathing. She was close to hyperventilating.

“Calm down,” Mateo told her. “He’s not going to kill her unless I tell him.”

They could hear Sandra sobbing.

“Now. Do you think you can answer my questions?”

She looked at him for a moment and then nodded, tears freely running down her cheeks. A choking sound emanated from her throat.

Mateo gave her a few seconds to compose herself and then asked, “Do the guards patrol the entire site?” He watched her closely.

She seemed to think about his question. “I think they check things about once an hour during the night.” And then she explained, “But just along the outside border, not throughout the facility.”

“How big is the place?”

“I don’t know.”

"What is the patient's name?" He wanted to test her. He knew it was Webster, but would she tell him?

"Webster," she said after a short hesitation. "Mike Webster."

"Good," he told her. "Now we're getting somewhere."

She tried to wipe her tears on her shoulder but failed; the rope was too tight.

"Where does he stay? What room number?"

She looked away. He could tell she didn't want to say.

"Where?" he shouted.

Startled, she relented, "He's not in a room. He's in a cabin toward the back of the property."

Surprised, Mateo thought for a moment.

"Is there more than one cabin?"

"Yes. I think there are three or four."

"Where is that map you mentioned? Something we can look at?"

"It's not here."

"At your office then?"

"Yes, on the wall outside physical therapy. We have to be able to show patients where they'll be staying when they're able to leave hospital status."

Mateo looked at her and smiled. "Are you up for a little trip?" he asked. "Because you're going to go and get that map for us."

## Chapter 37

Irene was snatched to her feet and forced back into the room where her mother and the other man were waiting.

"Oh, Mom," Irene sobbed. Her mother had a gash along the left cheekbone. The blood was already drying, leaving streaks on her face. There were droplets on her sweater, too.

"You bastards," Irene spat, glaring at both of them through her tears. "You'll get yours. I hope I can see it."

Oblivious to her anger, the young one said, "Here is how we're going to do this."

Irene stared at the man as he told her what he wanted. Concentrating was difficult. Dark emotions crowded her mind. There was no way to convey the hatred she had for these men.

But she listened. Irene somehow understood their only hope, both hers and her mother's, lay in doing what these men wanted.

"You are going out to your hospital to get that map," he told her. "Your mother will stay with us, but we won't be here at your house. We will be with you."

Irene stared, uncomprehending. "What do you mean you'll be with me?"

"We will follow you to your workplace and will watch you go in. Then we will park where we can see you come out. Do you understand so far?"

"Yes," she said. Irene focused on what he was telling her. She was also desperately trying to think of a way she might alert someone—if there was time.

Then he shocked her, closing most of her options.

"How far is your building from where you turn off the main road?"

Irene had to think. "Maybe a half mile."

"Okay. You will have five minutes from the time you turn off the highway," he told her. "Five minutes to get the map and be back on the highway." He obviously didn't intend for her to have time to alert anyone. "If you take more time than that, your mother will suffer. Do you believe me?" He reached over and turned her mother's injured cheek so she could see it.

Irene nodded.

Then Sandra looked at her. Irene mouthed, "I'm sorry." She shifted her glare back to the young man.

"I understand."

"When you come back on the highway, we'll follow you back here."

Irene remained silent.

"Now, take your mother to the bathroom and clean her up." he told her. "Pablo will go with you."

A name—now she had a name, for whatever good it might do!

He untied Irene while the older man untied her mother's feet. When the women returned from the bathroom, her mother's arms were untied, and they had Irene change her sweater. Irene realized they didn't want anyone to notice the cut if they were stopped. When the sweater was off, the rope appeared again and secured her mother's elbows loosely so that her hands were free at her sides. Another sweater was draped around her shoulders. It would be difficult to discern that her arms were tied.

It was time to go.

They went to the garage and got into the two automobiles. The young man put her mother into the front passenger's seat of the Suburban. The man she now knew as Pablo climbed into the back, directly behind Sandra. When they were ready, Irene was signaled to raise the garage door.

She backed out; the Suburban followed.

The trip took almost thirty minutes. Finally, Irene slowed, clicked on her turn signal, and pulled onto a gravel road. The GMC slowed and then continued on.

She was free—for five minutes.


Irene's heart rate was probably at 130 when she turned into the facility. She flashed her ID at the guardhouse and rushed on to the medical center. She could only hope she didn't run into anyone who wanted to chitchat. Taking the facility map off the wall would be difficult to explain if someone saw her and asked about it.

Glancing at her watch, Irene panicked. She had already used a minute of her time.


On the way out to the center, she had come up with an idea that might work. Irene had rummaged around in the front seat of the car and managed to secure a pen and a scrap of paper. It was an old grocery list but suitable to write a note to Webster.

Taking care not drive off the road, Irene wrote "They have my mother" on the paper. She folded it and wrote Webster's name across the outside. The note was in her hand as she sped into the parking lot.

She skidded into a parking space and rushed into the building. To avoid questions, she stopped at the nurse's station and quickly asked if everything was all right. Assured that it was, she explained that she was going to grab a couple of pictures from her office.

Then she held out the note to one of the nurses and said, "Get this to Webster for me." She added, "As soon as you can."

The nurse took the note, saying, "I'll take care of it, Dr. Dunn."

"I'm in a hurry," Irene said. "I left my mother at the drugstore." With that short explanation, she rushed toward her office.

As Dr. Dunn walked away, an emergency bell rang from down the hall and the nurse slipped the note into her pocket, promptly forgetting it.

As Irene passed the framed map outside of physical therapy, she lifted it off the wall and tucked it under an arm.

She had her keys out and quickly unlocked the door to her suite. Inside, she grabbed a landscape painting the same size as the map. With both frames in hand, she literally ran back to the parking lot.

Glancing at her watch, the five minutes were almost gone. She was going to be late. Not by much, but late. The thought of the men hurting her mother again terrified Irene. Surely, she would be given a little grace time. Then she remembered the cut on her mother's cheek and the scream.

Tossing the frames into the backseat, Irene frantically climbed behind the wheel. Gravel scattered as she sped toward the exit. Skidding out of the parking lot, Irene could see Bob as he walked toward their building. She punched the button to lower her window and yelled, "At the nurse's station!" She hoped he would hear, and the nurse would give him the note. He waved cheerfully and kept walking.

God, she prayed, help me. Please help me. I'm late.

~ ~ ~

The three individuals, each for their own reasons, watched the gravel road entrance to the medical center. She was late—they were all aware.

At just under seven minutes from the time the doctor had driven inside, Mateo saw her BMW skid out onto the highway. She was over the time he had given her, but he didn't think she'd had time to alert anyone. He had no doubt she understood the consequences.

He kept their vehicle several hundred yards back until they reached Highway 16; then he closed up to a normal distance. Mateo kept watch for anyone that might be tailing them.

Upon reaching the doctor's house, he stayed near as the BMW pulled into the driveway. He watched the garage door go up and closed the gap, following her in. She brought the door down without his having to tell her.

Mateo retrieved the map from the doctor's car and carried it inside. He set it on the kitchen bar and called her over to look at it with him. He was surprised to see that the Catawba River formed the rear boundary of the facility for several hundred yards. An idea began to formulate.

"Where does Webster stay, which cabin?" he asked. There were five cabins scattered around the grounds—all of them secluded.

"This one," Dr. Dunn said, pointing to the cabin farthest from the facility and closest to the river. Mateo made a mental note of its location. The gate where the guards concentrated most of their attention was approximately three miles away.

Mateo turned back to her. "I have to tie you up again now. My partner and I need to talk."

He walked her back into the family room where Pablo had placed her mother. She went toward the chair where they had bound her earlier, but Mateo stopped her. He motioned her to one like Pablo had used to secure her mother.

The young doctor stood as Mateo bound her hands. He knew it was uncomfortable, but she did not let it show. When he finished tying her arms, she sat down, allowing her feet to be secured.

"We'll get back to you," Mateo said. The men returned to the kitchen to complete their plans now that they knew where Webster was located.

Pablo was giving Mateo a free hand to run the operation and seemed to like what he saw. Mateo could think on his feet. Pablo obviously recognized that.

"Here's the plan," Mateo said. He laid out his thoughts for the next several hours. Pablo listened, nodding and asking several questions. When they were in agreement on the overall plan, Mateo took the map out of its frame and folded it.

"What do you want to do with the women?" Pablo asked in Spanish.

Mateo answered, also in spanish, his usually serious manner now even darker, "We must take no chances. The doctor knows too much about us. They've seen us and can describe us." He paused. "They must die!"

Pablo said nothing. It must be exciting, in a strange way, for the Merchant to watch Mateo make his decisions. Mateo thought Pablo was being reminded of himself when he was in his twenties.

Pablo volunteered to take out the women. "Do you want me to—"

"No, I will do it."

Mateo looked toward the room where the doctor and her mother were waiting. He put the folded map in his pocket, glanced at Pablo once more, and headed to where Irene and her mother were waiting.

Pablo climbed onto a barstool and waited. He knew what was going to happen. The Merchant had held the gun himself many times in the past.

The women's eyes followed Mateo as he entered the room. His weapon was one of the .22 calibers they had picked up in Atlanta. As he walked toward the women, Mateo could see them strain at the ropes. Still walking, he pulled the pistol from his waistband and shot the older woman in the forehead.

"Nooooo!" The doctor's scream was still in the air as the mostly silenced sound of the shot echoed lightly through the house. Her mother's chair had overturned, and she lay on her side, her face turned toward the floor. The daughter stared at her mother's body.

"You son of a bitch!" the doctor screamed. "You dirty bastard!"

Mateo stared at her, feeling no emotion. Killing the old woman hadn't bothered him. It was merely a part of the job.

"I did everything you asked," Irene said with bared teeth, though with less feeling now. "You could have left us here." She stared down at her mother, bound to the chair, blood spreading onto the floor. "You could have gagged us. No one would have known until you were gone." A tear glistened on each cheek as she glared at him.

The murderer said nothing, but as he stared at Irene, she shivered. His eyes were empty—blank. She had never seen such a complete lack of feelings on a human face.

She stared back, determined to look into his soul as he fired a bullet into her brain. Irene hoped the memory would haunt him.

He raised the pistol, pointing it at her face. Irene stared directly into his eyes, until the last instant. As his finger drew down on the trigger, she flinched. Her eyes involuntarily closed, and her head was turning away as the firing pin struck.

But her unintended try at escape was for naught. The bullet struck at the edge of her forehead, doing its damage. The force of the projectile and the jerking reaction of her body knocked her chair over onto the floor. Blood quickly covered her head and face, pooling on the carpet beneath her. Breath passed from her lungs as her body settled in on itself.

Mateo left the women's bodies where they fell. He was finished and would give them no further thought. That was his nature.

Pablo was waiting for him. They had been careful about handling things in the house, wary of leaving prints or other evidence. Pablo had wiped places they might have touched.

"Otra cosa? … Anything else?" he asked Mateo.

"Let's find the tall one!"

 **Chapter 38**

The men went out to the garage, and Mateo climbed into the Suburban. Pablo opened the garage door for him and then closed it, joining Mateo in their vehicle.

As soon as they were moving, Pablo called ahead to alert the others. A part of their planning was for the rest of their contingent to check out of the hotel, bringing the luggage. The equipment had been stowed in the Suburban when Mateo returned for Pablo earlier. Arrangements now called for them to meet at a remote location.

Mateo and Pablo were waiting when the men drove into their rendezvous point, a busy mall parking lot near their hotel. When the Ford had been wiped down, they removed the tag, loaded their bags into the big van, and everyone climbed in. Mateo drove them out onto the highway.

"One stop to make," he announced. "We need fishing gear and a couple of tackle boxes—casual clothing, too. We're going to rent a boat and go up the Catawba River a few miles."

The four men in back glanced at each other. This hadn't been mentioned previously.

"We'll be going after our target from the water," Mateo explained. "The medical complex where he's located backs up to the Catawba River. The entrance and along the front is guarded."

"What about the rest of the complex?" Tommy asked.

"There's a two-man patrol that rides through once every hour at night." Mateo said. "Maybe in the daytime, too, but that doesn't concern us. They scout along the perimeter. We'll watch for them and move in right after they pass next to the river. We have a map, so we know where Webster is located. He's staying in a cabin relatively close to the back of the property and away from the other residents. If we're cautious, we should be able to get in and out before anyone can come to help him or even know we've been there."

"I'll deal with Webster when we find him," Pablo said. "We won't be taking him with us."

Mateo glanced over; he could almost feel the hatred emanating from the Merchant.

Pablo added, "I'm looking forward to meeting him again, this Webster, or Michaels, or whatever he calls himself now. Tonight, will be a bad night for him."

Mateo pulled into a large Walmart. After killing the engine, he turned in his seat.

"Go inside," he told them, "and buy something you would wear to go fishing—and stay separated." He searched their faces to make sure everyone understood. "Try to be back in the van within thirty minutes. We'll stop at a couple of different places for everyone to change." He paused. "Any questions?"

Charlie leaned forward and asked, "How about some hunter vests? We'll need them to carry extra ammo and whatever."

"I'll get them. I'll pick up a couple of fishing rods and tackle boxes, too," Mateo said. "Pablo and I already have some clothes to wear. I'll buy snacks, too." He opened his door and climbed down.

With the door half open, he glanced back at Pablo, "You staying with the equipment?"

Pablo nodded as he pulled a small stone from his pocket and stroked the blade of his knife across it.

Tommy headed into the store after Mateo; the others followed at short intervals. After twenty minutes, Pablo saw his young friend coming toward the Suburban with a large plastic bag in each hand. Mateo tossed the bags into the back with the other equipment and then came around and climbed into the driver's seat.

"Did you find everything?" Pablo asked.

"Yes, everything's handled," Mateo said as he settled in to wait for the others.

They remained patient as the other men returned over the next few minutes. When everyone was back, Mateo started the vehicle and drove to the Interstate. He made three stops at convenience stores and fast-food restaurants for them to change into their new outfits. Once that was done, they were just six guys out for a late afternoon fishing trip.

Finally, they were headed out to find Webster.

Mateo and Pablo had put together a plan of action as they waited. José and Pedro, the men from the compound, would make the initial assault on the cabin. Charlie and Tommy would protect them from outside in case the guards or anyone else showed up. Pablo and Mateo would remain in the woods a few yards from the cabin as backup for the overall operation.

Hopefully José and Pedro would catch Webster sleeping in the cabin and hold him for Pablo. Other significant contingencies could be dealt with using the AK-47s. Pablo reminded everyone again that he wanted their target alive. He alone would deal with Webster.

A map Mateo had found in the glove compartment of the Ford showed a large marina a few miles from Exit 27 off I-85 West. That's where they were headed. The ride was quiet. Everyone was thinking of what the next few hours could bring.

It was late, and the afternoon sun was edging down past the horizon. By the time they reached the marina, it was five. Mateo parked and went into the office.

"Can I help you?" A young man was straightening up the place.

"You sure can," Mateo told him. "I need to rent a boat. I've promised some guys I work with I would take them for a ride on the river. They're from out of town."

"It's kind of late," the young man said. "We close at six."

"Couldn't we bring the boat back later and tie it up wherever you tell us?"

The attendant thought about it. "I guess," he told Mateo, "but I'll have to charge you a full day's rent."

"No problem," Mateo said. "The company's footing the tab."

"What size boat do you need?"

"Well, there are six of us," Mateo told him. "Give us something fairly fast. We'll just be riding for the most part, but we're carrying some fishing equipment, too. We might want to stop and wet a hook."

The man filled out a form, and Mateo paid with cash, asking for a receipt so the clerk wouldn't be suspicious. When the paperwork was completed, they walked out of the office and over to the boats. Pablo and the others were standing outside the Suburban. They joined the attendant and Mateo when they came outside.

The boat that had been chosen looked about twenty feet long. Pablo and Mateo glanced at each other, and Pablo nodded. It would do nicely.

The attendant showed Mateo a few things about operating the boat and then went back into the office. Mateo backed their vehicle as close as possible to the wharf. They loaded their equipment and fishing gear and then parked and locked the truck. Everyone climbed aboard and found a place to sit.

Mateo was a boating enthusiast, so he became the designated driver. He started the engine as Charlie cast off the lines.

Mateo backed the boat out of its berth and eased toward the channel. From there they turned north and headed upriver.

With a final glance back at the marina, Mateo opened the throttle and steered out into the middle of the waterway. They needed to find the riverbank that bordered the facility where Webster was staying before dark.

With a hand on the rudder control, Mateo pulled the map of the compound from his pocket, handing it to Pablo. He opened it to the area where they were going.

With the map positioned in front of him, thoughts of the doctor and her mother played across Mateo's mind. He wasn't emotional about killing the two women because he knew there was no other way. Left alive, they could have identified him and Pablo. The authorities would have had alerts out on them long before they could have gotten out of the country.

"How far?" Pablo asked, breaking into his thoughts.

"Looks like six or seven miles," he said after studying the map for a few moments. Mateo passed the map to Pablo and concentrated on guiding the boat.

"Are there any landmarks that will help us identify where to go in?" Mateo asked.

Pablo smoothed the map and studied it. He glanced up the river and said, "There are power lines crossing the river a few hundred yards before we get there. We'll need to watch for those."

Everyone settled back to endure the ride. All six of the men had turned up their collars. The wind whipping up off the river was chilling, and the spray from the boat's wake was very uncomfortable.

The boat was fast, and after a reasonably short running time, they came around a slight bend in the river and could see power lines ahead. Mateo eased off on the throttle as six pairs of eyes tried not to stare off to the right as they passed under the lines.

It was relatively easy to recognize the medical facility's property. Signs were posted every hundred feet or so proclaiming "no trespassing—government land." A fence was visible in places. It was at least ten feet high with barbed wire at the top.

Mateo sped up and kept the boat moving at a good clip as they continued upriver. It was almost dark as they pulled into a slight break on the western bank of the river, about a mile north of the facility's location.

"Get the rods out and pretend to fish," Mateo told the men. Expecting everyone could use a bite to eat, he passed the snacks around. He had water and cokes, too. He didn't want them hungry when the action started.

They relaxed and watched the sky fade and dark approach. A few lights came on along the riverbanks. They had seen several boat landings on their way upriver, but there didn't seem to be any in the area where they were tied up. That was good.

When most of the light was gone, Mateo told Tommy to break out their equipment. The AK-47s were handed out first along with ammo for two extra magazines each. Then he handed a Kerr 9 mm to each of the men, again with extra magazines and ammo. Last to come were the hunting knives. Pablo already had his. Each of the other men loosened his belt and slid the leather knife holster on. The pistols went in their belts or in a pocket on the hunting vests they were wearing.

"Everybody set?" Mateo asked when they were finished. Everyone nodded—even Pablo.

"I'm going to take us back a little closer," Mateo said. He started the engine and then quietly moved them back out into the channel and headed south. After traveling several hundred yards, he pulled over, and they tied to a small dock, again on the west side of the river.

At Pablo's questioning look, he explained, "I noticed it on the way upriver," he said. "There's no house up on the bluff, so I figured it belongs to someone who only comes out on weekends. We ought to be okay here if we stay down and don't make too much noise. It's less conspicuous than tying up to the bank."

"Let's get some rest," Pablo told them.

"We better keep a guard," Mateo said. "I'll take the first hour. If we each take an hour, that will take us to one or two o'clock, when we can go in. Everyone at this medical facility should be asleep by then."

The men tried to get comfortable enough to rest, and the boat became quiet. Mateo noticed a restlessness among the group. As with most missions of this type, there would be precious little actual sleep before they climbed the opposite bank in search of Webster.

 **Chapter 39**

A call from Tom Manning came in early that afternoon. Jack Robbins answered it.

"Anything new?" Manning asked.

"Nothing."

"Our boy's been quiet for a few days. That scares me, but the good news is that no one else has been killed."

"At least no one we're sure of," Robbins replied. "Dr. Best called. One of the nurses who flew to Charlotte with Webster was murdered at the medical clinic a couple of nights ago. Howard said the circumstances made it appear to be a sexual attack, but they're still investigating. He's suspicious because she knew about Webster."

"That's sad, whatever the reason. Have you talked to Webster lately?"

"Not since yesterday. I've been busy and figured no news was good news."

"I think we should send Jackson over from the ambulance assignment. Let him stay with Webster for the next few nights." Manning was anxious.

"Sure, we can do that," Robbins replied. "Good idea. I'll make it happen."

"Thanks. It's just me. I'm anxious."

Robbins chuckled. "I'll contact Webster. If I get anything new, I'll let you know."

Robbins made the call. It was answered on the first ring.

"Webster here, Boss."

Robbins thought he sounded calm.

"Everything quiet?"

"Yeah. I think they only have a couple of patients up at the medical building. I'm taking it easy. No sign of our boys at this point."

Robbins told him about moving Deputy Marshal Jackson, and, although hesitant, Webster agreed. "I'll make a place for him."

Robbins concluded with, "Call me if anything gets strange."

"I will if I'm not too busy. You know things happen fast sometimes."

~ ~ ~

Webster and Bob spent a good part of the afternoon going over their plan to see if they had missed anything. They had discussed Robbins's call and the new man, Jackson, and had agreed on a place for him in their plans. Afterward, Bob went home to get some rest. Webster walked up to the medical building and found an empty room. He locked the door, climbed into the bed, and slept like a baby for two hours.

When he awoke, he tried Irene's number but got no answer. He asked about her at the nurse's desk and was surprised to find she had been out to the facility that afternoon.

"Did she say why she was here?" he asked the evening nurse.

"The day nurse said she wanted to get a picture from her office. She was in a hurry. She said she had left her mother somewhere and needed to get back to her." The nurse gave him an apologetic look.

Webster walked down toward the physical therapy office. He wanted to look at the facility map and was surprised to find it gone. He walked back and asked the nurse about it.

"The last time I noticed, it was there," she told him.

Strange, he thought.

On his way back to the cabin, Webster thought about Deputy Marshal Jackson in their overall defense strategy. They had placed Jackson over to the right of Bob and assigned him to cover the woods on that side. That would give them a larger field of fire. I hope Deputy Jackson likes to sleep in a hole in the ground, Webster thought, smiling. A nest had been prepared for Jackson. Webster walked over and surveyed the scene one more time.

Satisfied, he went back to the cabin and set out some fruit for his evening meal. He ate on the porch while enjoying the wildlife.

After he had eaten, Webster arranged the cabin in case their unwanted visitors showed up during the night. With that done, he headed for one of the rockers again. Leaning back, he listened to the hushed sounds of the evening.

A bat was flying a figure eight around the sides and front of the cabin. The tiny airborne mammal had established its path about twenty feet off the ground. Webster assumed the insect hunting was good at that altitude. He closed his eyes and realized he could hear the bat making its turns among the trees. Even with his eyes closed, Webster had practiced the skill enough now that any unusual sound caught his attention.

He checked the time, and at eight thirty eased out to his station for the night, carrying his and Bob's equipment with him. During their planning session that day, Bob had suggested one of them change his position to face more toward the river. They had decided it should be Bob because his location was farther toward the back of the property.

Webster had helped him make the change. Bob had even gotten down in place and become familiar with the feel of the new arrangement. They believed they were prepared if trouble should come. Webster carried Bob's weapons and other equipment and stacked it where Bob could put his hands on it in the relative dark.

The addition of Deputy Marshal Jackson would make them a more lethal force. Without doubt, they would be able to stand off two or three men. More than that could be a problem.

Jackson arrived at nine and had brought his own equipment, a rifle with night scope and a handgun. Webster settled Jackson into his new home for the night, briefed him, and returned to his own position.

A few minutes before ten, Webster heard Bob coming along the walking path from the medical building. Because of the dense woods, it was difficult to see more than thirty or forty yards in any direction in the general area where the cabins were located. At Webster's cabin, they were limited to even less, fifteen or twenty yards in most cases. The trees came to within fifteen yards all around the cabin, with scrub and larger bushes even nearer in some places.

Bob walked near Webster's location on the way to his own. Webster stopped him and whispered that he had already set out Bob's equipment and told him about the new man. Though they had set it up together that afternoon, Webster pointed out Jackson's location and reviewed their new fields of fire. Their conversation was short; Bob was ready to position himself for the night.

Webster could hear his friend as he stepped off the walking path and settled into the bunker. Bob was quiet, but Webster had a trained ear.

In a short time, everything became calm except for the normal night sounds. Bob gave a gentle tug on the string to let Webster know he was in place. Webster acknowledged with a tug of his own. They had not included Jackson in the watch chores since he was unfamiliar with the routine. To cover the situation, he had been given an alert string connected to Bob's position and instructed to key on Webster's first shot.

Bob had first shift tonight, so Webster rested his head on an arm and closed his eyes. He already had everything laid out in the front of his position and ready for use. The rifle, his pistol, and Bob's night-goggles were positioned so Webster could put his hands on any one of them without looking. Prepared, he finally dozed off.

At his own location, Bob positioned his equipment carried in much the same way as Webster had, but he was wearing the night goggles. He moved his head slowly back and forth, taking in everything, whether it moved or not, and familiarizing himself with the terrain. He looked for and found the new man's position. Confident, but alert, Bob continued watching for a potential enemy.

Much of his marine training had come back to Bob in the couple of nights he and Webster had been playing soldier. He smiled at the thought that they were playing; Bob was well aware the situation could become deadly serious. Webster had taught him about night sounds and he caught on quickly. He considered himself a fast learner, especially when the exercise involved guns and real bullets.

The time between ten and midnight passed slowly. Bob was tired as his shift ended. When his watch finally showed twelve, Bob gave a light tug on the string and then felt one in return. He wondered if Webster had already been awake.

Bob removed his goggles and positioned himself for some much-needed rest. He made one last check of his equipment, making sure everything was where it should be. Although he was anxious now, Bob closed his eyes and was soon in a light slumber.

Webster had just opened his eyes when Bob signaled him at midnight. He awakened with a strange feeling in his gut. It wasn't the first time. The sensation had served him well in the past, even saving his life on a couple of occasions. If his intuition was right, the strangers would come for him tonight.

Staying low, he slipped the goggles on and adjusted them. Then Webster eased up and viewed the area without hurrying. Noticeable movement could get you killed—day or night. The slower you moved, the better.

Nothing new caught his attention. Webster settled in for the long haul, that period of boring time that came just before seconds of sheer terror and panic. He'd been there, and he bet Bob had been there, too. Maybe Jackson as well.

Webster had a routine. He covered thirty yards or so in his field of vision.

Then he would cover fifteen of those yards again as he moved on. He repeated this maneuver until he had memorized everything in his field of vision. Anything new could draw deadly attention.

~ ~ ~

A few minutes after midnight, Mateo tapped Pablo on the shoulder, awakening him.

"Time to go."

Pablo nodded, yawning. He reached over, shook one of the other men, and motioned for him to rouse the others. Mateo climbed behind the wheel and prepared to move the boat.

When everyone was ready and had their equipment in hand, Mateo started the engine. He kept it idling, making little noise. He whispered for the lines to be brought in. The boat floated slowly out toward the middle of the river, the current pulling them into the channel and toward their destination.

The boat drifted, its engine at idle. Mateo gave it just enough power to steer as they floated downriver. Continuing that way, everyone watched for the area where they would go ashore.

Mateo peered through the darkness, assessing the four men they had gathered to help him and Pablo find their target.

Mateo had never met Webster. Their paths had never crossed, but Pablo had given Mateo his version of Webster's 'crimes.' The Merchant hated Webster more than Mateo had ever seen one man hate another. Pablo's passion for killing the man worried Mateo. Those kinds of emotions, when acted on, tended to make men careless. Although he wouldn't tell anyone, least of all Pablo, the situation scared him—and Mateo wasn't easy to scare.

Pablo saw the government signs coming up on their left and whispered to Mateo to ease on past the property. He pointed to the riverbank a couple of hundred yards past the last "No Trespassing" sign.

Mateo brought the boat in with a minimum of power, pushing it into the ground cover at the edge of the river. Charlie slid over the side and climbed onto the bank, quickly securing the bow to a small but deep-rooted bush. The stern drifted downstream and under vegetation growing along the riverbank.

Everyone scrambled over the side, securing their equipment as they moved ashore. Rifles were held at ready, and heads were kept low. The six men were experienced at this sort of potentially deadly operation.

Mateo took the lead. Pablo was next, with José and Pedro following him. Bringing up the rear were Charlie and Tommy. The men spaced themselves at ten-yard intervals for the trek to the cabin.

Mateo had memorized the map and knew they had a long walk ahead of them. Although Webster's cabin was closest to the river, it would still be difficult to reach. According to the map, the woods extended right up to the dwelling.

Their first obstacle was the fence. Mateo checked it quickly—no sign of electricity. They had brought bolt cutters and used them to cut their way in. A five-foot bush covered the hole. Five minutes and they were inside the facility.

As they had planned earlier, the men moved into the edge of the woods and hid themselves to wait for the guard patrol to make its one o'clock rounds.

A few minutes after they had taken cover, the lights of a four-wheeler came into view with two guards riding side by side. They were moving slowly, talking and one of them laughing as they passed the men they were being paid to keep out of the facility. The six men waited quietly for five minutes after the guards had passed before leaving their positions.

"Let's go," whispered Mateo, and everyone eased out onto the path the guards had used. They followed it for several hundred yards, staying at the edge near the trees and brush.

When he thought they had gone far enough, Mateo turned into the woods and, he hoped, toward Webster's cabin. He had warned everyone earlier to be as quiet as possible moving through the thick brush and trees.

~ ~ ~

Unseen by the group was a young boy clinging to bushes overhanging the river-bank. He watched as the men ascended the bluff above the river and cut a hole in the fence, and he kept an eye on them until they disappeared into the forest. The boy had been asked to watch for unusual activity on the river. He had seen the boat go upriver earlier in the evening. The six men onboard did not look like fishermen.

Kenney Dawkin had watched but didn't make a move of his own until the men had moved into the woods inside the fence. When they were out of sight, the boy lifted himself and hurried off toward the trailer park where he lived. Kenney retrieved two short lengths of pipe he had stashed away earlier. With the pipes in hand, he hurried to bushes near the tall chain-link fence. He was excited but careful.

The boy had every intention of fulfilling the promise to his new friend. Raising his head slightly, Kenney listened for sounds being made by the group of men who had gone into the woods.

Yes, he could still hear them. Kenney crouched down again to wait. The time was not yet right.

~ ~ ~

Mateo moved out with the others following. Though everyone tried to hold their ten-yard intervals, they found it difficult in the thickly wooded terrain. The night was extraordinarily dark; in the trees, it was impossible to see more than four or five yards out. The men edged closer together, unable to maintain their distances.

After twenty minutes, Mateo stopped and dropped to a knee. The others followed his lead. Despite the cool temperature, everyone was sweating. The men remained quiet as they attempted to catch their breath. At least the bugs weren't as bad in the cool weather.

After a couple of minutes, Mateo got to his feet, prompting the others to do the same. He started off again, slowly and quietly moving toward the cabin.

They came to a large pine tree that had fallen. It lay in their way; they would have to climb over it or work their way around.

Mateo started climbing. There were limbs all over, making it difficult to get through. Many were broken; there were sharp, jagged points that could puncture clothing and skin alike.

Once safely past the last limbs, Mateo dropped to the ground. He whispered for everyone to be careful and slipped off a few yards ahead to wait.

Pablo came next and made it past the broken tree without incident. Then came Pedro, who managed to get the tail of his vest hung on a limb. It took two of the men behind to free him. After an exhausting couple of minutes, he climbed to the ground and knelt near Mateo.

The fourth, José, was doing okay until he reached the highest part of the tree. He caught his foot as he attempted to go over the trunk. Off balance, he fell head-first into the brush and debris. On the way down, he reached out, hoping to slow his fall; his right hand struck one of the broken limbs. The ragged point speared his palm at the center. The crash was loud, and José, unable to help himself, let out a low, deep groan.

Mateo, crouched a short distance away, heard the man fall and the sound of his pain. He hoped the noise hadn't carried outside of their immediate area. Pablo shushed everyone, and they listened for anyone coming their way. The forest remained quiet.

After a couple of minutes, Mateo stepped back to the men gathered at the tree. Pablo was there, too. José was trying to extricate his hand from the limb. It was entangled. Two inches of shattered wood was sticking out of the back of his hand. José was in agony. Mateo jerked out his hunting knife, causing the other men to step back and José to almost pass out. Heavy sweat covered his face and drenched his shirt.

Mateo stooped and placed the sharp edge of the blade immediately under the man's palm. He cut through the broken limb. When José was free, Mateo easily removed the remaining splinter from his hand. Pedro quickly wrapped a handker-chief around the wound, stemming the bleeding. That was all they could do until they got back to the boat where Pablo had noticed a small first-aid kit. Though quiet, José's face was twisted in pain.

"Can you make it?" Mateo asked.

José grimaced but nodded. "Si, I will be okay, and I will keep up and do my part. Don't worry."

Mateo slapped his shoulder encouragingly before moving back to his position. The last two men had negotiated the tree while José was being attended.

Rotating his arm in a "Let's move out" motion, Mateo started toward the cabin again. Then pausing, he signaled for Charlie to change places with José, leaving the injured man to bring up their rear.

In the distance, as the men were making the change, they heard metal clanging—like chimes—as though a timepiece was striking three o'clock. The men exchanged questioning glances.

After a moment of interest and curiosity, Mateo turned and took his place at the head of the column. A few minutes later, he noticed the brush and trees were thinning. There seemed to be more light through the canopy, too. Mateo went another dozen steps and then dropped to a knee. The other men did the same. About a hundred yards away, they could see the side of a cabin through the trees. Its position relative to the walking trail assured Mateo it was Webster's living quarters.

Pablo eased down beside him, looking at the cabin and its surroundings. The forest ended within a few yards of the structure. They could see wood piled on the porch.

After watching the area for several minutes and seeing no movement, Mateo decided it was time to make their play. He waved for the two men who would be going in first.

When José came forward, Mateo put his face to the man's ear and whispered, "Can you do this?"

José stared at him and nodded, mouthing, "I'm okay."

Pablo was getting anxious. "Let's go," he said, louder than Mateo would have preferred.

Mateo motioned for the two outside sentries, Charlie and Tommy, to take up positions where they could handle anyone coming along the walking paths.

Pablo touched the shoulders of Pedro and José. They would be the first to go inside, searching for Webster. When they glanced at Pablo, he waved them toward the cabin. Mateo knelt a few feet away as the men crept toward the porch.

The operation was underway. Webster's hours were limited.

# Chapter 40

He heard them coming long before they came into view. The signal from the boy was loud and clear, giving Webster plenty of warning. Bob and Jerry Jackson had also been alerted to expect the boy's signal.

Webster had been listening to the movements of the men in the forest for fifteen minutes. The strange sounds came to him a short time after he heard the guards come through on their one o'clock rounds. A few minutes earlier, Webster had heard something fall and then a moan. Someone is probably hurt, he thought.

As soon as Webster was sure it was the men they were waiting for, he gave two sharp tugs on the string, awakening Bob. Already wearing his goggles, Webster watched as Bob remained absolutely still for the first few moments. Then he alerted Jackson and tuned in to the strange sounds, too. Ever so carefully, Bob slipped his goggles on and started to watch the woods where the sounds were coming from.

With Bob awake and alert and Jerry Jackson watching the forest, too, Webster began to search for their enemy. Then he saw several men kneeling at the edge of the forest. They were about sixty yards away, partially hidden by low bushes, and seemed to be concentrating on the cabin.

Webster watched and counted, attempting to determine their number and what weapons they carried. His location on the opposite side of the cabin placed the men where they would be coming directly toward him. The cabin was to the left and between Webster and the men. He counted five individuals kneeling and watching the cabin. He thought that was all before noticing another man a few feet away from the others. Six of them—more than he expected. Hope we can handle them, he thought.

He watched as two of the men moved up. They seemed to be listening to the individual up front, probably the person in charge. One of the men was whispering and waving his arms about. The leader bent forward and said something to him. Both examined the man's hand. That's when Webster noticed a bandage of some sort wrapped around the man's hand. That could explain the earlier sounds of distress.

After a short time, an older man with Spanish facial features eased forward and waved the two men toward the porch. Two of the others moved off toward positions that would allow them to cover the men going into the cabin. Webster was glad the structure had no back door. That forced everyone to come toward the front where they were visible to Webster and his team. The last two men stayed waiting where Webster had first seen them.

Something, a moment of recognition caused Webster to peer back at the older Spanish-looking man. Then it hit him—the Merchant—Pablo Perez. So that's who has been searching for me. Pablo, the Merchant himself, was crouching in the woods across the clearing.

Now it all made sense. Webster could finally put a name to those who had come for him. Now he knew who the younger man was, too—Mateo Mendez. Mendez was the Merchant's top lieutenant. No wonder people had died in Perez's quest to find Webster. Mendez was known to be a cold-blooded killer who operated without a conscience.

Although they had never spoken, Webster knew a great deal about Mendez. He was young but rising in the ranks when the federal police had raided Pablo's compound in Bogotá and killed his son, Juan. Based on the obvious, the young man, Mendez, was running this raid tonight.

Webster had been told he was blamed for Juan's death. There were even rumors Juan had tried to smuggle a letter to Webster, telling him to get out of Columbia. Supposedly, the letter said Webster was slated to die. The story was that Webster was turning Juan against his father. But the letter, if there was one, had disappeared.

Webster knew Perez had put a price on his head, but he was surprised that the Merchant would come himself. Being in the United States would be enormously dangerous for him. There must be something special to bring him here. Could Perez be angry enough at Webster to take such chances?

Webster was shocked to see the Merchant only yards away.


Bob watched the activity, too. One of the men who had moved out to cover the others had come within yards of Bob's position. He had held his breath as the man slipped by. When the individual was about twenty yards away, he settled down with his rifle pointed back toward the cabin. Bob knew he would have to take that man out first.

When Bob first saw the men, he at once zeroed in on their weapons. They were carrying AK-4pag7s. All six of them. Damn!

Webster and Bob had agreed that Bob wouldn't fire until Webster discharged his weapon or activated their little surprise, whichever came first. Jackson would key in on that first response, too. Webster wanted as many of the men as possible to go into the cabin at the same time. Both Bob and Jerry Jackson understood the need for waiting.

The three of them, Webster, Bob, and Jackson, would have to fire off the first shots and make them count. Webster had seen the AK-47s, too. The big rifles carried by the opposition could cut his team to pieces if the six men got the upper hand.

The first two men came out of the brush as Webster watched. Silently, they moved across the open space toward the cabin. The door had been left unlocked, as usual. They wanted whoever was searching for Webster to be able to get inside the cabin without problems.

Easing out of the brush, the men moved forward, carrying their rifles at the ready. They appeared experienced. When they reached the porch, one of them whispered to the other and that man leaned his AK-47 against the porch rail and drew a pistol from his belt. The individual with the bandaged hand nodded, and they both then stepped lightly onto the porch. Webster heard the old floorboards creak and watched as the men stood still for a moment.

When no sounds came from inside, they slowly moved to the doorway. The one with the pistol crouched down and cautiously tried the door with his left hand while keeping the pistol out in front. The second man held his rifle in the firing position as he stood peering over the shoulder of the first.

The door opened easily, and the man swung it quietly out of his way and stared inside. The glow from the fireplace gave off enough light to see into the cabin. Webster watched him hesitate before entering. He had glimpsed the shape of a body under the covers on the bed.

Then the men slipped inside the cabin and out of Webster's sight.

José and Pedro were puzzled. With all the unintentional noise they had made, they would have expected the person in the bed to have stirred. He hadn't.

They went over and shook the foot rail. Again, nothing happened. Then Pedro raised the covers. Surprised, he touched the blankets rolled to look like someone sleeping.

He looked at José, shook his head, and whispered, "Man, somebody's messing with us. Let's get out of here."

"Yeah, we gotta go tell Pablo."

They moved out on the porch. Pedro remained there as José hurried over to the men waiting at the edge of the woods.

"What's going on in there?" Mateo was still in charge.

"There's no one inside," José said to Mateo and then looked at Pablo, describing the scene in the cabin. "Just a bunch of blankets folded to look like someone sleeping."

"Shit," Pablo stood up and headed toward the cabin.

Mateo reached and caught his arm, pulling him down.

"Take your hands off me." Pablo swung back toward Mateo, his pistol already in his hand.

"Pablo," the young man said, "they're probably watching. This is a setup."

Pablo was angry. "They would have shot us by now. There's no one watching." His face had grown red, flushed, and they could hear him grinding his teeth. They were keeping an eye on the pistol. After a moment he seemed to calm a little. Then he motioned for the two lookouts to hold their positions.

"Now, let's see what's going on." Pablo marched off toward the cabin. He stopped on the porch and glared out at the woods surrounding them. He knew there could be someone out there but doubted it. Why wouldn't they have already made their presence known?

After a few moments, he turned and slipped inside, followed by Mateo and José. Not knowing what else to do, Pedro joined them.


Webster had watched everything the first two men did before they entered the cabin. He had also glanced back at Bob several times. The former marine was watching the cabin, too. But mostly, Bob was watching the man lying in the brush a few yards away. He had a pistol trained on the man. Bob would have to get off the first shot when the clash started. He would need to surprise the individual to get him and that dangerous rifle out of action fast.

Concentrating on the cabin, Webster continued to watch the activity there. One man had come back out on the porch and remained there while the one with the wounded hand rushed back to where the Merchant and Mendez waited.

The wounded man appeared to explain the situation—probably what they had found in the cabin—while the other two listened. The Merchant had gotten up and started for the cabin when Mendez reached for him. Perez pulled a pistol, and there was an angry exchange. After that, all three of them walked over to the cabin and went inside. The fourth man, who had waited on the porch during the exchange, followed them through the door.

All but two of the men were now in the cabin. The beams from a couple of flashlights could be seen casting light on the floor and walls inside. Webster had his cell phone in his hand and a number punched in. All he had to do was hit the send button.

"You said he would be here." Pablo's anger was directed at Mateo and was becoming difficult for him to contain. "You said he always sleeps here. That damn doctor lied, and you believed her."

"You were there, Pablo." Mateo tried to reason. "We had her mother."

Pablo was listening, at least.

"She wasn't lying. She said he sleeps here all the time. She was too afraid to lie."

Mateo could see Pablo thinking about it and starting to calm down. The Merchant glanced up and then reached out to touch Mateo's arm.

"They may be getting jumpy," Pablo said. "They had no way of knowing we were getting close. They—"

Boomm!

An intense light flashed through the cabin. It was followed instantaneously by bits and pieces of fruit carried on a numbing shockwave. Then came the thick black smoke. The little cabin shook on its foundation as glass from the three windows blew out into the surrounding woods. The blast threw the men around like toys in a box being shaken by a child.

The blast had come from the table in the middle of the room. A bowl of fruit had hidden an explosive device.

Pedro and José had been standing closest to the table. The bodies of those two were thrown into Pablo and Mateo, carrying them away from the explosion and to the floor. Weapons flew, and senses were jumbled and lost in the chaos.

No one was killed, but the bomb temporarily blinded, stunned, or punctured the eardrums of everyone in the little cabin. It had served its purpose.

Mateo was the first to regain some degree of consciousness. He'd had the good fortune to have turned his head to look out the door at the very moment of the explosion, and he had been farther from the blast than the others. He could still see some shapes, and, straining, he thought he could hear a little. Though stunned, his mind was quickly coming to terms with what had happened.

He had to get Pablo out of there.

Mateo found the Merchant more with touch than sight and lifted him onto his shoulder. As he started to move, Mateo kicked something heavy near a wall—one of the rifles. He grabbed it, hoping it wasn't damaged. He started toward the door with his burden, then changed his mind and jumped through a side window of the cabin.

With the body on his shoulder and a rifle in his hand, Mateo landed badly, turning an ankle. It hurt like hell, but he doubted if he had done any real damage. He tried it, thinking he could walk it off—or, in this case, run it off. Either way, they had to get back to the boat, even if it meant leaving the others.

Now was not the time to stand and fight. Everyone was on their own in getting back to the river. He started off through the woods. Direction could be considered once he and Pablo were away from the cabin.

Mateo's hearing was improving. He could hear shots now, some from an AK-47, some pistols, and others from another kind of rifle. He hoped none of them were aimed at him and Pablo.

 **Chapter 41**

When Webster saw the men enter the cabin, he smiled. He waited a few moments before making the call. Flipping his goggles up on his forehead, Webster placed his left hand over his eyes. He hoped Bob and Jackson weren't looking at the cabin.

Then he punched the send button.

Webster felt the concussion. Bob and Jackson would have, too. The difference was that Webster knew when it was coming. Unless his comrades had watched the men, all go into the cabin at once, they wouldn't have known the blast was imminent.

The shockwave and ensuing sound jolted Bob, though he had known what Webster was going to do. The one-time marine flinched, losing an instant getting off his first shot. He rushed to aim, drew a breath, released, and pulled the trigger—the same steps as pulling down on a rifle.

Crack! Through the goggles, Bob immediately knew he had missed his target. He had jerked his aim—just a tad—and instead of hitting the man, his shot struck the AK-47 in the area of the trigger housing. Bob could see splinters flying and was pretty sure the rifle was now too damaged to fire. That was the good news; the bad news was that the man now had a pistol out and was preparing for a payback shot.

The flash from Bob's first shot must have been visible because a bullet struck branches where he had been lying only a moment before. But Bob had done as Webster had instructed and was now in his second position.

He lined up for a second shot and squeezed the trigger. This time the bullet struck home. The man twisted, reaching for his shoulder. Bob rolled again and took aim. His target was now more concerned with his wound than with firing back. But Webster had instructed him to always finish the job.

Bob aimed carefully and controlled his breathing as he took up slack on the trigger. He was watching this time as the bullet struck Bob's target. The man jerked to his side and lay still. One down!

As Bob watched for further movement, there was a loud burping sound accompanied by a flash of light off to his left.

Dirt and branches flew. Too late, Bob realized he had not repositioned after his last shot. Someone had opened up on him with one of the AK-47 rifles, probably the other outside guard. The only thing that saved Bob was a dirt mound on that side of his position. But still partially exposed, he had taken a hit. The bullet had torn into Bob's left arm. It was broken, he immediately knew, but the bullet had not struck an artery. Thank goodness!

The low dirt bank had saved the arm and his life. The immediate pain was numbing, and the torn wound was bleeding badly. He was likely out of the fight.

Webster was too busy to consider Bob's situation. Only moments after the improvised stun grenade rocked the cabin, Webster fired his rifle at the second lookout. He missed because the man had rolled away to protect himself when he heard Bob open up on his comrade. Webster saw him when he fired on Bob's position. The weapon had burped a couple of other times, too. From the sounds, the AK-47 was set on full automatic.

There was no time for Webster to look in his friend's direction. He fired off a single shot to take the shooter's attention away from Bob. He then failed to heed his own training and stayed put.

In the instant before he could get off a second shot, Webster saw a muzzle flash and felt something burn along his shoulder. Fortunately, the man had reset to fire singles, probably with the intent of finishing off Bob. Webster rolled this time and aimed his own rifle. His arm was functional despite the shoulder wound. He could see the man through his scope and brought his aim down to the man's chest. They were facing each other—head-on. Webster realized he was looking into the muzzle of the man's AK-47.

As he fired, Webster saw a flash from the man's weapon and felt shockwaves as the bullet passed close to his face. At the same instant, his target's body slammed backward, and the weapon flew from his grasp. Webster could see where his bullet had entered the man's neck.

That individual would not be firing back. Yet, to be on the safe side, Webster changed positions one more time.

As the short firefight had progressed, Webster had tried to keep an eye on the cabin. No one had ventured out the door onto the porch. He did think he saw someone jump from a side window. Webster holstered his pistol, grabbed the two loaded magazines, and stuck them into his pockets. Then he snatched extra magazines for the rifle and stuck those into his belt.

Wearing the goggles, Webster got to his knees and went searching for Bob. He hoped his friend was not dead.

He found the big nurse, turned mercenary, moving along the edge of the woods toward him. Ever alert, Bob was using the trees for cover, moving from one to another, and trying not to offer a clear shot to anyone.

Bob was wearing his goggles, too, so Webster didn't worry about their taking aim on each other. He motioned for Bob to stay in the trees while he checked the cabin.

When Webster reached the porch, he listened closely for any movement inside; there was none. Carefully, he eased to the door. Peering in, he saw two unconscious men on the floor. The room was a mess, pieces of fruit everywhere—the walls, the ceiling, the furniture, everywhere.

Webster slipped in and checked the floor beyond the bed. Two of the men were missing. There had been four inside when the bomb went off. He went back to the door and waved Bob over to the cabin. Webster figured if the men were functioning and still in the area, they would have gotten off a shot at him or Bob by now. Their escape must have been the movement he saw at the side of the cabin. They must have jumped through a window after the explosion and escaped into the woods.

Webster checked the two men on the floor and didn't recognize them. That meant the Merchant and Mateo Mendez were alive and out there. Webster didn't look forward to following them into the darkness, but it had to be done. He checked his shoulder as he waited and found he only had a grazing wound.

Bob eased inside and looked around. He grinned at Webster. "Man, we sure know how to make a bomb."

"Yeah, we spoiled their little surprise." Webster had a big grin on his face until he glanced at his friend. Holding his bloody left forearm, the big nurse appeared ready to pass out.

Webster rushed to his side. "Damn it! What happened?"

"The second lookout hit me when he opened up on automatic," Bob said. "A round made it through the berm."

"Let's get a look," Webster said as he stripped a sheet off the bed. Tearing the material into pieces, he wiped the blood off Bob's wound and examined it. "Not too bad," he said.

Bob flinched as Webster pushed and probed. "The small bone's broken," he said. "I don't think it's splintered, though. Let's wrap it to staunch the bleeding."

"Where are the other two?" Bob asked, realizing there were only two men on the floor. "They were here. Did you see them leave?"

"I think they escaped after the bomb went off," Webster said, pointing to the side window. "I was too busy to go after them at the time."

"Damn! They'll get away." Bob shook his head in despair.

"If you can handle things here, I'll go after them. I know where they're headed."

Then Webster thought of Jerry Jackson. "Did you see any activity from Jackson's position?"

"Not after he fired on the second guard," Bob acknowledged. "He drew some heavy return fire. I hope he's okay."

"He's probably just holding his position," Webster said hopefully. Then he added, "I need to get going if I'm going to catch up with the other two."

"I'll check on Jackson and take care of things here," Bob said. "Be careful. Those damned AK-47s are cruel."

"You'd know," Webster agreed as he finished wrapping Bob's arm. "I think I'll take one of them with me." There were three of the big rifles on the floor along with several magazines of ammo. Webster picked up one of the rifles, checking to make sure it was loaded. Then he retrieved three of the thirty-round magazines and shoved them into his belt.

Bob handed him a tiny flashlight. "You may need this."

"Still got your cell phone?" Webster asked.

"Yeah. What do you need?"

"Call the guardhouse and let them know what's going on. Tell them to stay out of this area. There may be more shooting."

"I'll handle it," Bob said.

"Have you got some of those plastic ties?" Webster asked. "I'll get them on these guys' wrists and feet before they wake up. We don't want them running around when they come to. One more thing. Call over to the ambulance service and tell Amy Hogan what happened here."

He studied Bob. "Can you handle the phone with one hand?"

"I got it." Bob laid the phone down and started punching numbers.

~ ~ ~

After Mateo jumped out of the cabin window with Pablo, he quickly moved into the forest. He was disoriented initially and not sure how to get back to the boat. He did know he needed to get himself and Pablo away from the cabin as fast as he could. He kept moving for several minutes.

His hearing improved rapidly. That allowed Mateo to use the sounds of gunfire to guide him away from the cabin and back toward the riverbank. Though groggy, he knew if he could get himself and Pablo to the river, he could follow it to the boat.

Carrying Pablo and the rifle through the forest was difficult. Mateo had to rest often. He was limping; the ankle was painful, and it was starting to swell.

And he was worried about Pablo. The Merchant was still unconscious. During a pause to rest, Mateo tried unsuccessfully to revive his friend. He gently shook him and then rubbed his face. There was no response, and even in the sparse light, Mateo could see blood at both of Pablo's ears. That wasn't good.

Though weary, he tried not to stop. Each time it was more difficult to get the Merchant up on his shoulder and start again. Walking through the forest in the darkness and under these circumstances was almost impossible. He'd already had to climb over two fallen and decaying trees.

Mateo needed to find the river soon. They were certainly being pursued; staying quiet was virtually impossible. At least the woods were thinning. He could see more of the night sky now, but the moon seemed to come and go, clouds often covering it. At one-point, Mateo thought he could hear the river but decided his ears were deceiving him.

He stumbled several times, falling to his knees once. It felt as though he had carried Pablo for hours.

Exhaustion set in, and Mateo had to rest again. He eased Pablo's body off his back. When he had him stretched out on the forest floor, Mateo tried to listen for anyone following them. Even straining, he realized he still couldn't hear very much. But he did notice that he no longer heard gunshots and hadn't for several minutes.

They had to keep moving, so Mateo once again wrestled Pablo onto his shoulder. Then he started walking.

# Chapter 42

Webster went outside to the window where he had seen movement after the explosion. Using the small flashlight and exploring carefully, he could see broken twigs and limbs where someone had gone into the brush. A trail meandered through the trees, most often taking the path of least resistance, so it was easy to follow.

Keeping the flashlight's beam shrouded and using it sparingly, Webster watched for footprints and soon concluded only one person was out there ahead of him. Something didn't add up. Two were missing, yet Webster was certain no one had come out the front of the cabin. Where was the other individual?

Reaching a marshy area, Webster searched for the prints he'd been following. When he found them, Webster realized what was going on. The footprints were pushed deep into the wet ground, and the steps were short. He paused and considered the evidence.

"Hmm! There's two of them," Webster murmured aloud. "One's carrying the other." He smiled. That'll slow 'em down some.

He started off again, but this time he veered to his right, away from the tracks, and took a more direct route to the river. Webster had carefully studied the map of the facility and of the surrounding property. He thought he knew where they would have tied up their boat. From the direction the men were traveling, they would end up hitting the bank downriver from their boat. They would have to get through the fence, too. But so would he, and he didn't have any cutters. He'd just have to climb the damn thing.

Webster realized the men were probably having a tough time with their hearing. The blast in the cabin had likely done some damage. They might not be able to hear the river and use it to guide them. Too bad. That was their tough luck.

Webster was getting close. The trees were less dense now and the ground sandy. The moist odor of the river was heavy in the air. Webster could even hear the rush of the current as it trickled over rocks and sandbars near the shore.

Suddenly the fence was in front of him. It seemed too tall to climb, and there was barbed wire at the top.

Something made him glance down—a sound. Probably a lizard. Then he realized it was sandy there. Maybe he could dig out enough to squirm underneath the fence. He found a stout stick and started to work.

Five minutes later, Webster reached back and pulled his weapons through the opening he'd made. He was free to move on.

As he neared the waterway, the moon slipped out from behind the clouds for a moment revealing the far bank of the channel. A few more steps and Webster would be able to see over the bank to whatever lay below.

The moon was gone as quickly as it had appeared, but he had his bearings now. He had found the river but couldn't hear any other human sounds. He lingered for a moment, wondering if the men were out there. They might be taking aim on him even as he hunted for them.

Webster crouched down with the rifle out in front of him. After a couple of minutes, he stood and looked up and down the riverbank searching for the boat. Nothing—it was nowhere in sight. Then he moved a few steps downriver to see around some heavy vegetation and was surprised to see the boat's shape through the relative darkness.

He had lucked out. It was below him and forty feet upstream, hidden earlier by the brush. He listened again, but there was no sign the men were here. Satisfied he had reached it first, Webster moved to a spot above the boat.

He needed a safe place to settle down and wait for Mendez and the Merchant. He couldn't remain out in the open. He would be too vulnerable. Webster glanced back toward the trees twenty feet away. That would do it, a place to hide and still be able hear the men even if they came to the boat from below the bluff. The tree line would work for that.

Now he needed a firing position. Continuing to search, Webster noticed an old stump leaning against a boulder upriver several yards. He went to check it out. It was at the edge of the bluff and overlooked the boat. Perfect!

A tree had obviously broken and fallen over a long time ago. The trunk and limbs above the break had probably been swept downstream. There was plenty of room for Webster to snuggle down behind the boulder and stump while still having a clear view of the boat. He even took the time to lie down and try the position. Satisfied, he moved back to the trees and found a place to wait.

He sat back, listening to the night sounds. The two men would be coming to him.

~ ~ ~

Mateo finally came out of the trees and into a brushy area. The foliage was thick and would keep them hidden. He eased Pablo to the ground. Fallen pine needles and leaves provided a soft bed for the unconscious Pablo.

As Mateo stretched him out on the ground, Pablo moaned and then blinked his eyes. Mateo patted his cheeks, bending close and softly calling his name.

A few seconds later, Pablo opened his eyes and was able to keep them on Mateo, but it was obvious he was having a difficult time hearing and focusing his eyes. He recognized Mateo but was disoriented otherwise.

"Where are we?" he asked, his voice loud and urgent. "What happened?"

Mateo quieted him and tried to explain.

"We're in the woods,"

"Where?" Pablo asked. Again, he was much too loud.

Mateo held a finger in front of his lips, signaling to keep it down. He hoped Pablo would understand.

"Okay," Pablo said, his voice lower this time. He reached up with both hands and rubbed at his ears, grimacing as he did so.

He tried to sit up, and with Mateo's help, managed to gain an upright position. He closed his eyes, though, still dizzy. After a few moments, Pablo shook his head and then held his hands over his ears again. He stayed that way for a moment before looking at his friend.

"It hurts," he said

"You probably have a concussion," Mateo replied. "Let's find the boat and get you out of here. We have to reach help and get you out of the U.S."

"I can't hear you," Pablo said. "Where are we?" Pablo reached up and turned Mateo's face toward him. "Watch me when I talk."

Mateo stared at him and spoke slowly. "We're in the woods. I need to find our boat. Stay here. Do you understand?"

Pablo nodded and pointed down. He understood. He said it too, "Stay here."

Mateo nodded, picked up the rifle, and walked away. He was hearing better now and could tell the river was off to his right. He could faintly hear the water running along the riverbank.

He stopped to get his bearings and for the first time saw the fence. Not wanting to lose time, Mateo pulled the bolt cutters from his belt and clipped an opening. Stepping through, he turned back to the chore at hand, finding the boat.

Turning to where he thought the river sound was coming from, Mateo looked for a landmark. Even in the darkness, he could see two tall trees out in front of him on the horizon. One looked like a pine and the other some sort of hardwood. Looking back where he had just left Pablo, Mateo could see an extremely tall pine that looked dead. Maybe struck by lightning, he thought.

He headed toward the sounds of the river while keeping his path toward the trees in the distance. It was nice to be out in the open with some visibility. Mateo picked his way along, careful of broken trees and brush. The sound of the rushing water was getting louder. His hearing was returning to normal.

Suddenly he stopped. The river was right below him. He had almost walked off the bluff above the water. The chest-high brush had continued right to the edge. It took a few moments for his heart to return to its normal pace. Whew!

Mateo looked around in the relative darkness. He couldn't see the boat or anything else he recognized. There was a clear area on the bluff a few yards upstream. He worked his way there.

From the new location, he had a much better view in both directions. Mateo stood looking for something familiar—the power lines, the boat, a dock, anything. He thought about the direction he and Pablo had taken from the cabin. He was virtually certain they had come to the river at a slight angle until the last stop where he had left Pablo. That would put the boat back upriver. He looked around, and satisfied with his thinking, headed back to get Pablo.

Together, they could make a run for the boat.

 *Chapter 43*

Bob called the guardhouse, bringing them up-to-date and warning them to keep everyone away from Webster's cabin. They said they had heard shots and wanted to send some people back to help. He told them that could be dangerous and hung up.

He dialed the ambulance service number next, telling Amy Hogan, "Webster said to call you. The people you've been waiting for showed up at the medical center a little while ago."

"Who is this?" Hogan asked.

"Bob Ramsey. I'm a nurse at the facility, and I've been helping Webster. We've been preparing for the people you were expecting. I'm an ex-marine."

"Oh! Well that explains everything," she said in a mocking way. "Is Webster okay? Why didn't he call?"

Bob didn't like her tone. "I told you I'm ex-marine so you'd know I'm capable of helping your friend." He gave her a moment to digest his comment. "He's fine, but he's out in the woods looking for two of the men."

"By himself? Damn! That sounds like him," she said.

"Yeah, he left me here to watch the area where they came in."

"How many of them were there?" Hogan asked.

"Six."

"And Webster's after two of them? Where are the others?"

"Two dead, we think, and the other two are out of commission. I have them tied up here at the cabin."

"What about Jerry Jackson? Is he okay?" she asked.

"He hasn't shown up since the gunfire," Bob told her. "I'm getting concerned."

"Damn, I hope he's all right. Stay where you are. I'll be there in a few minutes."

Bob heard the phone click off.

He hoped she identified herself coming in so he wouldn't shoot her.

~ ~ ~

Hogan dialed Jack Robbins, listening to his cell ring twice before he answered.

"Robbins here." He sounded sleepy.

"Jack, its Hogan. They've hit Webster's facility. There were six of them."

"I was afraid of that," Robbins said. "Is he okay?" He didn't sound sleepy anymore.

"Sounds like it," she told him, "but the fool's out in the woods, in the dark, after two of them by himself."

"Get over there and see if you can help," Robbins said. "And hurry."

"I'm on my way."

~ ~ ~

Bob checked the two men in the cabin. For added security, he pulled the men's feet up behind their backs and tied them to the wrists. They wouldn't be going anywhere when they regained consciousness. The chore was difficult with only one arm, but he got it done.

He put on his NV gear and went out to check on Jackson and the other two men. Bob approached each of the enemy guards cautiously, but his care was wasted. Both had been on their last operation.

Then he went to check on Jerry Jackson. At first sight, Bob's heart sank. Jackson's position was bullet-riddled and the U.S. deputy marshal was dead. He had taken two hits in the chest. Jackson hadn't stood a chance. The big rifle fired by the second guard had been lethal.

There was nothing Bob could do. He returned to the woods in front of the cabin and waited.

~ ~ ~

Using the landmarks he had sighted earlier, Mateo located Pablo quickly and was surprised to find him on his feet. He was still rubbing his ears but appeared to be functioning better.

"Did you find the boat?" Pablo asked. He hadn't yelled that time.

Mateo moved close to him, "No, but I think I know where it is. Are you able to travel?"

"I think so. I'm still a little dizzy," he said, "but let's try it."

Mateo offered his arm to his friend, but Pablo shrugged it off.

"This way?" Pablo asked starting off in the direction of the river.

"Yes, that way," Mateo said and took a couple of quick steps to get in front. He needed to lead him to the opening in the wire and didn't want Pablo walking off the bluff when they got outside the fence.

When they reached the overhang above the water, Mateo turned upriver toward the area where he thought they would find the boat. Pablo followed him.

After a while, Pablo tapped Mateo's shoulder and asked, "How much farther?"

Mateo stopped and looked along the riverbank and then at the woods before answering. "A few hundred yards probably."

"Good," Pablo said. "I'm getting pretty tired. My head and ears are killing me. I need a doctor."

Mateo looked at Pablo and found himself feeling sorry for his mentor. Mateo had been surprised that his own injuries were so slight. He was pretty sure that neither of his eardrums had ruptured. His head must have been turned at just the right angle when the blast went off.

"Did we get any of them?" Pablo asked.

"I don't know."

"That bomb came out of nowhere," Pablo said as they walked. "We should have expected something when we found the cabin empty and those blankets folded under the covers on the bed."

"Yeah," Mateo agreed. "But they didn't tip their hand. They just watched us until we went into the cabin. Then they lit the fuse."

"Do you think any of the others got out?" Pablo was thinking again.

"I doubt it. José and Pedro were down when I grabbed you and jumped out the window. I did manage to get a rifle." Mateo stopped to bend down and rub his lower leg and foot. "Twisted my ankle. Hurts like hell."

"Hmm," was all the reaction he got from Pablo.

"We better keep moving. I'm surprised no one is following us." Mateo turned and started to walk away.

Pablo followed, rubbing his right ear as he tried to keep up.

A short time later, Mateo spotted the boat. He got Pablo's attention and pointed to it. They were almost directly above it. They might have seen it sooner, but the bushes where it was tied up were large. The boat had drifted under them and was almost hidden.

Mateo found a place for them to go over the bluff and climb down. He went first and then reached up and guided Pablo down. They had to jump the last few feet. It wasn't easy, but they were soon at the water's edge.

"Let me get into the boat and start it," Mateo told Pablo. "Then you can untie the line and push us off the sand. I'll help you climb in when we're afloat."

With Mateo watching, Pablo looked over the situation and then motioned for him to climb aboard. With Mateo in the boat, Pablo started toward the line.

He was reaching for it when, for the second time, the night erupted in a blaze of light and noise.

~ ~ ~

Webster had heard them coming before he could see them. The sounds of the two men walking along the bluff were distinct from other sounds in the area. After he first heard them, the two men stopped and talked for a short time.

Webster knew he was well hidden, so he stayed still and quiet. After their conversation, the men continued upstream. They were moving slow when Webster would have expected them to be in a hurry. When they came into view, he could see Mendez was walking with a limp. The other one, the Merchant, kept rubbing at his ears. Some blast damage there, Webster figured.

Near the boat, the men climbed down to the water's edge. When he was sure they couldn't see him, Webster prepared himself for the encounter.

He quietly flipped the rifle off safety, checked that a round was chambered, and then assured himself he had a full magazine. Only then did Webster cautiously move to the edge of the bluff and the cover he had found earlier. Once he was hidden and lying prone behind the stump and boulder, Webster slid his goggles down to take a look at the boat and the two men.

Easing the rifle barrel out near the middle of his cover, Webster smiled, realizing he had a field of fire that covered everything from the river to the base of the bluff. The boat and the men were in the middle of his range.

Webster reached down and pulled two ammo magazines from his belt, placing them in front of him. He peeped back at the boat and smiled again.

Time for some fun, boys.

Webster flipped his goggles up. There was enough light to zero in on his target. Mendez was in the boat now, and the Merchant was about to untie the mooring line. Webster aimed and pulled the slack down on the trigger. He snuggled into the rifle's stock so he could hold it steady on his target. Satisfied, he drew the trigger down the rest of the way and held it until the entire thirty-round magazine had fired. Webster quickly released the empty magazine, replaced it, and chambered a round. He then set the fire selector to single fire.

Then he flipped his goggles down to look at the damage. Perez was cowering behind a dirt ridge up against the bluff. Mendez, on the boat when Webster fired, must have taken cover somewhere on deck. He had disappeared from view.

Webster then looked at his target. The intent had been to sink the boat and trap the men. With the boat out of commission, there were three choices for them: upstream or downstream on the riverbank or climb up the bluff. There was a fourth choice, Webster guessed, but who would want to try and swim the river? It was wide here, and the current was fast.

As he watched, the boat started to list in his direction. Before it tilted too much, Webster glimpsed the area where he had aimed. There was a hole about a foot in diameter at the waterline. That boat would never be seaworthy again.

As he admired the results of his work, Webster lost track of time and of the second man. He had momentarily forgotten, too, that the men had one of the AK-47s with them.

# Chapter 44

Mateo had been about to put the key in the ignition when bullets began striking the boat. He had stowed his own weapon on the small ledge beneath the windshield when he climbed aboard. Grabbing it, he went over the side and into the river. The water was only waist-deep, and the bottom seemed firm. Hidden by bushes, he made his way to the bow. After a few moments, the barrage stopped, and the river was quiet. Mateo took a chance and peeked toward where the shots had originated.

Pablo had tried to hide himself under the bluff. Mateo could see him a few feet away and motioned for him to remain where he was. Pablo nodded and cautiously looked up to the area where the gunman lay waiting for them to show themselves. A rifle shot from above convinced him to remain where he was.

Mateo had had a hollow feeling in his gut since that bomb went off in the cabin. He had known all along that Mike Webster was someone he couldn't take lightly. Pablo had said as much. Webster was intelligent and cunning, and he was street smart. Those traits made him very dangerous as an adversary. With bullets flying and their lives on the line, the situation was about as adversarial as it could get.

Webster was up on that bluff, Mateo guessed. He carefully peered around the bow and tried to see the shooter. Although he couldn't spot him, Mateo thought he knew where he was located. He had seen muzzle flashes as he went over the side of the boat.

On the bluff and upriver several yards, Mateo could see an old stump butted up to a boulder. He was pretty sure the shots had come from there. Mateo hoped he was right because he would only have one chance. If he guessed wrong about the location, or if he missed, he and Pablo could die there on the river.

The shooter had choices. If he emptied another magazine into the boat, he could blow away the bow of the boat and Mateo with it or he could shoot into the engine and set the boat on fire. Either could mean the end for Mateo. With him out of the way, Pablo would be easy to pick off. The Merchant only had a pistol to defend himself.

Mateo took a deep breath, and with a touch of his finger put his rifle on full automatic. He had plenty of ammo, so it wouldn't hurt to blow a full magazine. Mateo eased the barrel around the bow, hidden, he hoped, by the bushes. His concern was that the man on the bluff had night vision goggles. He lined up as best as he could on the stump up on the edge of the bluff. If the man was behind the rock, Mateo knew he could miss him completely. He steadied himself and took the shot.

Rounds tore at the stump causing sizable chunks of solid wood to fly off and throwing splinters all over the place. A few bullets, two or three, zinged off the boulder, too, making strange sounds and sending pieces of rock into the bushes with sparks trailing behind them.

When the magazine was empty, Mateo quickly headed to the rear of the boat and changed out the spent magazine for a full one as he moved. He hoped he had done some damage to the man on the bluff because he sure didn't want him shooting into the engine compartment.

Everything grew quiet again. Mateo listened but heard no sounds at all coming from up on the bluff. The only sounds were the river and Mateo's own heartbeat. If anyone was alive up there, he figured they might be able to hear it, too.

Peering around and seeing no movement at the stump, Mateo headed back to the bow. Pablo had remained where he was and now watched Mateo for instructions. Again, Mateo motioned for Pablo to stay put.

Then he reached out and shook some bushes. Nothing! But that could mean the shooter lay waiting for him to come out of hiding. Waiting for the kill. He could see Pablo cringe as he tried to stay tight against the bluff.

Mateo tried it again, shaking the bushes more vigorously this time. Still nothing. Everything appeared quiet up on the bluff. He checked his equipment. His pistol was loaded and ready. He returned it to his belt. There was one more magazine for the rifle, and it was set on automatic.

Mateo looked at Pablo again, made a sign of the cross, and broke for the bluff. During the first two or three steps, he almost expected to hear the man's rifle burp again and feel the shots tearing into his flesh.

But death as he expected it didn't come.

That didn't slow him down. Even with the rifle in his grasp, Mateo went up the dozen feet of the bluff in record time. He completely forgot about his injured ankle.

Near the top of the climb, Mateo launched himself over the last five feet. Landing on one knee, he rolled into the bushes and crawled away. When he felt safe, Mateo became still and quiet, listening for anyone following him. The forest was silent. Even the creatures seemed to be waiting for more gunfire.

After several minutes, Mateo slowly rose to his knees and then his feet. As quietly as possible, he held his rifle in a ready position and started working his way back toward the bluff where the stump was located. He realized he was risking a death shot with every step.

Webster had lowered himself and was getting ready to roll away from his cover when bullets tore into the stump. He was actually moving when it happened. At a time like that, he knew that you don't act, you react.

The shots came from somewhere down near the boat; he wasn't sure exactly where. He was too low behind the boulder and the stump for the bullets to hit him, but chunks of wood and rock were flying everywhere. Something struck him in the back of the head as he turned to escape. That's when the lights went out.

Webster's body crumpled and he lay there unconscious. Blood matted the hair at the back of his head with the scull visible in one spot. He stayed where he had fallen, out of touch with the world.

He would not be firing back this time. Unconscious and prone on the pine needles, he couldn't see the man who frantically climbed up the bluff and went into the woods.

Mateo worked his way through the bushes to a location where he could see the stump and boulder. Without a sound, he raised himself to get a better view. There was someone on the ground. The man was still, the back of his head covered in blood. Mateo tossed a pebble off to the side near the individual. No movement!

Keeping his rifle pointed in that direction, Mateo cautiously walked over and knelt beside the stump, putting his fingers to the man's neck to feel for signs of life. He was okay. His pulse was strong and steady. He was breathing, too, at a slow and regular pace.

After checking him over and assuring himself that the man was out cold, Mateo stood and called out to Pablo. "Come on up. He won't be firing anymore."

"You shot him?"

"I don't think so. Probably a chunk of rock or wood from the stump struck him. Hurry up. We need to finish him and get out of here."

Pablo started up the bluff. As he waited, Mateo turned the man over on his back. He still wasn't sure whether it was Webster or not.

But the Merchant was sure. Pablo became infuriated when he saw the man stretched out behind the stump.

Pablo kicked the unconscious man in the ribs. "That son of a bitch!"

"What? What's wrong?" Mateo looked at Pablo and then back at the man on the ground. "This isn't him?"

"Oh yes, that's Webster," Pablo said. His hatred screamed out with each word. "This is the bastard we came here for." Then Pablo glanced at Mateo and declared, "You better not have killed him."

"He's alive," Mateo assured the Merchant with some anger in his own voice. "He's just unconscious. There's a big gash on the back of his head. Something hit him when I shot into the stump from down below."

Pablo's shoulders relaxed, and he appeared to settle down. Then he did a strange thing, Mateo thought. He reached into his pocket and brought out a folded and worn set of papers—an old note or a letter.

"Let's set him against the rock and wake him up," Pablo said. "I've been waiting a long time for this." Pablo had an evil grin on his face as he spoke. Mateo shivered at the sight.

"We better tie him up before we move him," Mateo said. "I'll get some line from the boat. You watch him while I'm gone." He stepped around the boulder and started to climb over the bank.

With one leg over the side, Mateo glanced back. "We need to hurry. Others will come. They must have heard the shots."

"Yeah, yeah. Just get the rope."

"The boat's ruined. We'll have to walk out."

"Go. And hurry," Pablo said, motioning Mateo toward the boat.

Pablo kneeled a few feet away and watched Webster. His hatred would have been evident to anyone watching.

From a dozen feet below the bluff, Mateo heard the Merchant's harsh words. "He's going to wish he had never heard my name."


Mateo returned with a length of rope and tied Webster's arms and wrists together. Then he moved to his feet.

He motioned for Pablo to help, and they lifted the still unconscious man and sat him against the boulder. Webster's head hung forward, his chin resting against his chest.

Mateo stepped back and tried again to make Pablo move it along. "We really need to hurry. There's going to be more people out here looking for us."

Not appearing to care, Pablo laid his pistol on the rock and crouched down beside Webster.

"Wake up, Mr. Undercover."

Pablo suddenly slapped Webster and spit in his face. Then the Merchant waited.

Getting no reaction, he turned to Mateo. "He tried to turn my son against me.

He killed Juan." The pages were wadded and twisted in his hand.

Mateo suddenly understood why Pablo hated the man so much. He had heard the story from others, but Pablo had never mentioned it—until now.

Mateo showed no reaction, nor was one needed. Pablo was really talking for Webster's benefit.

Pablo said, "This bastard became a friend to Juan and wormed his way into my house. He sat at my wife's table, ate my food, and all along was telling his people all about us." He glanced at Mateo saying, "He turned my own son against me.'

Obviously unable to contain himself, Pablo slapped Webster again. Then he pulled the big hunting knife from his belt. Mateo stayed clear. Pablo's anger could turn from Webster to him in the blink of an eye.

Still looking at Webster, Pablo continued talking. "One night in Bogotá, they came for us at my estate. The tall one was with them. They shot me, but I managed to escape with a couple of my men. As we drove away, I saw them shoot my son off the roof where he had gone to escape." He glanced back at Mateo. "I also saw the federal police put this bastard in a van to carry him away. They were slapping him on the back and laughing."

"Were the rest of your people in the house?"

"Yes," he said. "My wife and others—uncles, aunts, even my wife's mother. Family! You understand?"

Pablo looked at Webster again. "They killed my son that night, and my wife never forgave me. She won't even let me talk to her."

Mateo slowly shook his head. Then he stepped away from the confrontation. He would let Pablo have his revenge. Afterward, he would try to get the old man away from there alive.


Webster tried to open his eyes. He raised his head and slowly focused on his surroundings, gazing at the younger man first and then at Pablo Perez. He focused on the Merchant.

"I wondered who was searching for me. I'm not surprised it's you. How did you find me?"

Pablo grinned. "The pretty doctor! The one that's been taking care of you told my young friend here." He motioned at Mateo, an evil twinkle in his eyes. "He was very persuasive with her."

Webster's heart almost stopped. Oh, God! Irene and her mother.

"Did you … Are they …?"

"Are they what?" Pablo grinned. "Did we hurt them? … Did we kill them? … You don't think we would leave them to tell their story, do you?" He paused, allowing Webster to imagine what must have happened to the women. The old man laughed and pointed to Mendez. "With his pistol, my young friend here made sure they wouldn't be talking to anyone."

Webster saw it in Pablo's eyes. He was telling the truth. They had shot Irene and her mother.

"Auhh!" Webster drew his knees and feet to his chest and struck out at Pablo. He hit him a glancing blow, yet managed to plow Pablo back into the bushes.

The Merchant was caught by surprise. He came up angry, so angry he had to do something. Before Webster could protect himself, Pablo jumped to his feet and rushed him. He raked the point of the hunting knife down Webster's face, leaving a cut and a trail of blood that quickly began to drip onto Webster's chest.

Jerking his head back, Webster glared at the driven, vengeful old man. His hatred had now added Irene and her mother to the list of people who had died at his hand—and he wasn't finished.

"You killed my son!" Pablo screamed. He came up with the papers again and shook them in Webster's face. "I trusted you and you took my boy from me."

Controlling his own anger, Webster said in a quiet but forceful voice, "No, Pablo. You killed Juan! You did it with the life you chose to live."

Pablo growled and raised the knife to slash at Webster's neck. Mateo took a step back, watching.

Webster's eyes closed, and he turned his head, waiting, in that moment, for the cold steel to do its evil errand.

Waiting for death!

 **Chapter 45**

The blade was in its downward arc when, from out of the fading darkness, a bullet struck the old man's arm. The knife, flashing toward Webster's throat a moment before, broke from the fingers that held it and flew over the stump and down beyond the bluff.

Mateo spun toward their attacker's position while reaching for his pistol. He almost had it free when a second shot was fired, this one striking Mateo in the thigh. It twisted him around and down, his weapon torn from his grasp, too.

Pablo, using his left hand, clawed for his own pistol as he scrambled away from the rock. The shooter's third round struck his shoulder, throwing him back and to the ground, the pistol still in his belt.

Both men stayed where they had fallen. Pablo glanced at Webster first, an angry look still on his face. Mateo was watching the location where the shots had come from. He figured the guards from the medical facility had caught up with them. Pablo's eyes were drawn to the area of the gunfire, too.

From his leaning position against the boulder, Webster tried to see through the receding shadows to his benefactor. Thick bushes near the edge of the trees parted and a form stepped out. Someone holding a rifle moved toward them. The three men waited and watched, believing it had to be someone from the medical facility.

They saw her at the same time, each of them with their own first impression. As though back from the dead, she stood there, blood crusted on her blouse, in her hair, and along her face. She was carrying Bob's rifle. Smoke still curled from the weapon's barrel.

Mateo spoke first—shock, even wonder, in his voice, "You …"

Pablo turned on Mateo. "You said you killed them. Both of them!"

Without noticeable emotion, Mateo told him, "I thought I did."

Webster, bound and unable to move, said, "Irene! They told me they shot you and Sandra."

She ignored him, staring only at Mateo.

"Oh, you murdered my mother," she said to young killer. "I was lucky. Your bullet only knocked me unconscious." She paused, then continued. "That's extremely unlucky for you."

She stepped over and picked up Mateo's pistol, tossing it out over the bluff.

Then she said, "Pull the knife and toss it over near Webster, handle first."

Mateo watched her. He was slow to respond, prompting her to shout, "Do it now, damn you!"

Mateo followed her command.

"And you," Irene said walking over toward Pablo, "do you get your rocks off by slapping an old woman?"

He started to reply, but her foot struck his face, cutting off his words.

"You and your violent young friend here made my mother's last few hours a living hell. Now, I'm going to return the favor—only it won't last as long for you."

Pablo and Mateo exchanged worried glances. Pablo ran his tongue across bloodied lips.

Webster watched Irene's face and listened to her words. He could visualize her intent. He couldn't stop her, but he had to try.

"Irene, don't do it," he said, trying to get her attention. "Let the courts deal with them."

Her eyes finally turned to Webster. "I'm not about to take the chance some sharp lawyer will get them off," she told him. "My mother was a good woman. She didn't deserve what they did to her."

Irene had finished talking. She stepped back and fired a shot into Pablo's right knee.

He screamed, "You bitch! You stinking bi—"

The last shot struck him in the head, cutting short his final curse. The Merchant slammed to the ground and remained still. Pablo had gone to join his son.

She turned toward Mateo.

"Irene, for your own sake," Webster implored her, "don't. They're not worth it."

It was as though she hadn't heard him. She walked over near Mateo as he sat on the ground holding his leg.

"You shot my mother and me while we were defenseless and tied to chairs," she told him. "I'm going to give you a better chance than that."

Mateo watched her, a sliver of hope in his eyes.

Webster couldn't believe what he heard next.

"Get up," she told Mateo. "I'm going to give you a two-minute head start."

Mateo stared at her, his eyes large, disbelieving. He obviously didn't think he had heard right. A head start—but with a broken leg?

"What about my leg," he whined, all show of machismo gone. "I can't run."

"Then hop," she told him. "That's better than you gave my mother and me."

He seemed to recognize that she meant it. Webster almost believed her, too.

Mateo crawled to the stump and climbed to his feet. He looked at Irene one more time and then started to hop away.

He made two agonizing steps before he heard her call to him.

"Hey!"

He stopped and turned, balancing by holding onto the boulder.

She stood there smiling at him. "I was just kidding," she said. "I would never let you go. I hate you too much." She tilted her head apologetically and then blew away the knee on his good leg.

She killed him with a burst of fire that ended only when the rifle was out of ammo. She pulled the trigger two more times before she threw the weapon down.

Irene stared at Mateo's body for several seconds and then turned her eyes downward for another moment. Only then did she turn back to Webster.

"I'm sorry you had to see that," she said. "You can turn me in now, or arrest me—whatever you have to do." She paused. "She really was a good woman, my mother. She would've liked you." She smiled at him, but there were tears in her eyes. She rubbed at her face with the back of her hand, all emotion gone, her shoulders rounded and tired.

When she walked over and picked up Mateo's knife, Webster rolled over, presenting his back to her. She sliced through the lines, freeing him.

Rolling back and sitting up, he rubbed his hands and arms. It took a couple of minutes for the feeling to return. While he was rubbing his legs, Irene checked the injury on the back of his head and the gash Pablo had cut on his cheek.

"Some stitches will take care of those," she said, dismissing the wounds for the moment.

Webster stood up and checked Mateo and Pablo. They were beyond help. Irene's marksmanship had been very good. Depending on how you thought of it, she hadn't wasted a shot.

"How are we going to do this?" Irene asked.

"Do what?"

"The arrest!"

He stared at her for several seconds. "There isn't going to be one."

"But …"

He shook his head.

She stared at him, "You mean—"

Webster cut her off. "They were going to kill me, and you stopped them. They died in the process. End of report."

They heard a four-wheeler coming flat-out along the bluff. A short time later, it thundered into sight. It was Bob with Amy Hogan.

Bob had the golf cart pedal-to-the-metal at 12 mph. They skidded to a stop and both jumped out and looked around with their weapons drawn. Bob was holding his bandaged arm up, but he still looked dangerous with a pistol in his other hand.

Hogan spoke first. "You got them both?"

"You're fast at grasping the obvious," Webster said and smiled. "Actually, Dr. Dunn got them. They were about to kill me. She saved my life." With a sad glance at Irene, Webster added, "They killed Dr. Dunn's mother and shot the doctor, too."

"I'm sorry," Hogan said to Irene and then turned to Webster. "Is one of them our killer?"

"Yeah," Webster said, pointing at Mendez. "He was working for the older fellow. That's who really wanted me. His name is Pablo Perez."

Hogan reacted to the name. "The Merchant?"

"The one and only," Webster replied.

"Why?" Hogan asked. "So much killing, and, so far, no reasons why."

"He thought I caused his son to be killed at their home down in Bogotá. I was undercover at the time."

"I'm just glad we got him." Hogan appeared relieved. Webster understood all too well.

Bob walked over and looked at Webster and Irene, taking a moment to examine their wounds.

"From the looks of you two and your clothes, we need to get you both back to the medical center. You both need stitches, maybe a bunch of them."

Take care of them," Hogan said to the big nurse and ex-marine. "I'll stay here. Call for at least two CSI teams. I'll contact Jack Robbins and explain the situation to him. He's probably already on his way here."

Bob and his two patients climbed on the four-wheeler and headed back to the facility. Bob drove a little slower than on his way out.


As they drove away, Hogan opened her phone and hit the speed-dial for Robbins. He answered immediately.

"Jack, its Hogan. Everything's finished here as far as the action goes."

He at once asked, "Casualties?"

"Five dead on the facility," she told him. "Four bad guys and Jerry." She told him about Jackson and then continued. "One dead off campus, Dr. Dunn's mother. Several other wounds of various sorts, including Webster and Dr. Dunn."

"Are they okay?"

"Yeah, both just need stitches."

"I'll be there in an hour or so," Robbins replied. "Tom Manning and I are in the air now. I'll call you when we're on the ground."

# Chapter 46

Webster hadn't slept decently in several nights, and neither had Bob. First, they had stayed up waiting for whatever might come. Then it came!

Now it was morning, and people were all over the place trying to sort things out. Webster had talked with Jack Robbins and Tom Manning several times and with the crime scene people twice. He wanted some time with Irene, but that hadn't happened yet.

After a physician assistant stitched her up, Irene had gone back to her house where the investigators were dealing with both her and her mother's shootings. Webster was concerned about his friend. There was so much going on, and she was sporting a head wound and a concussion.

She was lucky, medically speaking. Irene had said she could remember turning her head at the last instant. She had called it a gut reaction. The movement had saved her life. The bullet had grazed the skull but hadn't entered the cranium. The CSI people found it lodged in a stuffed chair. The man who had shot her hadn't checked to make sure he had killed her. That hadn't been the situation for her mother.

Now Irene had to deal with getting her mother's body to Montana after the medical examiner released it. And she had to break the news to her dad; what a thing to have to call and tell him.

Bob received care for his wounds and met with Jack Robbins and the other investigators. With his debriefing completed, Bob was told to go home and get some sleep.

Before that, though, he had to try and explain everything to his wife. Webster wished him good luck on that one.

Early in the afternoon, Webster told Robbins he needed some rest. He was past the point of exhaustion. Jack told him to find a quiet place and sack out. He said they'd talk later.

Webster caught a ride up to the medical building and asked the head nurse for an empty room. She took him down to the end of the hall where he was less likely to be disturbed and set him up with an extra pillow, two blankets, some juice, and a pitcher of water.

After taking a shower, he put on some clean shorts and slept for ten hours.

When he awoke at two thirty the next morning, Webster turned on the news and then dozed off again. He slept for five more hours.

Sunshine was coming through the window when he awoke the next time. Webster yawned, stretched, and then stretched and yawned again. Then he swung his legs off the bed. The time on the clock surprised him when he noticed it.

Donning a hospital robe and slippers he found in the closet, Webster splashed some water on his face and looked at himself in the bathroom mirror. The cut on his cheek with its small dressing looked simple enough. He ran his fingers through his tousled hair, careful about the larger bandage on the back of his head. He looked at himself again. That'll have to do, he thought.

He walked down to the nurse's station. Bob was there, along with Hogan.

"Look who's finally decided to bless us with his presence," Bob said to Hogan.

She turned and seeing him, smiled. "How's the head and face?"

He returned the smile. "Fine. Where's Jack?"

"Out at the cabin," she told him. "He's trying to tie up some loose ends before he and Tom Manning fly back to Washington."

"What kind of loose ends?"

"Well, for starters, how the two of you came up with a bomb."

"Oh, that!" Webster and Bob exchanged glances.

"Yeah, that," Hogan commented. Then she added, "And why you went off after those two killers without waiting to take some people with you."

"Thanks for the heads-up. I'll try to have some answers when I see him."

"I'd start working on it." She nodded toward the hallway behind him. "Here he comes."

"Morning," Robbins said as he walked up. "I have a couple of questions for you two." He included Bob as he gave them both a withering look.

"Excuse us for few minutes, Hogan."

Robbins started down the hall and motioned for the two men to follow him. He found a small meeting room, led them inside, and closed the door. He got right to the point.

"Where the hell did you guys get a bomb?"

They looked at each other and then Webster answered, "We made it."

"You made it?" Robbins sounded doubtful. "With what?"

Webster looked at Bob again. "Well … we both knew a little about what we needed and how to do it, so we just improvised. Bob picked up some supplies, and we put it together at the cabin."

Robbins looked at them and shook his head. Webster got the impression that Robbins might not want to know much more than that.

"So, you both knew a little about it." He gave each of them a stern look and said, "It's a damn good thing you didn't know a lot about it or you would have blown that little cabin right off its foundation."

Grinning, he then asked, "Whose idea was it to make it a fruit bomb?"

Without hesitating, Webster and Bob each pointed at the other. Robbins cracked up. The two bombers thought it was funny, too.

~ ~ ~

The first thing on Irene's agenda when she returned home was to deal with the sheriff's people. Her mother's body had already been taken away. The crime team was quietly going about their work.

As soon as she could, Irene called her father. It was one of the most difficult calls she had ever made. Her father answered after a couple of rings.

"Hello?"

"Dad?"

"Is that you, Irene? Is something wrong with your mother?" Her mom and dad worried about each other when they were apart.

"Yes, Dad, it's about Mom. I have some bad news." She choked for a moment and then said, "Mom's gone."

"What do you mean she's gone?" he asked, but she could hear it in his voice. He knew what she meant.

"She's gone, Dad. She died." She didn't want to tell him what had happened on the phone, but she knew she had to give him some sort of explanation.

"How? What?"

"Dad," she started, "some really bad people came looking for a patient we had in the medical center where I work."

"Yeah …" he said. "What's that got to do with your mother?" He seemed to want to understand.

"Dad, they didn't know where the facility was located. It's not common knowledge, you know."

"Yeah."

"Well, somehow they got my name and the fact that I worked there. They came here to my house," she said. By now she was crying. "Dad, they made me show them the location, and they made me go out there and get them some papers."

"It's okay, darling," he said. "You did what you had to do, but what happened to your mother?"

"They held her while I went to the facility. I got what they needed and gave it to them." She sobbed again. "I gave them everything they asked for, and then, Dad … they shot us."

"They shot you both?" He sounded incredulous.

"Yes. Both of us. Mom was killed, but the bullet bounced off my hard head. It knocked me out and turned my chair over. There was a lot of blood. They thought I was dead, too. They just left us here in the house."

"What about the people that shot you and your mother? Did they catch them?"

"Yes, Dad. They caught them. They're dead." He didn't ask how, and she didn't tell him.

"Good," he said. "I'm glad. I know I shouldn't be, but I am." He added, "The bastards!"

"I understand, Dad. I'm glad, too." He really didn't need to know the circumstances.

"I'll be there," he said, "as soon as I can get a flight. Where can I reach you?"

"Call my cell," she told him. "I'll keep it with me. Do you have the number?"

"It's on your mother's desk. I'll let you know when I'm going to arrive." Then he said, "I love you, baby. You can't always stop bad people from doing bad things."

"I love you, too, Daddy." She hadn't called him Daddy since she was a little girl, and he was a much younger man.

Irene couldn't stand the thought of trying to sleep in the house where her mother had been murdered. She packed a few things and drove to a hotel. She didn't call the medical center or anyone else. She wanted to be alone.

Around ten thirty the next morning, she finally called Webster. When he answered, Irene asked, "Would you buy me some breakfast?"

"Sure," he said. "Are you okay?"

"As okay as I can be."

"I'll dress and borrow Bob's vehicle."

She gave him directions and hung up.

Webster walked into the hotel a short time later. It was a meeting she didn't look forward to. Irene doubted if he did either.

# Chapter 47

Irene met Webster in the hotel's restaurant. Webster didn't say anything as he sat down at the table. He just reached over and took her hand. She gripped his with both of hers as she looked into his eyes.

Though she tried, Irene couldn't keep her tears at bay. One lonely teardrop crept down her cheek. He reached out with a single finger and gently brushed it away. That was all it took. She fell apart.

They were seated in a booth; he was across from her. Webster eased out and slid in beside her. Irene looked up at him, tears now flooding her eyes as he slipped an arm around her.

"I'm sorry," he said, holding her close. "They were after me—not you and your mother."

"You aren't responsible for animals like that."

"I know," he said, "but that doesn't change the way I—"

"Don't." She put a hand over his lips, stopping him from saying those things. "Just sit here and hold me for a minute."

He did what she needed.

The waitress sensed something and left them alone until Webster summoned her.

"Two coffees, and bring the lady a couple of scrambled eggs and some bacon and toast, please." He ordered some toast for himself.

"Yes, sir," the waitress said and was gone.

Irene was calm by the time their order came. Webster remained silent as she ate. She told him about the call to her father and how difficult it had been.

"How old is he?"

"Seventy-one."

"Healthy?"

"Overall? Like a horse," she told Webster and smiled. "He had bypass surgery a few years ago, and he's taking care of himself. More recently, he broke his wrist playing tennis." She grinned at Webster's uplifted brow.

"I don't know how this will affect him." She paused. "I just don't know."

They talked for a while and then the conversation finally turned to the bluff above the river and the things that had happened there.

"I shouldn't have done it, but I couldn't stop myself. The hate consumed me."

Irene gazed out the window and said without looking back, "My mother wouldn't have wanted it that way."

"Can I tell you something?"

She nodded.

"Any little misstep on that bluff, and they would have murdered us both. The young one, Mateo Mendez, had already killed half a dozen people before he got to you and your mother."

"I know, but—"

"That was all yesterday," Webster continued. "You can't change it. You have the rest of your life in front of you. Go live it."

"I know," she said again, "but …"

He gave her a moment and then asked, "By the way, where did you learn to shoot like that?"

That drew a smile. "I told you. I'm from Montana. We live in the woods." Irene grinned now. "Does that answer your question?"

"I'll remember never to make you angry when you're holding a gun."

"Not funny."

He thought about it. "Guess not," he said. "Sorry."

"Where will you go now?" she asked.

"I don't know. I'll have to go to Washington and talk it over with the powers that be. How about you? Will you be going back to the medical center?"

"I don't know. Dad will be alone now. I'll have to consider that."

After a while, Irene walked Webster out to the parking lot. The last time he saw her was in his rearview mirror. She was waving good-bye.

~ ~ ~

Back at the medical center, Robbins said he needed a few minutes of Webster's time and motioned him to one of the small conference rooms. Without leading into it, Jack handed Webster some pages encased in clear plastic sleeves.

"We found this on the bluff near the Merchant's body. It's a letter. I think it was intended for you."

Webster took it while keeping his eyes on his friend.

"Make yourself a copy, but don't remove the pages from their covers," Jack said. "Give the originals back to me. We want to check for fingerprints and DNA."

Robbins stood up and walked to the door. Webster watched him go before reading the pages. He didn't recognize the handwriting but knew immediately who it came from—the boy—Pablo's son, Juan.

"To my friend," it started.

"You must quickly leave. My father he is going to kill you. I hear him tell one of his men. He will probably shoot me also because I am tell you this. Leave now. Do not come back here anymore."

"Wow!" Juan was taking a big chance. Someone else, too, whoever had written it for him. Juan couldn't write in English.

"I will miss our friendship very many times."

The letter went on, speaking of things they had done, walks they had taken, conversations they'd had.

"Remember the time we went to the park down by river? Remember you tell me I may wish for to go to school in your country when I am big. When I say this to my father he become very angry. He say I must stay with him to learn for to take his place. He wish for me to make his business run for better. He want for me to be big boss someday."

Webster remembered all of it.

"Remember you say this may happen if I ask for too soon. I hope I have not make for you to be in dangerous because I am speak so fast. But I am now scared for you. I am afraid you be killed. I do not want you be gone but I want you be safe."

Webster could almost hear Juan's voice in the words. He would miss the youngster though they had only known each other a short time. Believing he had caused the boy's death by not getting back to the compound in time to get him out had been an error. If he had been there, they both would have been killed. Either way, nothing could be changed. But now, at least, the Merchant was dead, too. The old man's hatred for Webster had turned out to be a death sentence. Funny how things work out.

The message ended too quickly, the boy signing it in his own way: "Vaya con Dios, Your friend."

Webster sat for a few minutes in thought.

Juan, you knew something I didn't and tried to warn me. You didn't believe I could get you out. You didn't want me to come back for you.

You tried to save me instead.

Juan …

Carrying the letter in his hand, Webster went out a side door and found the walking path around the facility. He walked—he wasn't sure how long—until he found himself back near Kenney Dawkins home and the place where they had first met.

Dust and noise permeated the area. Activity on the other side of the fence was widespread. A transformation was taking place on the old pick-up baseball field and surrounding area. A bulldozer and other equipment were moving back and forth, making the area into a real park. In addition to the ball field under construction, Webster could see crates with assorted playground attractions sitting here and there. The kids from the trailer home neighborhood were watching, fascinated.

One boy stood apart and glanced in Webster's direction. Kenney Dawkins walked over and leaned against the fence, one foot on the wire at knee level, his fingers grasping the wire above. Webster held his distance and didn't wave, thinking it better to not get too attached. He gave a slight nod to the boy and then turned to go back to the medical center. As he began walking back, the boy yelled out to him.

"Hey!"

Webster continued.

"Thanks!"

Webster waved this time, but without turning back. He smiled; the Author had already called in a favor or two.

 ## Epilogue

Back at the medical center, Webster found Jack Robbins and handed him the letter.

"Don't you want a copy?"

Nah! Got it here." He tapped his forehead.

Jack started toward the door to the parking lot. "I'll be in touch tomorrow. We need to get you into a new situation before you get rusty."

"Yeah, like I got rusty this time, huh?"

At the door, Jack turned and casually mentioned he had given Webster's cell number to an old friend. He didn't say who. The door closed too quickly behind him.

~ ~ ~

Webster was sitting in one of the rockers that evening when his phone rang. He answered without checking the caller ID.

"Hello?"

"Webster?" A soft, woman's voice …

"Yes?"

There was a pause.

"Help me … please!"

Another pause.

"This is Cary. …

www.ingramcontent.com/pod-product-compliance
Lightning Source LLC
Chambersburg PA
CBHW071521110726
47908CB00003B/914